THE
WARNING

T. DAVIS BUNN

A
JANET
THOMA
BOOK

THOMAS NELSON PUBLISHERS
Nashville
Printed in the United States of America

Published in Nashville, Tennessee, by Thomas Nelson, Inc., Publishers.

Unless otherwise noted the Bible version used in this publication is THE NEW KING JAMES VERSION. Copyright © 1979, 1980, 1982, Thomas Nelson, Inc., Publishers.

Scripture quotations marked KJV are from the KING JAMES VERSION of the Bible.

Scripture quotations are also taken from the HOLY BIBLE: NEW INTERNATIONAL VERSION. Copyright © 1973, 1978, 1984 by the International Bible Society. Used by permission of Zondervan Bible Publishers.

This novel is a work of fiction. All characters, plot, and events are the product of the author's imagination. Any financial information or advocacy contained herein is purely fictitious.

Library of Congress Cataloging-in-Publication Data

Bunn, T. Davis, 1952–
    The warning / T. Davis Bunn.
       p. cm.
    ISBN 0-7852-7516-9 (pbk.)
    I. Title.
PS3552.U4718W37 1998
813'.54—dc21   97-40781
                                                                          CIP

Printed in the United States of America.

1 2 3 4 5 6 QPK 03 02 01 00 99 98

This book is dedicated to
Irven and Joanna Hicks
Twenty years ago, a young man ventured into
a Christian bookstore for the very first time.
Joanna introduced him to Christian fiction,
and Irven to contemporary Christian music.
Their patient sharing changed the course of his life.
He would once again like to say

Thank you,
Dear Friends

"Where there is no vision, the people perish."
Proverbs 29:18 KJV

⊣| ONE |⊢

Forty-One Days . . .

☐ The first Wednesday after Labor Day, Buddy rose from the nightmare like a drowning man fighting for the surface of the sea. Gasping and struggling and groping, he came awake with a hoarse shudder. It took a moment to get his breath under control before he could swing his legs to the floor and sit upright. He remained there, sitting on the side of the bed and gripping his chest against the sudden pain.

As he padded toward the bathroom, his wife asked quietly, "The dream again?"

"Yes." Buddy shut the door, stripped off his sopping pajamas, and washed his face. It had become a nightly routine. He glanced at the clock. Five o'clock in the morning. No chance of getting back to sleep.

When he came out, his wife was already up. He could hear her moving about the kitchen downstairs. He returned to the bath, ran himself a shower, and then dressed. The final words whispered through his mind the entire time, shreds of a dream which would not let go. *Forty-one days.*

He entered the kitchen to hear her say, "I'm calling the doctor first thing this morning. I want her to see you before you go to the office."

Buddy shook his head and finished knotting his tie. "What can Jasmine tell me about nightmares?"

"It's more than a nightmare, and you know it." Molly did not raise her voice. Molly seldom did. She was the quietest woman Buddy had ever known. But she held her opinions with silent conviction and protected her family with iron strength. "It's been more than two weeks now. Every night you wake up gasping and screaming and wet."

"She'll want to give me some pill." Jasmine Hopper was both their family doctor and a friend from church. "You know how I hate pills, Molly."

"Well, maybe this time you'll just have to take one." She turned to him and asked, "Eggs?"

"Why not." The wall clock read a few minutes to six. "I'll need something substantial to see me through to lunch."

"I spoke with Clarke Owen yesterday. Our prayer circle is going to start praying for you." She moved to the refrigerator and said as she returned to the stove, "Anne and Trish were over yesterday. They are going to talk with their Bible study groups and ask them to pray as well."

"For Pete's sake, Moll. You might as well have told the whole world." Clarke Owen was the assistant pastor and a close family friend. Anne and Trish were Buddy's two daughters-in-law. Good girls, but they did love to talk. "If they know, the entire town will be talking about it by dinnertime."

"A little prayer won't hurt."

"This is a whole lot more than a little."

"You're always so independent. Standing there as though nothing ever bothers you. Well, something is wrong, and I'm worried. I decided to ask almost everybody I know to help pray us through this."

Buddy stared across the counter at his wife. That was a very long speech for Molly. She was given to using one word where other women would use twenty, and to using silence most of the time. "You mustn't worry, honey."

"But I am worried. I see the way you hold your chest when you wake up. I hear how you gasp for breath, as if you can't get anything into your lungs." She brought over his plate and set it down in front of him. "Night after night I hear this. I know how you wake up soaked with sweat, how you have to lean on the wall to steady yourself when you rise."

"Aren't you having anything?"

"I'm too anxious to eat." She knotted the dish towel in her hands. The scar that emerged from her robe and covered the left side of her neck and chin was flushed with distress. "Promise me you'll call Jasmine today."

"All right." There was too much concern in her eyes for Buddy to refuse her anything. "But I'm telling you, nothing is the matter with me."

"And I'm telling you, there is. Are you having trouble at the bank?"

"Nothing to speak of." Buddy lowered his glance to stare at his food. "I'm not getting along with the director, but that's nothing new."

"You've had bad bosses before. None of them have ever bothered your sleep."

This one is different, he wanted to say, but he did not want to trouble her further. Besides, the new vice president responsible for their branch was not the reason for his nightmares. He was certain of that without knowing exactly why.

Buddy finished his breakfast in silence, accepted a topping off to his cup, and got up from the table. "I'll just go sit in the den for a while."

"Buddy—"

"If Jasmine can see me, I'll go by on the way to the office." He stooped to kiss his wife's forehead. "Don't worry, honey."

"But I do, you know." Molly gripped his wrist with surprising strength. She raised a gaze full of appeal. And fear. "I know you want to shrug it off and say this will pass. But it's gone on too long."

Nothing he could say would calm her fears. So he nodded and kissed her a second time, and left her for the quiet of the den and his morning Bible time.

□

Yet when Buddy entered his den, it felt as though the nightmare was there waiting for him.

Living shadows seemed to creep out of the corners, whispering with the same voices that turned his spirit to jelly at night— voices he never clearly heard, except for those final words,

Forty-one days. But he knew whatever else they were saying was bad. Very bad indeed.

He started to turn and flee, but he was fearful that if he did he would never return. Which was ridiculous. The den had been his little corner of the house since before the boys were born. Yet now it was an alien place.

Buddy forced himself forward. The leather settee by the back window was his morning abode, and he was determined to conquer this silly anxiety and take his place. His big Bible sat on the side table. He fastened his attention on the Book and forced his legs to carry him forward. He almost fell into his seat. He set his coffee cup on the cork mat and then had to use his handkerchief to mop up what he spilled.

Buddy tried to still his shaking hands as he lifted the Bible. He was studying Genesis again, having decided to read the Bible from start to finish for the first time in years. He leafed through the pages, waiting expectantly for the familiar peace to arrive and his world to settle back to normalcy. Yet today it did not happen. Instead, the nightmare's lingering edges crept closer, the sense of foreboding so strong he could almost smell it.

He found his place and focused upon the page. What he found there so startled him that he clamped his eyes shut. Praying aloud he gripped his chest, trying to push the sudden clenching pain away.

□

The sky was pristine blue as Buddy drove the quiet streets of Aiden, Delaware. Yet a sense of thunder echoed in the distance. Buddy saw a neighbor wave at him, and he returned the salute. But he could not recall who it was. His mind remained fixed upon what had happened in his den. He stopped at a light and prayed once more. But this time there was a difference. The words seemed to come both from him and from beyond him. *Show me what this means*, he prayed. It was a strange experience to feel that the words were more than his own. He had never felt what others called a movement of the Spirit. Never seen any need, for that matter.

Buddy was a contented man, happy just to plod along with his own peaceable form of faith. Yet this brief prayer had come from somewhere beyond his own mind, for Buddy had no real desire of his own to know what was bothering him so. In truth, he simply wanted it to go away.

The car behind him honked politely, and Buddy opened his eyes to see the light had turned green. He gave a little wave and started forward. At that moment, the brief prayer popped back into his mind. *Father, show me what all this means. Show me what it signifies. Help me to see clearly what is intended.*

This time the prayer's impact was so strong that he was forced to put on his signal and pull over to the curb. He shut his eyes, wishing he could shut his ears as well. Once more whispers gathered around him. Once more he sensed reality being peeled back. The normalcy of his life was being stripped away.

With trembling fingers Buddy pulled the slip of paper from his shirt pocket. On it were scrawled the words he had found in his Bible that morning. His hands were shaking worse now than then.

That morning in the den the words had reached across and gripped him by the heart. They had risen up and magnified until he could see nothing else. The words had blotted out the sunshine, the birdsong, and the sound of Molly in the kitchen. There had been room for nothing but their pounding force. He had written them down, not only because he wanted to remember them but also because he needed to do something to nullify their impact.

Now Buddy was forced to prop his hand on the steering wheel to reduce the trembling while he reread the passage. There in the midst of his morning routine, halfway between his home and the bank, the words came alive once more. They reached across the distance, shouting to him with explosive force from the forty-first chapter of Genesis, a passage he had read dozens of times before and never noticed. Yet this time they drained the morning of color and sound:

> *God has shown Pharaoh what He is about to do. . . . seven years of famine will arise, and all the plenty will be forgotten in the land of Egypt; and the famine will deplete the land. So the plenty will not be known in the land because of the famine following, for it will be very severe.*

Buddy prayed once more. Anything to make this anxiety leave him alone. *Show me what this means.*

When nothing happened except an easing of the pain in his chest, he opened his eyes and put the car back in drive. As he put on his blinker and checked for oncoming traffic, he sent another quick prayer heavenward. This one asked God to keep him from going insane.

─╢ TWO ╟─

□ "Okay, you can sit up now." Dr. Jasmine Hopper cut off the EKG machine. "How long have you had these chest pains, Buddy?"

"Hard to tell. Maybe a couple of weeks. No longer."

Dr. Jasmine Hopper was a woman of substance in every sense of the word. She was dark haired and big boned, with hands that would have suited a man, long-fingered and supple. She pulled the wires from their connectors, then began stripping the tabs and the tape from his chest. "Turn around and let me get to those on your back. Have you been under any undue pressure at work?"

"None to speak of."

Her gaze rested on him as she coiled the wires in a bundle. "What about at home? The boys doing okay?"

"The boys are fine, Jasmine. Their wives are fine. Their children are fine. Molly is fine."

"Something certainly isn't fine." She slid the long paper streamer through her fingers and tore it out of the machine. "No, leave your shirt off. I want to have another listen after I've studied the readout. I'll be right back."

The door closed behind the doctor. Buddy sat on the edge of the examining table. The room smelled faintly of some biting odor, sharp and clean. Buddy looked at his reflection in the long wall mirror. He straightened his shoulders and pulled in his gut. Even so, there was no escaping the fact that somewhere along the line middle age had sneaked up on him.

His black hair was graying but still pretty thick. Thick and straight, other than the bald spot at the back that he could usually ignore since he could not see it. He was a small man, standing just under five-foot-nine. His height had always been a disappointment, especially since his father had towered over the world. Six-foot-six his father had stood, and strong as an ox. Buddy had taken after his mother, a sparrow of a woman. It was hard to tell from whom he had gained his quiet nature, since both his parents had been tight with their words. But all his life he had wished he could have had at least a little bit more of his father's strength and height.

Buddy's father had come from the old country. That was how he had always referred to it. At the turn of the century, it was one forgotten corner of the Austro-Hungarian Empire. Then it was called Czechoslovakia for fewer than thirty years. After that the Nazis overran it and took all but the name. When Stalin assumed power he replaced one form of tyranny for another.

With democracy came independence, and the old country split in two.

Now the old country was Slovakia and the Czech Republic, and Buddy did not even know from which part his father's family had come. His father had almost never spoken of what he had left behind. His father had been nine when his own father, Buddy's grandfather, had pulled up the family and brought them to America. As far as Buddy's father had been concerned, it was America first and last. Whenever the old country had been mentioned in the news, Buddy's father had listened with a sort of bemused satisfaction, very glad in his silent way to be here and to be an American.

His father had been a handyman and carpenter and cabinetmaker. Buddy was the first of their family ever to graduate from college, the only occasion in Buddy's entire life when he saw his father cry. When Buddy had left for his new job at the then Aiden Bank, his father had been so proud he could have burst his shirt buttons. A picture of Buddy taken that first morning, dressed in his spanking new suit and tie, had stood on his parents' mantelpiece for as long as they had been alive.

"There is no indication whatsoever of any cardiac arrest." Dr. Hopper interrupted Buddy's musings as she shut the door behind her. She pulled the stethoscope from her pocket and fitted the earpieces into place. "Let's have another listen."

Buddy submitted to the quiet inspection, breathing as instructed. He was glad beyond words that his worst fear had proved to be groundless.

When she finally straightened, Jasmine went on. "I can't find a thing wrong with you."

"You don't sound very pleased about it."

"You say you've been having severe chest pains for the first time in your life. Generally this can be traced to some specific physiological change or new source of stress."

"I can't think of anything."

"Yet Molly says you've been having nightmares that leave you dripping wet and gasping for breath. Do the chest pains come with the dreams?"

"Yes." Able to be honest about it, now that it was not life threatening. His father had died from heart failure, keeled over three days before his sixtieth birthday. "Every night."

"You have had the same dream each night? For how long?"

"Just over two weeks." And each night the mysterious count-down continued. *Forty-one days*. But no need to mention that.

"You can put your shirt back on now. Can you tell me what the dream is about?"

"Ordinary things." Buddy hid his sudden discomfort by turn-ing and reaching for his shirt. He ducked his head to fasten the buttons. "I'm in the bank and then on the street downtown. Nothing that should scare me."

"Try to remember. Did anything out of the ordinary happen the first day? The day of your first nightmare?"

Buddy thought back. "Well, yes, but nothing that serious. The monthly business forecast arrived. The bank subscribes to it; all the bank's managers receive a copy."

"Bad news?"

"No, as a matter of fact it was all good." Too good. That had been his reaction. Buddy recalled it clearly. Strange how he could have forgotten that until now. But that had been his reac-tion the *instant* he had read the headlines.

Inflation was back under control, the statement had read. Interest rates were on the way back down. Employment figures were stable, factory orders in good shape, consumer confidence sound, housing starts up for the third month running. It looked to be a banner autumn for the stock market and a great final quarter to the year.

But Buddy's response had been entirely different. The paper had seemed alive in his hands. And despite the rosy forecast, he had felt a rising sense of dread. It had seemed as though barriers separating him from the future were being rolled back, until before him lay only bleakness and sorrow.

He looked up to find Jasmine Hopper watching him closely. This was one of the qualities that endeared Jasmine to her charges and made them friends as well as patients. She would stand and wait with them, working not just to treat the ailment but also to find the cause. "Something bad?"

"No. Well, yes. But not . . ." He stopped. There was no way he could put into words what he had felt that day.

Her eyes narrowed at his inability to continue. "Buddy, I could give you a prescription that will help you sleep. But I don't think that's what you want."

"No," he agreed, definite on that point.

"Do you have a psychiatrist you could speak to? I could suggest one if you like."

His mouth opened and closed a couple of times before he could manage, "I don't think that's necessary."

"What about one of our pastors? Somebody you can trust with your darkest secrets?"

"Yes."

"Something is trying to work its way out. That's my guess. Talking to a trusted professional is perhaps what you need to put all this behind you."

"I'll think about it."

"I want you to do more than think. I want you to act." She moved for the door. "And if the chest pains grow any worse or start appearing at other times, I want you to call me immediately."

"All right."

"For that matter, make an appointment to see me next week, regardless." She nodded and gave a brisk smile. "Remember me to Molly."

⊣| THREE |⊢

☐ When Buddy arrived home that evening, his older boy, Paul, was sitting at the kitchen table. Somehow his father's height and strength had managed to skip a generation, bounding straight over Buddy's head and landing in his son. Nobody had any idea where his son had obtained his blond looks, however. Paul looked like a giant Swede—hair almost white, skin reddened by twenty minutes in spring sunshine, eyes the color of an early morning sky.

Jack, his second boy, was stamped from Buddy's mold. He had the same small build, the same intent air, the same dark hair and eyes. Jack was a lawyer with one of the local firms, a member of the town council, and a quiet bastion of their community.

Paul was as gentle as he was big. Both Buddy's boys were. Their gentleness had been a source of great concern to Buddy when the boys had been younger. Buddy had pushed them as hard as he could manage, trying to instill in them a need to excel and to do the most with what they had.

"Hello, Son."

"What did the doctor say, Pop?"

"Clean bill of health." But Buddy's eyes were not on Paul. They were on his wife. The scar that began just below her left ear and spilled down her chin and disappeared into her high collar was red as a beet. This was a signal of strong emotion. Anger, happiness, sadness, distress, joy—it did not matter. Whatever Molly felt, if she felt it strongly, was displayed the length and breadth of her scar. Molly was so quiet that this was often his only signal that she had been hit hard by something while he had been away. And right now it was blazing as if lit by an internal fire. "Anything wrong?"

"No, not wrong." Paul had a glow of quiet satisfaction about him. He set his mug down. "Mom tells me the dreams are still bothering you."

"From time to time." Buddy kissed his wife and studied her gaze. He saw a gentle joy in her eyes. He sighed silently with relief. Whatever had her so worked up was good. "But my health is sound, and that's what matters."

Molly asked, "And your heart?"

"Fit as a fiddle, according to Jasmine." He accepted a mug and seated himself across from his son.

"That's good, Pop. Real good. We've been worried."

"No need." He took a sip and gave thanks for the umpteenth time for having been blessed with two quiet and well-behaved sons. He did not know how they would have coped with loud or rambunctious children. He and Molly were simply not made for confrontation and anger. In their twenty-nine years together, he did not think he had ever shouted at her. Not once. It was just not their way. "Dr. Hopper wants to have another look at me at the end of next week, but she thinks everything is all right."

"I'm glad you talked with her," Molly said. "But I'm still worried about those nightmares."

He nodded, not wanting to go into that. He was glad his son was there; he was glad that something else in the air kept them from dwelling on what he still did not understand. "What brings you over today?"

Paul and Molly exchanged a look that filled the room with shared anticipation. Paul turned back to him and announced, "We've decided to expand. We're going to set up a second store in the new shopping mall."

This should have been the best possible news. Buddy had been after Paul for years to start a second shoe store. But his son was naturally cautious. Running one successful shop had been enough. Even when Buddy had walked him through the statistics and the calculations, shown him how he was being overcharged for his product, and pointed out to him how fragile his outlook was with just one source of revenue, his son had held back. Until now.

Yet Buddy felt none of the pride and satisfaction that he would have expected. Instead he felt a sense of danger.

Molly prompted Buddy with her words. "Son, that's wonderful."

Paul fiddled self-consciously with his mug. "I'll be coming in tomorrow to meet with you, Pop. I just wanted to let you know in advance that we're going to do it like you said. Keep our savings in place and borrow what we need, so we can write off the interest."

The words wrapped around Buddy in a veil of dread. "I'm not sure that's a good idea."

Paul's eyes widened in surprise. "But why, Daddy?"

It was the first time Paul had called him Daddy in years. Why, indeed? Buddy could not explain it, even to himself. Yet the dread continued to build, like floodwater rising to surround him. "I'm not sure now is a good time to saddle yourself with more debt."

His words were met with absolute silence. Molly slipped into the chair beside her son. "You've been after him for years to start that second store."

"I know I have." He rubbed his palms together, wiping away the dampness. He asked Paul, "Could you put off the decision for a while?"

"I suppose so." Paul was watching him strangely. They both were. "For how long?"

Despite his strongest efforts to keep it at bay, the pressure continued to mount. Once more an unseen force seemed to push at him and to squeeze his mind and his heart so tightly he could scarcely draw breath. "Two months," he managed. His voice sounded weak to his own ears. "Wait two months."

Paul looked frustrated. "And then?"

The idea popped straight into his head and exploded with the force of a skyrocket. Buddy said, "I've decided to sell the ridgeline."

Both his son and his wife gaped at him. "What?"

"Tomorrow. Those developers were back again yesterday. They want to build a hotel."

"But, honey." Molly's voice sounded as weak as his own. "You've always said that was for our retirement."

The ridgeline was a strip of land Buddy had bought soon after his first son was born. The bank had offered their employees low-interest mortgages, which had been a relatively cheap way for the bank to ensure employee stability. Instead of using the money to buy a larger home, however, Buddy had purchased the ridgeline from an aging farmer. The land totaled almost forty acres and overlooked the town and the interstate. Every year or so, some developer approached him with another deal.

"It's time to sell, that's all. We'll still have the cash." Buddy kept his eyes on his son. It was easier than meeting Molly's troubled gaze. "Wait two months. If you still want to go ahead, I'll lend you the money interest free."

Molly asked quietly, "What's wrong, honey?"

He could not put her off any longer. And he owed Paul that much, dashing his son's hopes as he had. "Nothing I can put my finger on. Nothing I can give any name to. But I've had the feeling for more than two weeks now that something is going to happen. Something bad."

There. It was finally out in the open. Words to clothe the rising dread. "Something awful," he went on, "an economic downturn or cyclical correction. I know everything looks rosy right now. And I feel like a fool for being so worried. But I am."

Buddy studied each of their faces in turn. "I have the strongest feeling that we're headed into the worst recession any of us has ever experienced."

He sighed with sudden release. The act of speaking had eased the pressure as inexplicably as Paul's announcement had brought it on. He steeled himself for their criticism.

Yet the ensuing quiet held none of the condemnation Buddy had feared. In fact, his son's face seemed to clear up and relax. Even Molly's concern eased.

Paul said, "It makes sense, Pop."

"It certainly does," Molly agreed.

Both of the men looked at her in surprise. Molly dropped her gaze. "Oh, I don't know the first thing about economics, but you'd be surprised what people say to a quiet person. Maybe they think they're safe, that I don't understand or won't repeat what I hear. And they're right. But I do hear things, and what I hear I take in. There isn't a single woman in my Bible study who isn't worried about money. Not one."

"It sure is strange," Paul agreed. "People have good jobs; they're making good money. But everybody's afraid."

"They buy things they don't want," Molly continued in her quiet way. "They go into debt and hate themselves for it."

"As if they can't control their own actions," Paul added.

"Or they sense that something is happening and feel powerless to do anything," Molly agreed. "Running faster and faster after something they'll never have."

Buddy stared at his wife in absolute astonishment. "Of all the things I might have expected you to say, this would have been the last."

"People are frightened of tomorrow," Molly said.

"I am too," Paul confessed. "I've put it down to nerves over starting another store. Like you said, Pop, everything *seems* to be fine. But what my mind says and what my heart tells me are two very different things."

There was a moment's silence before Molly asked her husband, "Does this have anything to do with those nightmares of yours?"

"Yes," Buddy replied, and he realized he was also admitting it to himself. "But it's not just the dreams. There have been other things. In the office, and during my quiet times."

Molly's gaze was level, deep. "Has the Lord spoken to you?"

Hearing the words he had been afraid to think left Buddy floundering. He opened his mouth, closed it, and finally managed, "I'm not sure."

⊣| FOUR |⊢

Forty Days . . .

☐ The nightmare came again just before dawn. The dream was as bad as usual, the awakening as wrenching. Molly watched him rise, go to the bathroom, and return wearing fresh pajamas. This time she said nothing; she only lay her hand upon his shoulder as once more he settled into bed. But as Buddy drifted off to sleep again, he thought he heard a hint of murmured prayer.

The half-heard whispers remained with him through his shower and breakfast and prayer time. He heard them again on the way to work. They were there with him in the car, vague murmurs that were more than lingering tendrils of a bad dream. Yet try as he might, pray as he would, he could not seem to work it all out.

□

Upon entering the bank Thursday morning, Buddy felt every vestige of the dream and the uncertainty disappear, which was strange, since the nightmare's first scene was always in the bank's main foyer. Even so, the night's distress was pushed aside by what he saw as soon as he walked through the big main doors.

Aiden was a middling town abutting the steep hills lining Delaware's inner border. It was too far from the big cities of Washington, Philadelphia, and Baltimore to have ever known the explosive growth that gripped much of the surrounding regions. Buddy had never minded. He had grown up here and had never wanted to live anywhere else. He liked the quiet attractive little town just the way it was.

The bank where Buddy worked was almost one hundred fifty years old. Seventeen years ago, however, the Aiden Merchant Bank had been taken over. The Valenti Banking Group had swallowed many such small banks, allowing it to dominate local markets. At the time, Buddy had been the bank's assistant manager and had wondered for weeks and months if he was going to keep his job. But Buddy had earned many friends within the local market, people who made it clear to the newly imported branch manager that their business would leave with Buddy.

In time, the incoming managers recognized that Buddy was the genuine article, a local man with local savvy. They sweetened his paycheck, for other banks were also seeking to make inroads into communities like Aiden.

A year later, Buddy was offered a major promotion and the chance to take over loan operations at another branch in another small town, one where they were having trouble making contacts within the local business community. Buddy turned them down flat. Eighteen months later came another offer. This time, Buddy told them the only way he was leaving Aiden was in a pine box. They got the message and left well enough alone.

But the Valenti group had a strict policy that each promotion required a move. Every man or woman on the rise thus came to know different divisions and different branches. And equally important was the fact that a person who was shifted around did not put down deep roots. Their first loyalty remained to the bank and not the community—which was exactly why Buddy refused to move.

This was also why he was so enraged upon entering the bank. These people were more than citizens of his hometown. They were part of his extended family. And Buddy's first glance was enough to tell him that one of his group was in dire trouble.

He had been concerned from the outset about hiring such an attractive and vivacious woman for the job of teller. But bank teller jobs were some of the lowest paid in town, and when the job market was tight, it was not always possible to hire people with families and thus greater stability. This was exactly what Buddy wanted in anyone who was going to be handling the bank's money day in, day out.

But Sally had seemed a proper kind of young lady, despite her bubbly personality and good looks, and the public liked her. Some of their older clients waited until she was free so they could stand and flirt a bit. Buddy did not mind in the slightest, so long as the bank was not too busy. After all, these clients' money kept their bank in business. If they enjoyed chatting with a cute young teller, that was fine and good.

But it was not a client who was making the teller's giggles ring like chimes through the bank's quiet air. Leaning across the partition that separated Sally's station from the next was the bank's new manager, Thaddeus Dorsett.

Since the takeover by the Valenti Banking Group, Buddy had endured eleven branch managers. Eleven in seventeen years. But Thad Dorsett was the first one since Valenti had itself been acquired by the famous New York tycoon Nathan Jones Turner. Thad Dorsett was also the first manager Buddy had ever genuinely disliked.

Thad Dorsett was a trader, imported from the financial markets of Chicago, the first one Buddy had ever met face-to-face. Buddy knew the bank now had a policy of promoting managers up from the ranks of their traders. And on paper this made sense. After all, traders were now responsible for more than half the bank's total profit. Buddy tried not to let Thad's background affect his thinking, but it was very hard. Buddy held a strong aversion to traders and all they stood for.

In their first conversation that previous winter, Thad's gaze had lingered on the silver cross in Buddy's lapel. He had smirked a little with the corners of his mouth, as though seeing the cross had confirmed something Thad had either heard about or expected to find. Then he had said, "You know, I actually attended seminary."

Of all the things Buddy had expected to hear from the new branch manager, this was the last. "You did?"

"One semester. Never even took my finals. I did it for dear old Dad, who was a preacher. And my grandfather. And the one before that, for all I know. It was all I heard about when I was growing up. This family tradition." His smile was larger this time. "But after I got there, I decided I'd rather serve mammon than heaven."

Buddy had felt like he had just swallowed a mouthful of quinine.

Now he walked across the lobby's parquet floor, under the huge brass-and-smoked-glass chandelier, and through the little gate separating the bank's office area from the main chamber. His secretary, Lorraine, was already at her desk. Her face was clamped into a harsh line, which was very strange, as Lorraine had one of the sweetest natures Buddy had ever come across. But she was staring at Thad Dorsett as he hummed his conversation across the partition to where Sally was smiling and setting up for the day. And Buddy remembered four months earlier, when he had come in and found Lorraine weeping bitterly at her desk, while Thad Dorsett whistled and chatted with one employee after another, pretending that nothing was wrong and that he had not just broken the heart of Buddy's secretary and very good friend.

Buddy walked straight over to where Thad was standing and said, "Can I have a word with you?"

Thad was slow in turning. The movement was a silent warning that he was not in a mood to be disturbed. He had a lot of moves like this, tight looks and silent signals. The branch employees were frightened by this outsider and normally kept their distance. But Thad also possessed a remarkable magnetism. Thad's gaze finally came around, and he said coolly, "It can wait, Korda."

But Buddy did not let him turn back around. He put an emphasis to his words, one he had not used since his boys had reached manhood. "*Now,* Thad."

Buddy walked back to his office. Passing Lorraine's desk, he exchanged a glance. Her eyes still bore the pain and sadness of a woman betrayed. Buddy stiffened his resolve. Which was helpful, because Buddy was no good at confrontation. He hated it, in fact. He would go around the block backward to avoid an argument. Yet there he was, picking a quarrel with his own boss. Buddy stood by his desk and watched through the glass wall as Thad approached.

Buddy's office was in the corner of the bank, with two walls of waist-high oiled wood and then tall panes of glass rising to the ceiling. Only the manager's office was completely enclosed. Yet Buddy loved the openness of his office, loved the way he could observe the entire operation. The glass, which had been put in when the bank was built, had beveled edges with hand-carved vines and flowers rising up each side. Over the past century and a half, the panes had gradually begun to warp. As Thad approached, his appearance waxed and waned, like a colorful apparition that was not entirely genuine.

Thaddeus Dorsett was the picture of a modern-day buccaneer, and he told anyone willing to listen that he was wasting his life away in Aiden. He was twenty years younger than Buddy and on the bank's fast track. His hair was dark and so thick it bunched and waved even when tightly slicked back. His face was angled and strong. His eyes were such a light green that in the morning sun they appeared flecked with gold. Thad had learned to use them well, and even now he opened them in a parody of innocence. "You had something that couldn't wait?"

Buddy had seen that innocent look before. It was Thad's way of covering a fast-moving mind. Sunlight streamed through the back window and turned Thad's eyes the color of a big cat's.

"The Valenti Bank has a strict policy against fraternization between managers and staff."

"Fraternization, what a quaint word." He cast a wide-eyed gaze about the room. "It suits you, Korda."

"I want you to stop flirting with Sally, Thad. It's a dangerous sport, and it disrupts the bank's smooth running."

"My, my. Aren't we on our moral high horse today?" Thaddeus Dorsett stepped closer, trying to use his superior height to intimidate. "In case you haven't noticed, Korda, you're speaking to your boss."

Buddy resisted the urge to step back. "If you don't stop this now, I'm going to report the matter to the head office."

"Report what?" Thad sneered. "That I was taking time before the bank opened to be nice to our newest employee?"

"I wasn't planning to report Sally," Buddy replied. "And I would substantiate my report with another one from Lorraine."

Like a veil dropping silently to the floor, Thad's round-eyed innocence slipped away. In its place rose a silent rage. Thad took another step closer, until Buddy could smell the coffee on his breath. His gaze was feral, his tone furious. "That's just the kind of spiteful attitude I'd expect from a backwater imbecile like you, Korda."

Buddy held to his course but could not keep the quaver from his voice. "Lorraine approached me last week about lodging a complaint, and I said—"

"I don't care what you've been sermonizing to your secretary." Thad wheeled about, stalked to the door, and stopped long enough to throw back, "For your information, Korda, Lorraine was chasing me."

Thad slammed the door hard enough to make the panes rattle. Buddy said to the empty room, "That's a lie. I was watching, you know." Then his strength left him, and he slumped into his chair. He hated confrontations. He really did.

A soft knock brought his head back up. Lorraine entered, her face wreathed in concern. "Would you like a cup of coffee?"

"Not right now, thank you." He glanced at his watch and rose to his feet. "I've got an appointment with some developers at their offices."

As he passed by Lorraine to reenter the main chamber, she patted his arm. "You did the right thing."

"I hope so," he sighed.

"Believe me, you did."

Something in her tone halted Buddy. He looked at his secretary and saw wounds that still had not healed. Lorraine went on, "He will do anything and say anything to get what he wants. Anything at all."

"I'm very sorry," Buddy said quietly.

"You know what they say." Her mouth twisted in a sad smile. "Big-city ways and small-town girls are a terrible mix."

□

Buddy walked back through the bank and entered the day's gathering heat. The developers' offices were about two blocks away. When he had called that morning from home to say he was ready to sell the ridgeline, the developer had instantly replied that he would prepare the contract for him to sign. And the check. It was the smoothest real estate transaction Buddy had ever heard of. Odd how something like this could seem so strange and yet so right at the same time. As though his actions were guided by something far greater than himself.

As he crossed the street, the nightmares that were behind his decision to sell the ridgeline struck him with the sunlight. The only words that had been clearly audible returned to him, as though the whispers had penetrated the day and his wakened state. *Forty days.*

Buddy clasped his hand over his heart and hurried onward. He could not help but wonder how he had remained perfectly all right through such a confrontation with his boss yet now was being attacked by a dream.

☐

"Don't even think about it," the voice on the other end of the phone commanded. "Put it out of your head."

Thad Dorsett stared out his sunlit window. "But Keith—"

"I'm telling you to forget it. Have you spoken about it with anyone else?"

"Not yet." The harsh tone confused him. Keith Wilkes was Thad Dorsett's chief sponsor within the branch. He was also senior vice president and the man who had personally hired Thad away from Chicago Mercantile. "Why?"

"Because you might as well shoot yourself in the foot as complain about Buddy Korda. Do you know how many branch managers he has ushered through since the original takeover?"

"Keith, the guy is so far over the hill he's sunk in the valley on the other side."

"Eleven. Eleven branch managers who are now senior executives. One of whom is now the bank's executive vice president, and another is a member of the board. All of them remember their time with Buddy as a real training ground. Do you hear what I'm saying? This guy may be as aggressive as a bath towel and a throwback to the last century, but he is also very well connected."

Thad had not expected this. "Keith, you don't have to work with the guy every day. He's a total waste of time."

"And I'm telling you that complaints like this will earn you nothing but enemies! Do you have any idea how hard I had to fight to get you this post?" Keith had to take a moment to get his impatience back under control. "We've been through this how many times? It's bank policy that every senior executive has to spend at least a year in a local branch. Buddy's branch has the lowest level of bad debts and the highest return on dollars spent. Staff turnover is low, morale is high, and business is growing."

"It's also like living in a crypt. This place has all the life of a funeral parlor."

"Then have yourself a few weekend trips to New York. I'm telling you, bank execs take a close look at your performance at the branch level. And being on Buddy's team is almost a guarantee of success."

"It's not Buddy's team, it's *mine*. And I want to fire the guy."

Keith's tone turned razor sharp. "You do that and the only way you'll restart your career will be through reincarnation."

"Can you at least shorten my assignment here?"

"I doubt it, but I'll see. In the meantime, put up with the guy. Laugh at his small-town ways. Everybody else does. But don't complain. It's suicide, I'm telling you."

Thad Dorsett kept his calm until the phone was back in place. Then he allowed his rage to build, a flood that turned his vision red. He hated being told what to do. Hated even more having his plans thwarted, especially by some small-town wimp in a suit straight from the fifties. Buddy Korda, what a name. With his starched shirt and dark tie, he looked like an undertaker and talked like a pallbearer. Never raised his voice. Never spoke back to him, not once, until this morning.

Thad was so angry he shook. A little fun never hurt anybody, and that's all he was after with these small-town girls. A little fun. Something to spice up the time until he could be up and out of here.

Thad bundled up the page he had been scribbling on, clenching it tighter and tighter until it was a solid ball the size of his thumb and threw it at the trash can. Nobody got in his way. Nobody. Especially not some assistant manager in Podunk, Delaware. He was trapped in a town nobody ever visited, much less called home. If he had known it was the bank's plan to stick him out here in the boonies for a year he would never have taken the job. A *year*.

Thad bounced from his chair and began stalking the floor. There had to be something he could do, someone who would understand. He stopped, staring sightlessly at the window. Perhaps he should contact Nathan Jones Turner's office directly. Spell it out. Thad was a trader, used to a trader's life. Cut him a break or risk losing one of their fast-track managers. Perhaps even talk to a couple of headhunters beforehand, make sure word got back to headquarters in New York. Something definitely had to happen. He was suffocating in this place.

⊣| FIVE |⊢

☐ Buddy was so tired that evening he could scarcely finish dinner. When Molly shooed him away from the table and ordered him to bed he did not object, not even when he saw the clock on the mantel read seven-thirty.

Buddy stopped to lean on the wall twice as he climbed the stairs. He undressed in a stupor. The doctor's visit, the quarrel with Thad, the daily bank stresses and strains, two and a half weeks of bad dreams and not enough sleep, the talk with his family and having his concerns finally out in the open—all the recent strains left him exhausted. He was asleep before his head hit the pillow.

There was no escaping the dream. Not this time. He was too tired. There was no normal drifting into the dream either. Buddy fell like a stone.

And yet, and yet. The dream was different this time. Very different. Sharper. More carefully defined. So crystal clear it did not seem like a dream. His every sense was heightened above the norm.

Not only that. The dream was no longer a nightmare. How he could be so certain the instant it began, he did not know. But it was not a nightmare anymore. At least, not a nightmare for him.

Buddy stood in the bank's central hall. Just like every other entry into the dream, he did a slow sweep of the grand old chamber. Only this time the scene was far more vivid. Dust motes danced lazy circles in the sunlight streaming through the top of the side windows. The blinds on the bottom halves of the tall windows were closed, as they always were until about a half hour before opening time.

Old Carl, the bank's morning guard, leaned against the wall just inside the main doors. He was no longer needed, what with the bank's modern security system. But Buddy had insisted that Carl be kept on, a bastion of the service and the heritage the bank stood for. In his dream Buddy raised his hand in a half wave but was not surprised when Carl did not respond.

What did surprise him, however, was the fact that Carl did not move at the sound of weeping. Generally he was on the spot whenever someone needed assistance, be it customer or clerk. But Carl just stood there, staring into space with a bemused expression, bemused and so shaken that his features made him look even more aged than he already was. His cap was pushed back on his balding head, and he stared across the chamber at nothing.

Still the weeping went on. Buddy made a gradual revolution. Everything seemed to be in slow motion, as though an invisible hand were guiding him, silently urging him to take everything in deep.

He saw that the wall clock showed ten minutes until opening time. Normally the venetian blinds would have been opened on all the windows by then. Yet the bank remained partly shrouded in shadows, while light through the windows' top half-circles sent beams of brilliance lancing across the room.

This was as far as he had ever continued in the dream. By this point, the sense of pressure had squeezed him from sleep like a seed shot out between thumb and forefinger. That tension was still there, but it was no longer directed at him. Which was very strange, for he could now sense a wrath behind the pressure.

His turning continued until the back half of the bank came into view. Lorraine sat at her desk, her eyes pressed into a handkerchief, her shoulders shaking hard. Buddy remained unmoved by this sight. Normally he would have rushed over and demanded to know what was the matter. Now he only continued to turn. And he realized that it was not only Lorraine who cried. Every one of the tellers was weeping.

The bank director's door was wide open. No one was inside. Nor was anyone in Buddy's office, which gave him a brief moment of relief. Even from within this protective cocoon, he would not have wanted to come face-to-face with himself in a dream, especially if he was to see himself crying. For somehow he knew a tragedy had struck. Not a dream affliction. Something real. Some cataclysmic event had buffeted the bank, and it was a genuine comfort not to find himself there sobbing with the others. It was very selfish. But it was also very true.

The slow circle continued until he faced back toward the bank's main doors just in time to hear the clock strike nine.

Carl pulled himself together enough to fumble with the lock. Buddy wanted to remind them to open the blinds and get ready for business, but he could not speak. He could only watch as the locks were released and the door slammed back, sending Carl sprawling onto the floor. The old man did not move. He remained where he was as a flood of humanity streamed inside.

Shouting, screaming, pushing, fighting, and clawing toward the teller windows. Hundreds and hundreds of people. People Buddy had known all his life, their faces distorted until they were strangers. Foreigners who were gripped by universal terror. They pounded fists upon the counter and teller windows, waved checkbooks and canes and papers in the air, screamed words that were lost in the crush as still more people pressed through the doors.

Buddy wanted to stay. He wanted to help, to find some way to calm them. He had never felt so horrified in his entire life. And yet, and yet. It was no surprise. Somehow he had sensed this from the very beginning. As though the instant the very first nightmare had attacked him, he had known this was what was behind it all.

Disaster.

But the invisible hand did not allow him to linger. Instead, he rose and floated over the crowd, passing through the tall main doors. Over the heads of those still fighting to get inside, across the street filled with even more people, beyond those who stood weeping and watching on the opposite sidewalk. On into the heart of his little town.

Aiden was as alien as its citizens. Gone was the cozy atmo-
sphere he had known since childhood. Vanished was the feeling
that here the world was a slower, kinder place. In its stead was
an impression of *burden*.

The pressure was clearer because it was directed away from
him. The force seemed to begin directly behind him, shooting
out over his shoulders and his head, filling the world with wrath.
Yet it was more than anger. It was an all-powerful force, filled
with unimaginable sorrow. A strength so overwhelming nothing
could stand in its path. Wrath and sorrow. Determination and
vengeance. And it was here. In Aiden.

The roads were filled with cars that had simply stopped, as
though the drivers had vanished and the cars had continued until
something impeded their progress. Their doors were open and
flapping in the hot autumn breeze. People clustered here and
there, or moved aimlessly. In and out of doorways, up and down
the sidewalks and the streets. Or they sat head-in-hand on the
curb. Even from this height Buddy could see they were weeping.

□

"Buddy? Honey?"

He rose to a seated position and swung his legs to the floor.
"It's all right."

In the bed beside him, Molly lifted herself on one arm. "Sweet-
heart, are you crying?"

He rose and shuffled toward the bathroom, wiping his streaming eyes with his sleeve. "It's all right, Molly. Go back to sleep."

He closed the door but did not turn on the light. He leaned
on the wall next to the sink. There was enough light from the
window to show his outline in the mirror. The clock on the shelf

glowed, but his eyes were still too blurred to read the time. It did not matter.

He turned on the faucet and washed his face. There was no need to undress, for there had been no sweats with this dream. But it had not been a dream. Buddy did not know how he could be so certain about something like that. But he knew. This was no dream. It was a message.

The whisper came then, no longer simply a memory from the vanished dream. He heard the words so clearly they might as well have been spoken aloud. *Thirty-nine days*.

As he dried his face he knew what he had told his wife was totally, utterly wrong. Things were not all right. They never would be again.

⊣ SIX ⊢

Thirty-Nine Days . . .

☐ The limousine turned up Broadway and halted once more in midtown Manhattan traffic. Nathan Jones Turner fumed to his assistant, "The mayor has one. So does the governor. I'm more powerful than either one. If they don't think so, I'll be happy to put on a little demonstration."

"Sir, I've spoken to both their personal aides. There's some city ordinance that outlaws police motorcades for anyone except visiting politicians and dignitaries."

"They don't think I'm a dignitary? They think somebody from the other side of the Atlantic's got more clout than me? I'll show them just how much clout I've got if they keep me sitting here." He leaned forward and shouted through the half-open portal, "Get the lead out! You think I pay you to keep me sitting still?"

"I'm doing the best I can, Mr. Turner."

"It's not good enough!" He pounded on the armrest hard enough to make his assistant wince. "If you can't find a way to get me there faster, I'll find someone who can!"

To the driver's immense relief, an ambulance chose that moment to sweep around the corner, turning on both lights and siren. The driver eased over just far enough to permit the ambulance passage, then swept back inches from the rear bumper, cutting off a taxi trying for the coveted spot. He sailed down the block, the ambulance now forging a path for them both.

Nathan Jones Turner settled back. "That's better. Nothing I hate worse than sitting still."

"Yes, sir," the assistant agreed, pushing forward the file he held in his hands. "If you'll take a look at this—"

"Sitting still is for peons. You call the governor and you tell him that right to his face. Tell him if he's going to try to make Nathan Jones Turner sit still, he'll find somebody else sitting in his chair. You tell him that."

"Yes, Mr. Turner. Sir, you said you wanted to study the closing positions in Tokyo."

"I've read them already. Put that thing away." He drummed his fingers on the window. "You say they both refused me a police escort?"

"Point-blank, sir."

"Put them down for my box at the next Jets game. I'll have a word with them personally."

"Yes, sir. That'll be the season opener next week." To sit in the private box of Nathan Jones Turner, especially when the Jets finally had a chance to return to the Super Bowl, was one of the most coveted invitations in all New York. Turner was the team's largest shareholder, and he treated it like a personal fiefdom.

Nathan Jones Turner, the son of a middling Hollywood movie producer, had taken an inheritance of some ten million dollars and turned it into one of the largest privately held fortunes in America's history. *Forbes* magazine was consistently wrong in judging his wealth, but last year had accurately placed his stock and bond holdings *alone* at over a billion dollars. Besides that, he owned a hotel chain, a Wall Street brokerage firm, some Manhattan real estate. And the Valenti Bank.

His only two hobbies were his father's old movie production company and the New York Jets. He had been married five times to four different women and had fathered seven children, all of whom he had long since disowned. He was seventy-one years old and worked an eighteen-hour day.

He was pompous, rude, and tremendously overbearing. He could be courtly, however, when it suited him. He also possessed the ability to focus on a person with a force that people claimed was physically palpable. When he liked an idea he adopted it as an original thought. He managed to hold on to talent because he paid better than anyone else, but in return he expected his staff to demonstrate slavelike devotion. Dissent was an unforgivable error. The only person allowed to have a temper around Nathan Jones Turner was Nathan Jones Turner.

Most of his time he spent working from the Turner farm in Connecticut. Located just forty miles from Manhattan, the farm was a six-hundred-eighty-acre spread with almost a mile of coveted private beach.

But today's meeting required his personal presence. Nobody tried to transport the senior staff of a brokerage house away from Wall Street while the market was in session. Not even Nathan Jones Turner.

The Turner Building anchored the corner of Wall Street and Broadway. It had been built in the twenties, redolent of art-deco foppery, and was the second highest building in that part of town. Only the Chrysler Building was higher. Turner would have preferred to buy the Chrysler Building, but it wasn't for sale, and it didn't stand on Wall Street. He responded by pretending the Chrysler Building did not exist.

Greed might have lost much of its eighties allure elsewhere, but not on Wall Street. In today's financial markets, an investor could win or lose more quickly than a bettor at any racetrack or casino—and lose far more. This was the mad world of modern money, where billions changed hands every hour, and where gambling had become the norm.

This was the real reason Turner came here at all—to feel close to the action, to drink the energy, to get a sense of the market's pulse. It was as close as Nathan Jones Turner ever came to taking any drug. He neither smoked nor drank and seldom took anything stronger than an aspirin. When he felt the need for a fix, something to push him to a higher limit, he wallowed in the thrill of chasing money. And the power of controlling its course.

Before the limo pulled to a halt, three senior executives scurried out to welcome Turner. He ignored their greetings and marched straight to the elevators.

Nathan Jones Turner hated elevators. He managed to ride in silence by gritting his teeth and clenching his fists. His staff had long since learned that anything said during an elevator ride was not heard. So the ride was made in absolute silence. The one nice thing about riding with Nathan Jones Turner was that the elevator halted for nobody. The security guard responsible for the bank of elevators was on notice that if an elevator carrying Nathan Jones Turner stopped on any floor except the one where he was getting off, the guard was out of a job.

They finally stopped on the sixtieth floor and headed for the double doors at the foyer's far end. The secretary stationed there merely stood and smiled a nervous welcome as Turner and his entourage entered the lair of Larry Fleiss.

Larry Fleiss was one of the world's most successful traders. Which was why Nathan Jones Turner willingly paid him almost six million dollars in annual salary and double that in bonus. He was certainly nothing much to look at, and his personality was hardly any better.

He looked like a bespectacled slug, clad in a wrinkled white shirt and beltless trousers. He remained safely ensconced behind his huge U-shaped desk, not even rising for Nathan Jones Turner himself. Instead he glanced over, waved the entourage in, then turned back to his monitors. Someone on the speakerphone was shouting, "It hasn't changed positions since I was in your office."

"Yeah, well." Fleiss gave a laconic shrug. "You had the chance to say no before we got started."

Fleiss hit the switch and set down the coffee mug, his eyes tracking the group as they seated themselves. "How's it going, Mr. T.?"

"You tell me." Nathan Jones Turner tolerated such ill manners from no one but Fleiss. It was one of the prices he paid to keep the man behind the powerboard. That was Fleiss's name for his desk. The powerboard controlled the flow of the bank's and Turner's own money every day. Fleiss was rumored to spend more time at his desk than even Turner himself.

"Market's nervous this morning. Needs a tweak." Fleiss had the hoarse voice of an adrenaline junkie. His gaze constantly shifted back and forth, from Turner's face to the scrolling blue screen set in his side panel. The front of the blond-wood desk was bare save for a coffeemaker, two mugs, a pitcher of fresh cream, and an empty leather blotter. The desk's two long extensions, however, looked like imports from a flight control tower. They contained seventeen television screens, six phones with multiple lines, two computers, and a constantly scrolling news service. "Given a strong kick it could go either way."

"That's the same thing you told me last week."

"Nothing's changed, Mr. T. Everybody seems to be waiting for someone to tell them which way to jump."

Instead of waiting respectfully for Turner to respond, Fleiss punched a speed-dial number and demanded, "Anything happening post ten o'clock with your stuff?"

"No, looks like people have been kicked around too much." The voice on the other end shared Larry Fleiss's dislike for small talk. "The only sure bet is yen. It keeps falling like a stone."

Nathan Jones Turner kept his inscrutable mask intact. But inwardly he tasted bile.

Hastily Fleiss clicked off and tried to cover. "Problematic. Real problematic. People are just waiting for somebody to point out a direction."

"Is that—" Turner started but changed his mind. He turned to the others encircling him. "Leave us."

When the pair were alone, Turner went on. "Is that what's behind our own problems?"

"Partly. It's gotten worse since last week."

"I'm well aware of that," Turner snapped.

A tic surfaced under one eye. "Worse even since yesterday. The currency market's moving directly against us."

"Then get out."

"I've covered us as best I can. But the fact is, we're exposed."

"How much?"

"Down another eighty mil."

"*What?*" Turner half rose from his seat. "Since yesterday?"

"It's going to get worse before it gets better," Fleiss said. "Not much, but some."

"I thought you said we were covered."

"I've done all I can. If we got out now, we'd have to drop another thirty, maybe forty, before we could walk away. Any sale of that size would catch the market's attention. So what I did, I matched our sells with buys. Our floor is now set at twenty mil below where we are now."

"But if you've set a floor," Turner said, hating the sense of not having an adversary he could face and destroy, "that means we've set a ceiling as well, doesn't it?"

Fleiss's flabby shoulders shrugged once. "Best I could do. To stay uncovered is too risky. To cover means to cut off our upward chances, unless you want me to start all over and buy—"

"No." Turner resisted the urge to rise and throw his chair through the window, watch it fall upon unsuspecting heads sixty floors below. "What about the analyst who pushed us into this rotten mess?"

"It was an honest mistake. She's my best trader."

"Not anymore." Snarling the words, wishing he could destroy this worm as well, knowing he couldn't afford it. Especially not now. But he knew this analyst-trader was Fleiss's protégé. The one good thing to come from all this was finally having a reason to get rid of that woman. She had remained a barrier between Turner's spies and Fleiss. Turner hated the fact that he could not observe Fleiss's every move, observe and learn. Fleiss was a lone wolf, operating in solitary secrecy. The woman had been Fleiss's fire wall, keeping everyone else at arm's length. At least now Turner had a chance to move in someone who would report on Fleiss's tactics. "She's history."

A flicker of defiance, then a shrug of acceptance. "No problem."

"There better not be. I don't just want her fired. I want her destroyed." Good. Fleiss understood how close he was to the dagger himself. "I want you to make sure she can't get a job as dogcatcher in this town."

"You got it."

Turner took a breath, glad he had ordered the others to leave the room. "So what is our total exposure?"

"From this trade or overall?"

He gritted his teeth. The question burned like acid. "Overall."

It was Fleiss's turn to hesitate. A trace of fear appeared in those dead eyes, then, "Almost a quarter."

Two hundred fifty million dollars. A year's profit from all his nonfinancial operations lost in the space of one week. Turner rose and walked to the window. An unacceptable loss at an impossible time.

Until this present deal, Turner had never invested his own money into the futures markets. He was content to act as go-between, hiring the traders and taking a rake-off from every transaction. Turner saw himself as the shopkeeper who had followed the miners to the gold rush of the last century. He was the one who accepted their claims when the cash ran low. He was the man who stood on the front porch and watched them whoop and scream as they tumbled off the boat, staking money that burned holes in their pockets. He was the one who sold them everything they needed and turned a handsome profit at the same time. Then he watched them stumble back in after the money was gone, the claim had paid out, and they were down to their claim papers and their tools. He bought those as well, stowing them away for the next fool to take off his hands, taking his share coming and going, staying safely out of the fray.

Until now.

Turner rapped his knuckles on the glass, staring out at a fog-shrouded morning. The problem was the market, not him. He had stood by and watched traders turn fifty thousand into a million dollars, a half million into twenty, a million into serious money. The market was skyrocketing and people were making money hand over fist. Suddenly his own safe percentage had seemed too small.

Five weeks earlier, a luxury hotel chain had come up for grabs. He had always wanted to own a nationwide chain of first-class hotels. But the hotel market was booming like everything else, and it was a seller's market. The owners had stated that all bids would be cash only. No stock trades, no options, no bank paper. Cash.

The problem was, all of Turner's money was tied up in the other acquisitions. The only cash he had on the books was property of the Valenti Bank. And because it was a bank, its cash reserves were capped by federal law. He couldn't just dip into them.

He made a fist, wishing he could grind those bureaucrats into dust. Federal regulations on banking practices hung like a noose around his neck. "How are the pension funds?"

Larry Fleiss cleared his throat. "I'm not sure we should go that route again."

"Don't tell me the obvious." Turner kept his tone casual. "I want to know their status."

"Stable. No alarms raised."

"Good." Those pension funds were why he had acquired the Valenti Bank in the first place. Valenti was repository for seven of the largest corporate pension funds in the east. Like the big insurance groups, pension funds tended to spread their capital among a select group of investors. They were restricted to blue-chip investments and were left more or less alone. Pension funds sought security, not explosive growth. As long as the quarterly balance report showed steady returns, expectations were satisfied.

He had milked the pension funds for the cash required to buy the hotels. Strictly illegal, but that only mattered if he was caught. It was a temporary switch, or should have been.

Fleiss had come up with the plan of actually taking out *twice* what had been required. Half to pay the 50 percent down payment for the hotels. The other half for what should have been a surefire investment in futures options. Japanese yen, Fleiss's protégé had urged, it was time for a major upswing. A quick in and out, 100 percent profit in ten days was the prediction. Enough to slip the entire amount back into the pension fund and have the hotels added to his real estate portfolio. Everybody wins. Or they should have.

Turner walked back over and seated himself. He could not keep the sigh from escaping. "Whoever would have thought that the yen would do such a nosedive."

"If it's any consolation," Fleiss offered, "you've got the best of company. Word is that people took a bath up and down the Street."

"I didn't get where I am today being part of the herd," he snapped. "All right. Here's what I want you to do. Take out the same again."

Fleiss could not hide his astonishment. "Another three hundred million?"

"You hid it once, you can do it again." Masking his nervousness with customary harshness. "Only this time, you're going to find me a sure thing."

"Right." Fleiss resumed his customary stillness, watching and listening. "Whatever you say."

"What I *say* is this," Turner snarled, leaning across the desk. "You had better not let me down a second time. Do I make myself perfectly clear on that point?"

SEVEN

Thirty-Eight Days . . .

☐ Saturday morning, when Buddy told Molly that he wanted to spend his day in prayer and fasting, she did not object. Even so, he felt a need to explain. "I feel that the Lord has been close by. I know that may sound strange, what with the strain of the past couple of weeks. But that's how it feels. Now, anyway."

"I don't think it sounds strange." She was going to Bible study, dressed in her navy blouse with the high, frilly collar and her grandmother's cameo fastened at the neck. A light dusting of powder covered the worst of her scar not hidden beneath the blouse. "I'm glad you're doing it."

"You are?"

"It is a good thing to draw near to the Lord in confusing times. I'm glad to hear you say you feel like he's been close by. You need him right now."

He nodded agreement. "It's more than a feeling, Molly."

She did not ask what he meant; she did not pry. It was not her way. She simply said, "I'm glad."

When she was off and the house was quiet, he shut himself in the den. There was no need to ask to be left undisturbed. A closed door to the den meant he was to be left alone.

The den was a long room that ran the length of the house next to the garage. Elm wainscoting ran around three walls, a Christmas gift from his father. There was a big picture window looking out over the backyard. Buddy's desk was situated so that he could sit and watch birds flit from the feeder to the birdbath. It was where he did his morning Bible readings.

But today, when he sat down and picked up his Bible, the chair did not seem right, not fitting, in a strange sort of way, as though it had grown uncomfortable.

Buddy thought he understood. He slid down to his knees, and instantly the discomfort vanished. He pulled over the Bible, propped it on the seat of the chair, and read whatever caught his attention. He shut his eyes, prayed a little, but there was no sense of having much to say. He did not feel that he was there to talk to God. Rather, he felt that he was there to listen.

He settled on the Psalms and found a rhythm in reading a passage then shutting his eyes and letting the words sink in deep. Whenever his knees grew tired he stood up and walked around, carrying the Bible with him, stopping whenever he felt it was time to turn back to the Lord.

The hours passed. The outdoor Saturday noises dimmed, the birdsong and the dogs and the children and the lawn mowers. Now and then the phone rang, but Buddy felt no need to answer it.

Around midday his attention began to wane. He was down on his knees at the time, and it seemed the most natural thing in the world to stretch out on the rug and let the drowsiness sweep up and over him.

When he awoke the shadows were beginning to lengthen across the backyard. He felt mildly hungry, especially since he hadn't fasted in years, but not too uncomfortable. He went back to his knees, rubbed the sleep from his eyes, and reached over to reopen his Bible.

An authority seemed to descend upon him and the room and the day and the world. One that had been waiting just beyond his field of awareness, waiting for him to open his eyes and return to the position of prayer. One that was so strong the afternoon sunlight dimmed to insignificance.

The power was absolute, so strong that it could move with complete gentleness, speak in utter silence, and still dominate his being. In fact, had the power not been silent, Buddy knew with utter certainty that it would have shattered his mind.

He did not know how it was possible for silence to communicate in words. Nor did it matter. There was no room for objective questions. In that moment the silence spoke to him, and he heard with faultless clarity.

It is coming.

Buddy could not control his reaction. Sobs wrenched his body. Every dark shadow was illuminated, every failing, every mistake, every sin. All that he had not done, all that he had done for any motive but the purest. His whole life, his entire being, was revealed with perfect clarity. He was shamed to weeping submission.

At the same time, the power of Christ's sacrifice was incandescent. So far had his sins been separated from his eternal forgiveness that the Spirit saw them not. As far as the east is from the west, that was the distance separating his imperfections from the perfect One.

It is coming.

The sobs wrenched him still. He could not help it. The communication was planted within his mind and soul along with an absolute sadness. An immutable determination. Buddy had no doubt that the horror he had seen in his dream was indeed coming. He was totally convinced. It was indeed coming.

He raised his tear-streaked face to the unseen ceiling, and whispered, "When?"

Thirty-eight days.

He moaned aloud. The pronouncement was as powerful as the pounding of a funeral bell. Hardly more than a month. It was no time at all. "How long will it last?"

Seven years.

He clutched his chest, not in pain, but terror. Seven years of famine. Seven years of devastation. Seven years of need.

You must warn them.

"Who?" He could only manage a croaking sound, but he had no doubt that he was heard. He was not speaking aloud for the Spirit, but rather because the pressure required release. "Whom do I tell?"

All who will listen.

He almost cried the words, "What do I say?"

But there was no reply. Not this time. Instead the Presence began to recede, and with it the sense of overburdening sorrow. Buddy was instantly on his feet, aching with the absence of what was now disappearing. He raised his voice and shouted out the back window, "But why *me*?"

The response was a whisper, certain and steady and commanding.

All who will listen.

⊣| EIGHT |⊢

Thirty-Seven Days . . .

☐ As usual, Buddy arrived at church a half hour before the first Sunday service. He was both deacon and usher, and the group liked to gather for a little prayer time before the day began. Afterward he accepted his sheaf of bulletins and stationed himself by the side doors. This was as public a profession of faith as Buddy had ever cared to make—smiling and greeting the people, trying to make them feel welcome, having a friendly word for every newcomer.

Only today his smile was a little strained, his greeting not as heartfelt as usual. Each passing face seemed a silent accusation. Should he tell this one? And if so, how? Surely God hadn't chosen a man as shy and reserved as he was to stand up in front of the entire congregation.

"Buddy, how are you this morning?"

"Hello, Clarke. Fine, fine." Clarke Owen was the church's assistant pastor and a friend. When the old preacher had retired, they had passed over Clarke and offered the pastorship to a dynamic young man. Attendance and membership had rocketed as a result, but Buddy still preferred the quieter ways of the older man.

"No, you're not and don't fib on a Sunday." Molly stepped lightly up the stairs, halting next to Clarke. "Good morning, Pastor Owen."

"You look pretty as a picture this morning, Molly."

Molly blushed crimson. One hand reached up to hide the scar rising from her high starched-crinoline collar. But she forced her hand back down and clenched her purse. She turned to Buddy. "You need to talk with him."

Clarke stepped aside to allow people through the doors, then returned to say, "Why don't you come by my office after the service, Buddy? We'll have us a little chat."

□

Even before Buddy had settled in his seat, Clarke Owen asked, "Now what's this I hear from Molly about nightmares?"

"I've sure been having them." The church office on a Sunday after services was a good place for sharing confidences. Outside Clarke's closed door were the sounds of people hurrying off, sounds gradually replaced by the stillness of a big empty place. "Every night for more than two weeks."

"Do you want to tell me about it?"

Clarke was the perfect man to discuss this with, and Molly was a gem for having paved the way. He was a graying man in his early sixties, far too mild-mannered to have ever made a dynamic sermonizer. Yet he was adored by the parishioners, the one they always turned to in times of stress and strain. Clarke was a steady listener who knew the value of an open heart.

Even so, Buddy did not answer him directly. "What would you say if I told you I thought maybe God was giving me a message?"

Clarke leaned back and eyed him over steepled fingers. "Is that what you think?"

"I don't know." The calm was a comfort to his soul. Here he could be honest, and honesty was what was called for. "Well, yes. Yes, I think He is."

"Buddy, I've known you for how long, thirty years? You've been a deacon for most of that time. You've seen us through two building programs, loaned us the money, looked after our accounts, done just about anything we've asked you to. You never look for thanks; you never ask for the limelight. You are one of the most selfless servants I have ever had the honor of knowing."

Buddy looked askance at the pastor. This was the last thing he had expected to hear. "Clarke—"

"Hang on a second. You should know by now never to stop a pastor in mid-sermon. Now then. I know you to be a good husband and father. You are also known throughout the town as someone to approach with a financial problem. Half the houses in these parts are owned through mortgages you have personally written. You have the ability to help people see what they can and can't afford, and you do it without offending them or making them feel that you're prying or trying to take advantage. You're the only banker I've ever met who counsels people *away* from debt if they can possibly help it." Clarke allowed a small smile to break through. "Have I forgotten anything?"

"I feel like you've been talking about somebody else," Buddy replied. "Somebody I just wish I was."

"Natural modesty is a fine trait, so long as it doesn't keep you from being all you can be." Pastor Owen paused a moment and then finished, "Or all the Lord wants you to be."

Buddy stared at his old friend. "Does that mean you believe me?"

"I haven't heard what you think you've heard. But I have to admit that my natural inclination would be to say yes. If Buddy Korda tells me that the Lord has given him a message, and if the message stands up to scriptural inspection, I'd be inclined to accept it as truth."

Buddy found the same question welling up that had remained unanswered the day before in his den. "But why *me*?"

"Why *not* you?"

"Because I don't like people noticing me." The mere thought of it was enough to make his hands damp. He wiped his palms down the legs of his trousers and went on. "I'm a nobody, Clarke. I'm a second-rate bank clerk in a small town midway to nowhere. I don't know the first thing about talking to people."

"Ah. Now we're getting somewhere." Pastor Owen reached to the desk for his Bible. "We're really facing two parts to your question. The first part is why would the Lord choose you to receive a message from on high. The second is why would He want you to pass it on."

"I guess that's it." Relief was so strong it made his eyes burn. Not only was he dealing with a solid man of the church who believed him, or at least was willing to, but here was also someone who had the ability to put things into perspective. "That's it exactly."

"Fine." He handed Buddy the open Book, pointed to the bottom of one column. Start right there, First Corinthians, chapter twelve, verse four."

Buddy found his place and read aloud. "'There are diversities of gifts, but the same Spirit. There are differences of ministries, but the same Lord. And there are diversities of activities, but it is the same God who works all in all. But the manifestation of the Spirit is given to each one for the profit of all: for to one is given the word of wisdom through the Spirit.'"

"Okay. Now I want you to stop thinking of this as something that is going to make you declare yourself as an old-style prophet. Instead, see this as simply one more responsibility in your life as a believer. You have been given a *message*. And the message is for the *common good*."

Buddy saw where this was headed and tried to steer away from it. "You don't even know what the message is yet."

"Hear me out." Pastor Owen was not to be distracted. "Now, if the Lord has indeed given you the gift of a message, how can it be for the common good unless you share it?"

"It can't, I guess," Buddy mumbled.

"Exactly. How this is to be done is not for you to determine, do you see? If the Lord is truly behind this, then He will show you exactly where and how the message is to be shared. If He had wanted somebody who would have sprung directly into the limelight, appeared on television, and declared the message to the world, He would have gone elsewhere. If He has chosen you, then He has chosen you with some special purpose in mind. Simply keep your eyes and ears open, Buddy. He will open the doors if this is indeed His will."

Clarke Owen stopped there and waited long enough for Buddy to have a chance to object. When Buddy remained silent, Clarke asked, "Do you want to tell me what you think you heard?"

Buddy took a deep breath and let it out. He set both hands on the open Bible. He took another breath. "I think there's going to be a major financial collapse. An economic disaster. Followed by a time of commercial famine."

The pastor remained stock-still, his gaze steady. "When?"

"Just over a month." Buddy's voice cracked under the strain. He swallowed and tried again. "In thirty-seven days, the third Tuesday of next month."

Buddy waited for the soft voice to calmly dispel his fears, to echo all he had told himself through the previous night's sleepless hours. How it was natural in such unstable times to be worried. How things had often been far worse than now, and somehow disaster had been averted. How every economic indicator now said that things were good and getting better.

Instead, Clarke nodded once. A slow up and down, and then he said, "I think you should share this with the deacons."

"Clarke, no, I—"

"You know there's a finance meeting tonight. I want you to tell them what you've just told me." Before Buddy could object further, Pastor Owen lowered his head. "Now why don't we join together in prayer and ask the Lord to show us exactly why He has spoken to you, and what it is He intends for us to do."

⊣| NINE |⊢

☐ It seemed the longest afternoon of Buddy Korda's life.

As soon as lunch was over, he fled to his study. Sunday afternoons usually began with a nap on his couch, but today he started wearing a path in the carpet, pacing from the window to the door and back again. The idea of standing in front of the church's deacons and declaring he had received a message from on high was appalling.

Then a thought struck him. And he stopped in his tracks. His first smile of the day spread across his features. An expression of pure bliss.

Buddy walked over to his desk. He seated himself and pulled over his pad. He had always liked to have important points down in writing. He ignored the feeling that he was trying to make a deal with God. He was a banker and had a banker's eye for details. He simply wanted to get his understanding down in black and white.

A sign. That was it. He needed a sign before he gave himself up to this. A sign.

He wrote a contract, at least in his mind. On paper he simply put down a few terse words, numbering them one, two, and three. But in his mind it was set down as firmly and precisely as a loan document. He was asking for three signs. If a man as strong as Gideon could ask for two, then Buddy Korda needed at least three.

First, his darling shy wife would not only agree to go with him and be there in public at his side, but she would suggest it herself. Second, his wayward brother would not only return to the church, but he would offer to work with Buddy on this. And third, every single member of the finance committee would agree that Buddy Korda had received a message from God.

Buddy folded the paper and slid it into his top drawer. He released a contented sigh. If the signs did not appear, he was going to be able to walk away from this with a clear conscience. The first two signs were pretty impossible, but the third was straight from a fairy tale. The finance committee couldn't be unanimous over how much coffee to serve for the Wednesday night Bible study.

Buddy leaned back in his chair, thoroughly satisfied with the world.

□

He found Molly working in the kitchen. "You busy?"

"No more than usual."

"I think it's time I told you what's been going on."

His wife had a quiet way of moving, as though she wanted to pass through life without disturbing a single blade of grass. She glided over, pulled out a chair, and seated herself.

Buddy laid it out flat. No inflection, no embellishments. The nightmares and the pains and the Bible passage. He finished with the previous day's prayer time. Then he stopped and waited.

After lunch Molly had changed from her Sunday clothes to a housedress, one with a stiff collar that reached almost to her chin. All her dresses and blouses and nightgowns had high collars. They helped to hide her scar.

Molly was a naturally shy person. To have such a vivid scar only amplified her natural reserve, turning it into almost a phobia. She had spent much of her life hiding from public inspection. Even if Buddy had been determined to go ahead with this crusade, he could never have asked his wife to join him.

And yet, when she finally spoke she said, "I knew it was something like this. Even before you told Paul to wait with the new business, I knew."

"You did?" His voice sounded dull in his own ears. "How?"

"I don't know. But I did. And I knew it was something I was going to need to do with you."

Her eyes were brown, like her hair had been before age had turned it to strands of silver. Buddy stared into them now, looking straight into her heart. He felt shocked beyond speech.

"I've been praying about it all week. And the only thing I've felt come to me is how happy I've been these past few years, with the boys grown and busy with their own lives."

Buddy wanted to ask, What about how you are with strangers? What about the bad days, when you ask me to drive you to the shopping mall and walk around with you so you don't have to be around strangers by yourself? He wanted to ask her all these things and more, but not because he was interested in her response. No. There was too much honesty in Molly's words for him to be less than fully honest with himself. He wanted to push her away from where he felt she was headed.

"I was glad to be a mom," Molly confessed. "But I'm much happier being a grandmother. It means I can concentrate on being a wife again."

She had often said this to him these past few years. The words had come to be an intimate confession just between the two of them. Buddy waited for her to finish with something like, I don't want to leave this now. He even wanted to speak and say the words for her, because he most definitely did not want to be any-where but here. Yet the words simply would not come.

She looked around the kitchen. "I like being just the two of us. I like being here with you at home."

He reached over and took her hand. He wanted to push away what he was hearing, what it might mean. But the love that welled up in him for his wife gentled away his ability to object.

"It's home the way we like it, quiet and cozy." She looked around again, sad this time, as though she was already saying good-bye. "I'll miss it."

He finally managed to force out the words, "We're not going anywhere." Yet even before the words were out of his mouth, Buddy knew they were wrong.

Molly did not answer him. Instead she simply reached over and placed her free hand on top of his. She sat there, looking around, looking at him, and then back again at their home. Her gaze was quiet and searching, seeing beyond the walls and the years, saying farewell to all that was and once had been.

Buddy hung his head. Never had the message seemed more real than at this moment. Nor the calling more dire.

Finally he rose from the table. Molly's gaze lifted with him. "Where are you going?"

He looked down at his wife. He answered, "I have to go see Alex."

⊣| TEN |⊢

☐ Buddy found Alex where his older brother spent every Sunday—at work.

Buddy drove under the banner announcing that the dusty lot was home to Korda's Fine Used Cars. He stopped and stared through the sun-dashed windshield to where his elder brother stood with a couple beside a car festooned with bunting and balloons. Alex was waving his arms about, which meant he was closing a sale. Buddy had spent a lot of time watching his brother and wishing things had turned out different than they had.

His brother was bigger all around than Buddy. Taller, wider, broader. Bigger smile, bigger hands, bigger heart. Alex Korda was one of those people who never learned to adjust to the real world. Buddy had known this long before Alex had gone through what Buddy had always called his change of life.

When Alex was eighteen he had fallen head over heels in love with a girl down the street. She, too, had claimed to love him, which was all the impetus Alex had needed. He had courted her and wooed her, or so everyone had thought. Especially Alex. Together they had set a date for the wedding. Two days before they were scheduled to be wed, the girl had left town. No word, no nothing for almost a month. Then a letter had arrived, and she had confessed to having fallen for a drummer in a band that had passed through town.

Alex had done exactly as she had requested, which was to walk over and pass the news on to her distraught parents. Then he had packed a bag and left town himself.

He had been drifting ever since. Oh, he had returned to Aiden six months later. But he had not been the same Alex. The smile was still there, the hearty voice and the friendly hello. But the man behind it had never returned from the horror of seeing his dream dashed on the rocks of reality.

There had been other women. A lot of them. And in between the ladies there had been an on-again, off-again love affair with the bottle. Three years earlier, Alex had finally sworn off the booze for good. He had joined AA and regularly attended the meetings. But he had never returned to church, never again set foot inside the doors, not even to see his two nephews get married. As far as Alex was concerned, when his fiancée had walked out of his life that day, she had carried God off with her.

Buddy sat in his car and waited for Alex to shake the couple's hands and send them inside to where his assistant sat ready to draw up the papers. Buddy reflected that there was still a chance he might get away with doing nothing.

Alex sprinted over to Buddy's car and opened the door. "You gonna sit there all day?"

Buddy climbed out and said what he did every Sunday. "Missed you at church this morning."

Alex gave his easy laugh, seeming to all the world a happy-go-lucky dreamer. "You're the second person who's told me that today."

This was new. "Who was the other?"

"Ah, now. That would be telling." He checked his watch. "Do I have the date wrong, or did we plan things different this month?"

"No, nothing's changed." One Sunday a month, Buddy came out and checked Alex's books. Another Sunday, he invited his brother for a family dinner. The other Sunday afternoons, Buddy simply telephoned for a long chat. They saw each other fairly often during the week, but the Sunday contacts were Buddy's way of reaching out. Buddy had been praying for Alex since Alex had disappeared, which was forty-four years ago. "I've got something I need to talk with you about."

"Come on inside then." Alex walked with the rolling gait of a big man. He was tremendously strong and possessed the jaw of an ox. No wonder the ladies swooned over him. Walking alongside, Buddy felt dwarfed by his brother and saddened by the missed opportunities. Alex had so much to offer the world. So much goodness. So much heart. Buddy found himself sighing a lot whenever he spent time around his brother.

Alex led him into the long trailer converted into an office. Couples were seated in front of both desks used by Alex's salesmen. Alex gave the entire room a cheery wave and led Buddy down the narrow hallway. The trailer smelled of antiseptic cleaner and old coffee.

Buddy followed Alex into the back room. On the side wall were three letters framed and hung like diplomas. They were from the sales managers of the three main car dealers in Aiden, all offering to buy Alex's stock and hire him as manager of their used-car divisions. He was that good.

Alex spotted the direction of Buddy's gaze and warned, "You're not going to start on that old thing again, are you?"

"No, that's not why I'm here." The fact that Alex was already on the defensive cheered him, and the fact that it cheered him made him feel guilty. Buddy shook his head to clear it. God knew him well enough to know that he would not want to take on the task of messenger. There was nothing wrong with being honest. And the truth was, he more than half hoped the signs would not arrive.

"What's got you so worried, little brother?"

So Buddy told him, in the same unadorned manner as he had used with Molly. Laying it all out, skipping nothing. He even paused a few times, waiting for Alex to give his big booming laugh and cut him short. The laugh was Alex's way of dealing with things he didn't like. The sound, as strong and dominating as he was, left little room for anything else.

But Alex did not laugh. His dark eyes seemed to deepen as he listened. No, listen was not the right word. He *drank* in the words.

When Buddy finished, silence filled the room. Which was extraordinary. Alex seldom permitted silence to linger when the two of them were together. There was too much chance Buddy would start in on all the things Buddy wished his brother would do, like make more of his life and his talents. And return to God.

Alex rose from his chair and walked to the room's only window. He stood with his back to Buddy, his fingers laced behind his back, and stared out at the yard full of cars. "I've got some news of my own."

There it was, the sudden change of subject, the move to something safer. Buddy was caught by the hope that Alex was not going to help him, then an accompanying twinge of guilt. "What's that?"

"Been wondering when I was going to tell you."

"Tell me what, Alex?"

One hand raised to part the blinds, as though Alex felt the need to get a better look at one of his cars. "That I've got cancer."

Buddy was on his feet before he realized he had even moved. "Alex, oh, my God, tell me it's not true."

"Wish I could, little brother." Alex angled his body away from Buddy's approach so that his eyes were almost hidden from his brother. Almost, but not quite. "Went in for that checkup you and Molly have been on me about. Look where it got me."

Buddy reached out his hand, stopped just short of touching Alex. "What kind is it?"

"I've forgotten the fancy name. In my lymph nodes." He grimaced toward the window. "Haven't been feeling myself lately. Nothing definite, just aches and pains now and then, here and there."

Alex had never been sick a day in his life. Just like his father. Buddy fought back a rising sense of nausea. He could not imagine a world without his brother. "Are they going to operate?"

"Can't. Wednesday they did one of those scans where they slide me inside a giant tin can, I can't remember the word now."

"MRI scan." And he had not been there. He had not even known. "Alex—"

"The stuff is everywhere, Buddy. Throat, under my arms, in my gut. Every lymph node has little bumps. They showed me." He turned around now, and let Buddy see what was there in his eyes. "I've got another couple of tests, and then they start me on chemotherapy at the end of the week. It doesn't look good."

Buddy did the only thing he could, which was to hide from the horror by taking his brother in his arms. Anything but stand there and see death's shadow in those dark eyes.

They held on for a long moment. When they finally released each other, neither could meet the other's gaze. Alex walked back around his desk, snuffling and wiping his face on his sleeve. "You know what I was thinking while you were telling me your news?"

"What?"

"That I wish there was something I could do to help."

The words felt like a stab to his heart. Buddy had to cover his eyes with one hand. "Oh, Alex. I feel like I've been the one to make you ill."

Alex huffed a short laugh. "What are you talking about now?"

"I made a bargain with God." The words were a moan. "I told him I'd go out there and warn the world if He gave me three signs. Molly would have to say she wanted to go public with me. You would have to offer to help out. And the entire church finance committee would hear me out this evening and say the message was real."

When his brother did not respond, Buddy looked up to find Alex grinning broadly. Alex asked, "Did Molly say she'd be there with you?"

"Right after church."

Alex's chest started shaking with silent laughter. "Sounds to me like you've done sunk your own ship."

"This isn't funny!" Buddy had to clamp down on his own case of shakes.

"Then why are you laughing?"

"I'm not. Well, maybe I am. It's better than crying, I suppose. Of all the things you could tell me."

"You don't know which surprised you more, me getting sick or me wanting to help, am I right?"

"How can you be laughing about this?"

"It's the way I've handled everything else in this crazy life."

"Crazy is right." How on earth he could be laughing was utterly beyond him. "Alex—"

"I want to help you, Buddy. I really do. I've been lying awake at night thinking things over. How you always said I wasted my life."

"If there were any way to take back those words, I'd do it," Buddy said vehemently. "I should've had my mouth washed out with lye."

"The words were true just the same. I want to do something good for somebody else." A trace of the shadow returned. "While there's still time."

"Alex, hearing you say those words is like a knife in my heart."

Instead of replying, Alex slid over a yellow legal pad, pulled his pen from his pocket, and started making notes. "We'll make this your command center."

"What, here?"

"Where did you plan on having it? You can't use the bank, that's for certain."

"I hadn't thought that far."

"Well, you'd better. They're not going to be very pleased to hear their manager start warning about a financial collapse."

"Assistant manager." But his mind was trapped by the realization that going public meant exactly that. "They won't be pleased at all."

"'Course, we're not planning on calling them up and telling them what you're doing in your spare time." He made rapid notes. "Anybody who wants to hear what you've got to say can call or fax us here."

Each word Alex spoke made the whole affair that much more real. "I feel awful."

"You look awful. You look like you need to go lie down before your third big sign comes true tonight." Which was good for another chuckle. "Boy, did you ever get it coming and going."

"Alex, I'd do anything—"

"Just stop right there. You didn't cause this illness." Alex raised his eyes from his note taking. "Did it ever occur to you that your God might have *suggested* these signs to you?"

Buddy did not know which was more startling, the thought itself, or to hear it come from his brother. "He's your God too."

"He might have known you'd need something like this to get you up and moving. If it's my time, well . . ." Alex stopped, momentarily silenced by the rising shadows. He pushed them back down and focused once more on his brother. "I want to help you do this, Buddy."

"Then you will." Buddy forced himself to his feet. "I'd better be going."

"Call me tonight when you get back." Another smile. "Tell me how it went."

"All right."

"Buddy." Alex waited until Buddy turned back around to say quietly, "There was something else I was thinking while you were telling me about this message. I was thinking that God couldn't have chosen a better man."

⊣| ELEVEN |⊢

☐ Buddy arrived at the church still numbed by his brother's news. He had left Molly teary eyed and heartsore, trying hard to put on a brave face for him. But she did not need to be brave. Buddy was too worried to care much one way or the other.

He entered the church's main conference room to an argument. One so unexpected that it almost shocked Buddy from his cloud. The church's two pastors were squared off at the front of the room. The others present clustered in silent little groups, staring in confusion.

Pastor Allen demanded of his assistant pastor, "You are *certain* this is a good idea?"

"Yes, I am. More than that, I feel it is divinely inspired."

Pastor Allen shook his head, clearly irritated. "I have to tell you, Clarke, I think this is unwise. Very unwise."

"You weren't there," Clarke Owen responded. He held to his normal, quiet tone, but he was equally firm. Equally unbending. "You didn't witness what I did."

"We have too full an agenda already, as you well know." Pastor Allen was a tremendously dynamic man in his mid-thirties, with an athlete's taut build and a movie star's even features. He dearly loved the Lord and approached the pulpit as he would a goal-line drive. He was definitely the force behind the church's revival and growth. He was also accustomed to subservience from his assistant pastor. "We have more than half the year's budgetary items to cover, and we're only two weeks away from presenting it to the church. Not to mention the shortfall in our missions goal. Something will have to be cut, and you know how hard a decision that is."

"Buddy will not need much time," Clarke responded. He seemed utterly unfazed by the pastor's determined arguments. His calm was unruffled, his stance relaxed. "All it took was a few short sentences to convince me."

"Convince you of what?" Pastor Allen ran an impatient hand through his hair. "That Buddy has something of such divine importance that we have to interrupt the church's monthly finance meeting to share it?"

"I could not have said it better myself," Clarke affirmed.

Buddy stood in the doorway, taking in one impression after another. The fact that they were arguing about him would normally have been enough to force him forward, to make peace between them. But today he could not do it. He felt shell-shocked, numbed by too much too fast.

There came another niggling notion, one that he did not at first recognize. Then it hit him with a start. The room was full. Hastily he counted the heads clustered at the room's other end. Fourteen. All fourteen members of the finance committee were present. He tried to recall another time in the twelve years he had worked with the committee when that had happened and could not come up with a single occasion.

Then he noticed the way they were standing. The committee members were drawn from the church's senior deacons and elders, along with a smattering of very large donors. They were people of importance within the community, people whose success and age generated solid confidence in their opinions. And since they all had opinions about everything, they argued all the time. They were a pompous, contentious lot, these committee members, and this was the impression of someone who loved them dearly. Talking about money and how to spend it often brought out the very worst in them. Only the leadership of both pastors working in tandem kept them in line—Pastor Allen leading from the front, Clarke Owen soothing from behind.

But today the normal lines of contention had vanished. The conference table was a long, slender oval stretching down the center of the room. Normally a group of seven or eight sat at the table, while any others chose positions on the sofas and in easy chairs that lined the side walls. These positions reflected their leanings; they seated themselves near the persons they tended to back.

Agatha Richards, a tall angular woman in her early sixties and widow to one of Aiden's richest men, headed one such group. She liked to see the church as spearheading a push to the farthest reaches of the earth. Every cent not spent on missions was reason for battle. To hear that her precious missions budget was to face a cutback was normally enough to have Agatha loading for bear.

Lionel Peters was the other powerhouse, a man who measured the church's progress by the height of its steeple. In his mind, the missions outreach should be restricted to what could be accomplished within the church's own buildings. He and Agatha genuinely loathed one another. And yet, and yet. Buddy stood in the doorway and watched the two of them standing side by side, their shoulders and arms almost touching. Like all the others, their eyes were fastened upon the two pastors. Who never argued. Who never seemed to differ in opinion on anything.

"I want you to give this up, Clarke."

"I would be happy to," his assistant pastor replied, "if I was not so certain that this was genuinely something that God was instructing me to do."

Pastor Allen reddened. He started to say something else, then he noticed Buddy standing in the doorway. His lips struggled to form a welcoming smile, but he could only manage a further tightening of his features. "Buddy, hello. Good of you to come." He turned so as to fasten his full attention on Buddy. "Clarke tells me that you have something of *vital importance* to share with us."

"I don't know if I do or not." Buddy recognized the pastor's appeal for support. But he could not give it. Not then. "If it is, I think that's something you folks are going to have to decide for me. Because right now I'm too drained to care."

Clarke walked over. "Are you all right?"

"No, I'm not." Sorrow hung like a leaden weight in his chest. He passed his hand over his eyes. "I just learned Alex has cancer."

The entire room drew a collective breath. They all knew the story of Alex. Many of them had grown up with it.

Agatha was the first to reach him. "Buddy, I'm so sorry."

The pastor was one step behind her. His concern was deepened by what he had just been saying. "This is terrible. How can we help?"

Buddy looked from one face to the other and saw the sorrow and genuine concern. "You're doing it now. Thanks."

"Come on up here." This from Pastor Allen. His former resistance had vanished. "Are you sure you're up to this today?"

"I just want to get it over with."

"Fine, fine." Allen guided Buddy into the chair he normally reserved for himself at the head of the table; then he motioned for everyone else to take their places. "Let's just bow our heads and have a moment of prayer."

Buddy lowered his head with the others, but did not hear the words. Instead, as soon as his eyes were closed, he felt a sense of peace. The words came instantly to his mind. *Heal my brother,* he prayed. *I'll do anything you want. Just make my brother well.*

He raised his head to find all eyes on him, the entire room waiting patiently. How long he had sat there he had no idea. He looked from face to face, wondering what on earth he was doing there at all.

Then Agatha Richards reached over and took his hand. She had never been particularly friendly to him in the past. Her family were grown and scattered, and she lived for her missions and her church. She had always viewed Buddy with suspicion, for he had sought to play peacemaker alongside Clarke rather than declare himself solidly for one side or another.

But none of the former distrust was in her face now. Her sight had started to weaken after her husband's death, and she wore bottle-bottom glasses that made her eyes look impossibly big. She gazed at him with brimming eyes, her hand gripping his firmly. Then Buddy recalled that it was cancer that had taken her own husband, and he placed his second hand on hers for a moment before rising to his feet.

Even when standing, he still had no idea what on earth he was supposed to say. So he simply laid it out. He cleared his throat and launched into it without preamble. How he had suffered through more than two weeks of nightmares. How he had seen the Bible passage about a coming famine come alive before his very eyes. How he had fasted and prayed and had received answers. How he had asked for signs . . .

Right then, before he could tell them what the signs were, a chair slammed so hard against the back wall that Buddy jumped. He turned to see Pastor Allen standing alongside him.

The pastor's head was upraised, his eyes clenched shut. He was swaying slightly, his arms outstretched, his hands rigid.

Pastor Allen was not opposed to movement of the Spirit, but he himself had never been a demonstrative man. His sermons were often punctuated by loud *amens* and occasional clapping, while many in the congregation sang with hands outstretched and faces upraised. He remained unfazed, simply accepting it and waiting them out.

But not now.

His entire body seemed to vibrate, shaking like a tuning fork struck by a divine hand. His neck muscles were so taut they stretched like wire cables beneath his skin.

Buddy took a step back and then caught sight of the assistant pastor. Clarke Owen was sitting beside his colleague, seemingly caught halfway between laughing and crying. He was biting his upper lip, rubbing one hand up and down the side of his face, up and down, his eyes never moving from Pastor Allen's face.

"*Praise God!*" Agatha Richards rose in trembling stages, her eyes staring up unseeing at the heavens. She reached one hand toward what only she could envision and cried again, "*Praise be to the Lord Almighty!*"

"*Hallelujah!*" Lionel Peters was up now on the table's other side, his voice charged with emotion. "*Hallelujah, Amen!*"

Buddy kept backing away from the scene until he was pressed hard against the wall. He watched as one after another of the committee members began to rise and call and shout and lift their arms and close their eyes. He felt nothing except shock. He could not be the cause of this. It was impossible.

Clarke Owen rose to his feet, the last to do so. Calm in a joyful way, clearly in control and yet guided with the others. "Brothers and sisters," he called, and gradually the hubbub faded. "Brothers and sisters, let us pray together and give thanks."

Hands were joined, and Clarke began the prayer. A low murmuring ran in waves around the chamber. Buddy joined his hands with the others, yet remained isolated and untouched. It was impossible that he had caused such a commotion.

The prayer went on and on. Buddy scarcely heard anything at all. Three words resounded through his mind, over and over, a litany spoken to the confusion he felt surrounding and filling him.

Heal my brother.

⊣ TWELVE ⊢

☐ As soon as he was home Buddy retreated to his den. It seemed a center of calm in the midst of the storm. He did not do anything; he merely sat at his desk with the Bible opened and unread before him.

Molly came in to say good night. She studied his face for a long moment and then brushed the graying hair from his forehead and kissed him and left him without speaking a word.

The night gathered, and more than darkness crouched beyond the reach of the room's feeble light. Buddy felt overwhelmed by all that had happened. He opened his top drawer and took out the list he had made. Could that have truly been only a few hours ago?

Almost in reply there came a whisper, a silent response. Not in words, not this time. But a signal that was understood just the same. Buddy caught a sense of urgent need.

He slid from the chair to his knees. The Presence gathered and intensified. He took no pleasure from it and little comfort. The future was too formidable. Too close.

"Make this cup pass from me," he said, speaking with eyes closed. Clasping his hands to his chest, pleading with all his might. "Give it to someone better prepared."

The response was as clear as it was silent. A simple waiting.

He sighed, understanding the message far better than if it had been in words. He had asked for signs. They had been given. He was chosen. He had promised. He was called.

He wanted to make his brother's healing into another sign. Wanted to bargain. But he could not bring himself to do it. Why, he was not sure. But the wrongness was so absolute that Buddy could not negotiate. He could only beg.

He raised his clenched hands toward the ceiling, and pleaded, "Heal my brother. Please. Make Alex well."

The image was instantaneous in its arrival, as though waiting for this moment, ready in advance, prepared long before he was even born. It was that clear, that total.

Buddy saw his brother. Not with his own closed eyes. The image was far stronger than something of his own senses. He saw his brother in *entirety*. The Alex of all time appeared in his mind and heart—the young man, the brokenhearted lover, the fallen drifter, the drinker, the salesman, the hollow gourd who had turned his back on the church and refused to be filled. The hearty handshake, the empty laugh. The burly giant pasted around a life of chasing barren dreams.

With the image came a sense of seeing it not through his own memories at all. He was watching through wiser eyes, seeing a wholeness that was limited neither by time nor anything human. And with this observation came an overpowering sorrow. Anguish over a beloved child who had drifted away.

There was no time to give in to grieving. In fact, it did not feel like his own grief at all. Instead, his perspective began to expand. He did not retreat from his brother. Somehow he began to see Alex, and more besides, taking in the customers who came to Alex's lot, then all of downtown, then the entire town of Aiden.

The broadening did not stop there. The vista swept inexorably outward, carrying Buddy with him. No longer was there any question that he was seeing more than his own vision. No longer. The county, the state, the region, and onward. Farther and farther, on and on, until he was looking and feeling for an entire nation.

He did not stand at some great distance and look down upon his country. He was *joined*. The connection was *intimate*. Each person was there, each town and county and state and everything in between. How it was possible, Buddy did not know. But he saw both the individual and the total. And the sorrow would have overwhelmed him had the guiding hand not filtered it. For with the expanding vision had come a growing realization. It was not just Alex who was ill. It was not just for his brother that Buddy should be mourning.

The illness was an all-pervading malignancy eating at the very fabric of society. It came under a variety of guises, and was called by myriad names, but the source was the same.

The stain reached from shore to shore, from border to border. Buddy saw it all. He saw and felt a mother's anguish for a child who was slowly giving in to a deadly disease. He saw and wept for all the cancerous growths that had infected the body of his beloved country.

Here and there were islands of light, flickering candles of life. No words were needed now. No convincing necessary. For a reason that Buddy did not understand, he had been selected to speak with them. To carry the message and pass on the warning.

Suddenly the why behind his being chosen no longer mattered. The unspoken lesson had carried with it all the explanation he would be offered, all that really mattered. Buddy had been called. Despite all his failings and all his misgivings, no matter what anguish he himself might be facing in his own life, he had been *called*.

The perspective faded as quietly and gently as it had appeared. No indication of the force behind it, nothing of the experience's immense infinity remained. Instead, the room returned to focus. Buddy was back, and his life was changed forever.

The Presence whispered to him then, in words for the first time that night.

THIRTEEN

Thirty-Six Days . . .

☐ Monday morning Thad Dorsett entered the bank in a foul mood. He had taken his boss's advice and spent the weekend away. In Chicago, however, not New York. His first trip to New York would be as a king, not a weekend wanna-be. Still, Chicago held more than enough diversions to keep one returning veteran satisfied for a weekend.

Yet returning from the big city to Aiden, Delaware, was a bitter way to face another Monday. Thad grunted in reply to his secretary's cheerful greeting and poured himself a cup of coffee. His throat burned, his mouth tasted gummy, his tongue felt slightly furred. The insides of his eyelids seemed coated with sand from too little sleep and too many hours spent trying to have a good time. He stared out the bank's rear window, slurping his coffee and willing his body to wake up. The day outside was as grim as the town.

Thad was not so weary as to be blind to the way the bank's employees treated him, playing at being polite but not meaning a thing. He turned so that he could watch Sally at her till. Even she had started keeping her distance. He felt another set of eyes on him and looked over to where Lorraine sat behind her desk, watching him like a disapproving hawk. He stretched his tired face into a parody of a smile, but she did not even blink. No question who had been talking to Sally. As soon as he found a way to rid himself of Korda, that Lorraine was history.

Korda. The thought of that measly little guy getting in his way twisted Thad's uneasy stomach even tighter. And the way the others in the bank treated him, that was even more galling. Thad had seen it happen dozens of times. All the guy had to do was walk in the door, and every face in the place lit up. Like he was some kind of potentate instead of another small-town loser.

Thad couldn't stand to watch another of Korda's entrances. He carried his cup back to his office, saying as he passed his secretary's desk, "As soon as everybody gets here, have them come in."

□

Monday morning arrived dark and rainy. Buddy drove along streets he had known all his life, feeling as though he was saying farewell. He was not leaving, not yet. Yet the *when* no longer mattered.

He looked out his rain-washed windshield and saw his own future. The trees were still verdant with the weight of summer's leaves, but it was only a matter of time before autumn came.

Only a matter of time. Buddy listened to the windshield wipers snap back and forth, and wondered if there had ever been another moment when he had felt so helpless.

He arrived just as the bank's managers were filing into Thad's office for their regular Monday morning meeting. Buddy entered and slid into a seat in the far corner. He remained locked in his own private reverie through the report on accounts and outstanding loans. He said nothing as the previous week was reviewed. Nothing sank in very far at all, in fact, until Thad Dorsett rose and addressed the gathering.

"Interest rates have taken another rise, as all of you know. Or should know, if you're doing your job." He gave his dangerous little smile. "Unfortunately, too much of the bank's loan business is tied to fixed rates. This can only grow worse, as rates are predicted to go even higher. So here is what I want you to do. Make a list of all our customers with fixed-interest loans. Ignore the mortgages; we don't hold them anyway. Star all those who use their loan arrangements for rollover credit—the small businesses with salary accounts, that sort of thing."

Buddy was paying attention now. His focus was locked on the branch's manager, with his dark, swept-back hair and his tailored gabardine suit. Dorsett continued. "We're going to catch them in a double pincer. Starting today, no further increases on their loan balances will be permitted. And the rate of repayment will be increased by tripling their minimum monthly payments."

While this was still being digested, Thad went on. "Not only that, but we're going to issue each of these people new credit cards. We'll send them a personal letter signed by me announcing that as valued customers we are waiving our normal account charge and offering them our new Platinum Corporate Cards for free. With a twenty-thousand-dollar credit ceiling."

Buddy could remain silent no longer. "That's disgusting."

Thad did not seem surprised to hear from him. "No, Mr. Korda. It is highly profitable."

"Credit-card debt carries the bank's highest interest rate. Last week's rate hike pushed the accumulative over nineteen percent."

"Exactly."

"Those fixed loans and rollover credit accounts belong to our bank's oldest customers."

"Deadbeats who need waking up," Thad snapped, his face reddening.

"They aren't deadbeats," Buddy heatedly replied. "A lot of small businesses are being operated by the third generation of the same families. Businesses who started around the same time as this bank. They've trusted us with their accounts for over a hundred years."

"I remind you, Korda, that your loyalty should be to the bank and its policies. You—" He stopped at the sound of someone knocking on the door.

Lorraine poked her head inside, then said, "I'm sorry, Mr. Dorsett. But Mrs. Agatha Richards is here."

"Tell her I'll be right with her," Thaddeus Dorsett said. At the death of her husband, Agatha Richards had inherited three large companies and was now one of the bank's wealthiest customers.

"Mrs. Richards," Lorraine replied, "wants to see Mr. Korda."

Buddy felt as though he was propelled from his seat. "I'm going to write all my customers," he announced grimly, "explaining to them what's behind this scheme. I'll instruct them to destroy the cards and refuse to pay the increased minimum payment."

"Do that," Thad snarled. "Be sure to send me a copy. I'd be delighted to show our central office what sort of assistant manager I'm saddled with here."

□

"Can I get you a cup of coffee, Mrs. Richards?"

"No thank you, Lorraine." Agatha followed Buddy into his office.

"Mr. Korda?"

Hearing Lorraine call him by his last name was so surprising he turned back. "What?"

"Coffee?"

"No, no, I'm fine, thanks." He watched her softly shut the door, and wondered what had Lorraine acting so demure. "Why don't we sit over here by the window. What can I do for you, Agatha?"

"I just wanted to tell you how thrilled and moved I was last night."

"Oh." Buddy slid into the settee facing Agatha.

Agatha was not a gushy sort of woman. She stood an inch higher than Buddy but looked even taller, as she held herself rigidly erect. She gripped her purse in her lap and kneaded the top clasp with beringed hands. "I feel so *honored* to have been there at the outset. I've never been one to go in for gifts of the Spirit, but—"

"Agatha, please stop."

"I just can't tell you . . ." Her mind finally registered Buddy's quiet words. "I beg your pardon?"

"Stop. I don't know how to make it any plainer than that." He knew he was being too harsh, but he could not seem to help himself. "This is hard enough already without your gushing all over me."

"Why, Buddy Korda." His words caught her totally off guard. "I thought you'd be delighted."

"Well, I'm not." He could not bear to have her finish. "The last thing I want is for people I've known all my life to start treating me like I was some kind of—" He started to say, some kind of prophet, but stopped himself just in time. He finished lamely, "holy man."

Before Agatha could collect herself, there was a knock on his door. Lorraine timidly stuck her head inside and said, "Please excuse me, Mr. Korda—"

"Not you, too, Lorraine."

"I'm sorry, what?"

"Never mind. Never mind."

"Reverend Owen and Reverend Allen are out here."

"Well, show them in." Buddy rose to his feet. Agatha remained planted where she was, giving him an odd look. Buddy looked at her and said, "I suppose you told Lorraine all about it."

"I didn't have to." Her gaze did not waver. "The whole town is talking about you."

"Great. Just great." He walked over as the pair entered, and offered them his hand. "Gentlemen. Come on in and have a seat." He stopped Lorraine's question before it was spoken. "That will be all, thank you."

He waved them into seats and sighed as he sat back down himself. "What can I do for you?"

"Be careful what you say," Agatha said. "Buddy is in one of his moods."

"I do not have moods," he snapped.

Agatha Richards harrumphed. "Buddy Korda, I've known you all my life. And I know you can be the most quietly contrary man I have ever laid eyes on."

Buddy turned to the pastors. "Don't pay her any mind. She's the one who's being contrary."

"Now that is just not true. I simply wanted to offer you my help."

"No, you didn't." Buddy knew he should stop, but he did not feel able. "You came in here to sit at the feet of the wise man. Well, I'm sure not wise. And I'm not interested in your getting down on my carpet, no matter what the reason."

Clarke Owen halted Agatha's reaction with, "Actually, we came by for the same reason."

"If you really want to help me," Buddy snapped, angry despite himself, "you'd make this whole mess up and vanish."

Agatha was horrified. "You don't mean that."

"Oh, don't I?" Distress rose in waves. "Do you know what I hear when you start talking about last night? I hear the end of a life I've loved. Everything is about ready to be turned on its head, and I'm supposed to be happy. Now tell me exactly what it is that I'm supposed to be so all-fired delighted about."

There was a long silence, finally broken by Pastor Allen. "So you really think it's going to happen. This economic famine, I mean."

"Yes, no, I don't know." Buddy kneaded his forehead. "It's not only the famine I'm talking about. It's the *warning*. It's the fact that I've been chosen to go out and deliver this to people.

Only I don't *want* to go. Is that so difficult to understand? I *hate* traveling. I'm scared of airplanes. I don't like trains. My car is eight years old, and it's done less than twenty thousand miles."

He felt thoroughly unable to explain what he was feeling. His gaze landed on Pastor Allen who wore a troubled expression. Buddy said, "I sound ungrateful, don't I?"

"I should say so," Agatha huffed.

"Well, to be honest, I don't know what I have to be grateful for." Even so, the act of confessing was calming. He could feel the pent-up steam leaking out with his words.

"If you don't beat all." Agatha had difficulty finding the words. "Buddy Korda, the Lord has *called* you."

"That's right, He has. Now let's take a look at what exactly this calling is. I've been given a message of direst ruin. A seven-year famine is coming. That's my message. I'm called to go out and spread this message to anyone who will listen. I'm called to make myself a laughingstock in the business community, at least among those who won't believe me. And for those who *do* believe, I'll be bringing a warning that dashes every dream. I'll be telling them that their worst fears for the future will soon come true."

He felt like a deflated balloon, yet he was satisfied just the same. There was a genuine fulfillment in speaking the truth. And that was what he was going to do, he decided then and there. "I don't want this job. I didn't ask for it. I'm not a talker, and I don't like being noticed. The Lord's called me, and I guess I'm going to do what He's told me to do. But that doesn't mean I have to like it. Not one bit."

Agatha looked from one pastor to the other. "Are you just going to sit there and let him go on like this?"

Clarke Owen turned and waited for the chief pastor to speak. But Reverend Allen continued to study Buddy. Genuine uncertainty clouded his gaze.

For some reason, Pastor Allen's silence seemed to satisfy Clarke. He turned back to Buddy and said, "I have to tell you, Buddy, what I've just heard here only makes me more certain that the Lord has chosen rightly."

Agatha's mouth worked a couple of times, but no sound came out.

"Buddy, you're not a pastor. You're not called to lead a flock. You are called to give the world a warning. A message, Buddy. That is what the Lord intends for people to focus on. Not the messenger. Never the messenger. Do you see where I'm headed with this?"

"Yes," he reluctantly allowed. "Yes, I guess I do."

"Someone who wants to be the center of attention could very well get in the way of what God is intending here. He wants His people to hear a message, and to have it spoken with an authority that is so solid, so *certain*, that they will do as He instructs. They might not be anywhere near that certain if the message was to come from someone else."

Clarke paused for another glance at Pastor Allen. A knowing smile played across his features. "If the message came from someone with a talent for speaking and a heart for the stage, their attention might be on the *speaker*. But that's not what's intended here. The Lord wants people to focus on *Him*."

There was a moment's silence before Pastor Allen shifted in his seat and said quietly, "I agree."

The soundness of what he was hearing left Buddy locked in his unfolding destiny. "I'm so afraid."

"Well, of course you are," Clarke affirmed.

"Every word you say," Buddy went on, "brings my departure one step closer."

"Buddy, I'd like to tell you that you can go out and do your work and return home. I wish I could do that." Clarke placed his hands on his knees and leaned through the distance separating them. "But I can't. What I can say is that I'm proud of you. And I'm certain the Lord is too."

Pastor Allen rose slowly to his feet. "I suppose I'd better be getting on. I've got appointments back-to-back today. I just wanted you to know I'm behind you on this." His gaze fell not on Buddy, but on his associate. As Clarke smiled up at him, Pastor Allen went on, "Buddy, there's a meeting of the Businessmen's Bible Fellowship tonight over in Wilmington. They've asked me to speak. I think you should be there in my stead."

"I—" Buddy stopped as he watched Clarke reach out, grip Pastor Allen's arm, and squeeze it hard. His smile was exquisite. Buddy told them, "I don't know what to say."

Clarke dropped his hand and turned to Buddy. "Tell him yes. Let the Lord begin his work."

⊣| FOURTEEN |⊢

☐ The chairman of the Businessmen's Bible Fellowship in Wilmington, Delaware, tried hard to put a good face on it. But he was definitely unhappy with Buddy's appearance as their speaker. "We meet every Wednesday morning for a prayer breakfast. Once a month, we have these evening suppers. Usually it's on a Saturday, but we rescheduled to have our senator make the address—he could only come tonight. Then he couldn't make it, and Pastor Allen said he'd fill in. And now, well, I guess he had something come up too."

"No," Clarke said from Buddy's other side. "It wasn't like that at all."

"To be honest, I wasn't clear at all on why the reverend felt that we needed to hear Mr. Korda." He was leaning back in his chair so he could see Clarke, and paused long enough to offer

Buddy an apologetic smile. "Normally we get in some big speakers for these evening functions. The wives come, and we invite other people from the community."

"I am pretty certain," Clarke replied, "that you won't be at all disappointed."

The chairman looked as if he wanted to say something more, but settled on, "Maybe it'd be a good idea if you did the introduction, then."

"I'd be honored."

Buddy waited until the chairman had turned to speak with someone else, then muttered to Clarke, "I wish I was half as sure about all this as you are."

The room was part of a riverside wharf restoration project, with ancient timbers holding up the high ceiling. Every sound rebounded off the red-brick walls and polished floor. By the time everyone was seated and dinner was served, over a hundred people filled the long banquet tables. Every time Buddy looked up from his place at the front table, his stomach did flip-flops. A wave of laughter swept down one side, and it seemed as though the noise beat at him. Buddy pushed his plate away untouched.

Clarke set his utensils down and slid one arm around the back of Buddy's chair. "You'll do just fine."

"I wish it was over."

"I know you do."

"All of it. Not just tonight."

"Well, it's not. It's only just started. And you might as well get used to the idea and stop bellyaching."

The words were so surprising, coming from the quiet assistant pastor, that Buddy felt pushed an inch or two away from his anxiety. He stared at Clarke and was met by intense gray eyes. Clarke went on, "The Lord has chosen you, Buddy. You may not like it much, but it is still an honor. And more than that, what you have to say may be of vital importance."

Buddy gave a single slight nod. "You're right."

"Of course I am. God is not intending for you to go out and scare his church. He wants them to *prepare*."

Strange how being scolded could force him to a new level of calm. "There's a second part of the message about how to do just that."

"I did not doubt it for a moment." Clarke looked beyond him. "The chairman is going to call us to order."

Buddy sat through the opening remarks and the Bible reading and the prayer and the singing, scarcely hearing any of it at all. His heart beat a frantic pace. Finally Clarke rose at the chairman's nod and approached the podium.

"When I came to the First Christian Church in Aiden twenty-seven years ago, I did not know a soul. New assistant pastors are generally treated like a sort of third thumb at first—people don't have any idea what to do with them. Yet Buddy Korda went out of his way to make me and my wife feel welcome. In his own quiet way, he treated us like family. And that is exactly how we have considered him ever since. A member of our family."

Buddy's attention was caught by the side door opening, and he started at the sight of two people slipping in. His brother, Alex, was in the lead. Agatha Richards came in next. He stared as they slid into two empty chairs by the side wall. A more unlikely pair Buddy could not imagine.

"Buddy is assistant branch manager of the Valenti Bank in Arden. He has helped handle the finances of our community for more than thirty-five years. People tend to overlook him unless they need his help with something, because he prefers to stay in the background. To say that Buddy would rather not be up here tonight is like calling the Atlantic a fair-size puddle. But he *is* here, and he *does* have something to tell you. There is nothing I can say that will prepare you for his message, and so I am just going to sit back down and ask him to come forward. Buddy?"

There was some scattered applause and more than a little muted conversation as Buddy made his way over. He gripped the sides of the podium, feeling the grainy wood under his fingers. He looked out over the hall and remained silent. He was no longer afraid. That was not why he did not speak. He was silent because there before him in that sea of strange faces Buddy caught a glimpse of his own future. Traveling from place to place, passing on from church to Bible study to gathering, moving farther and farther from the town of his birth. Spreading a message of doom.

"Buddy." Clarke leaned over his empty chair, and gave his quiet smile. "It's all right, brother."

And suddenly it was all right. Perfectly all right. Buddy found himself abruptly sheltered within invisible wings of love, safe in the arms of the same Lord who had asked for his help. Buddy looked out over the murmuring crowd, and quietened them by simply starting with his story. How he had started having nightmares. How the Bible passage had risen up before his eyes. How the message had been given to him after a day of fasting.

He stopped there, expecting some back talk and mutterings. But the hall remained silent. Utterly still. So Buddy continued with how he had then asked for signs, looking directly at his brother as he explained what he had asked for. He felt anew the stab of pain over Alex's illness, an ache so deep that he caught his breath and stopped.

Which, as it turned out, was a very good thing.

A man seated at the center of the table to his right suddenly rose to his feet. It was a gradual change, almost as if the man was lifted up by invisible strings. But what raised the hairs on Buddy's neck was the expression on his face.

The man wore a look of blinding ecstasy.

One by one other people around the hall followed Buddy's gaze. The man remained as he was, hanging limply and yet erect. And as silent as the rest of the room.

Then it happened.

There came the sound of a rushing wind. A spark of joy so powerful it *leaped* from person to person and *rushed* through the room. From where Buddy stood, it looked like an instantaneous storm ignited the entire chamber. Some people remained seated, others rose and stood at their places. But no one spoke. Not a word, not a sound. Only the rushing wind. A deeply drumming crescendo of the power of God.

As swiftly as it came, it passed. In its place was a vacuum, interspaced here and there with the quiet sound of weeping. Buddy looked out over the crowd, waiting for people to resume their seats. He had not felt a thing. But he had seen it. And though he was sorry not to have had the experience anew, he was glad all the same. He did not think he would have been able to speak if he had been caught up once again.

"I have something more to tell you," Buddy said, and he waited until all eyes were once more fastened upon him. There was a new focus to the room, a desperate desire to hear what he had to say. Which was good. Because he then delivered the second part of the message. And that was far more surprising than the warning itself.

⊣| FIFTEEN |⊢

Thirty-Five Days . . .

☐ When Buddy arrived home from work Tuesday he was struck by a panic attack. Cars filled his drive and spilled out along the front curb. Then he recognized all but one of them and breathed a little easier.

He had hardly stepped through the doorway before he heard four voices squeal impossibly high and saw two white-blond-haired and two auburn-haired girls come racing from the kitchen. "Granddaddy!"

"A family gathering. Just what I need." It seemed as if the sun rose in his heart at the sight. "How are my princesses?"

He sank down and allowed himself to be engulfed by his four granddaughters. It was like trying to hold a basketful of wiggling puppies. Meredith and Macon belonged to Paul, his older son. They were almost exactly the same age as Jennifer and Veronica since Jack, his younger boy, had married while still in school, whereas Paul had waited to start his family. Buddy tried to envelop all four girls at once and wished there were some way to stop time from advancing. He would have loved to spend the rest of his days with these little angels, just as they were right now.

"You didn't hug me, Grandpa."

"Yes, he did. I saw him."

"Well, he didn't hug me enough."

"I cut my thumb. Will you kiss it?"

"I got an *A* on my coloring today. The teacher put it on the board for everybody to look at."

Buddy kissed the Band-Aid on one little finger, looked up to where Molly and his two daughters-in-law were watching and smiling, and said, "This is just the medicine I needed."

"Did you have a hard day?"

"Let's see." He rose to his feet, keeping his hands down low to hold the little forms close. "The entire morning was spent writing letters to three hundred customers telling them to oppose the bank's new credit-card policy. Then after lunch word filtered back to the branch manager about my speech last night. That's when things got interesting."

"Oh, Buddy."

"It occurred to me about then that it might be a good idea to take some vacation. I've got almost a month stored up." He looked at Molly. "I know we were planning to use it for that trip out West, but I don't think I could bear trying to handle the bank and this new work at the same time."

Molly gave him a quiet smile. "You were the one who wanted to go out West. Not me."

"I wanted to take you off somewhere."

"It looks like I'll be traveling with you now," she said, clearly at ease with how things were.

All six females were watching him—his two daughters-in-law and his four granddaughters—waiting to see his reaction. It was not the time to show worry. "Where are the boys?"

"Out back, keeping the company occupied."

"Company?"

"Wait, don't tell him yet." Trish was Jack's wife, as petite as Molly and as auburn-haired as her two girls. "I want you to see something first before you get all worked up." She raced back into the kitchen.

Buddy started to ask worked up about what, but the four granddaughters stuffed little hands in their mouths to stop their giggles and did excited dances in place. He put on his sternest face. "Jennifer, what on earth is your mother up to?"

"You'll see." She beamed up at him. "Something good."

"Veronica, you'd better tell me right quick."

"It's a surprise."

"I didn't have time to wrap it, Dad." Trish reappeared, flushed and flustered. "We just picked it up from the framer's on the way over here."

Trish did scrollwork and etchings for a number of the local shops. Buddy watched as she rushed over, hugging a frame to her chest. "What have you been up to, Daughter?"

This brought forth another paroxysm of giggles from the four little girls. Shyly, Trish raised the frame for him to see. "I hope you like it."

A simple, gold passe-partout framed three different pastels and bestowed a sense of colorful depth. At its center, words were scrolled in rich blue and edged in gold. They came from First Corinthians, and said:

> *Pursue love, and desire spiritual gifts, but especially that you may prophesy. He who prophesies speaks edification and exhortation and comfort to men. He who prophesies edifies the church.*

"I'm very proud of you," Trish said quietly.

"I don't know what to say," Buddy told them all.

"We'll hang it in your den," Molly suggested.

"We're all proud of you, Dad." Anne, Paul's wife, was a statuesque blond whose warmth drew people like a flame. She gave Buddy a quick hug. "I'll go tell the boys you're here."

He looked up from the picture and asked, "What was that about company?"

"Alex called and asked if it was okay to bring him around," Molly replied. "I said yes."

"Bring who?"

"A reporter," she answered. "From *The Wall Street Journal.*"

□

"I find it surprising that somebody from *The Wall Street Journal* would come all this way to talk with me," Buddy said.

"I've been in Wilmington working on another story." He ground his cigarette in the house's only ashtray, which was why he was sitting on the back porch. Molly was allergic to tobacco smoke. "You know the Chemtel Corporation, of course, they're the biggest employer in this area. They were in the final stages of acquiring a local company."

"I think I heard something about that."

"The sale price was somewhere in the vicinity of a half billion dollars. This morning the chairman of Chemtel called it off. He gave several reasons, but he said in a private interview with me that the most important explanation was your speech last night."

"I see." Buddy was seated beside his elder son. Paul's silent presence was comforting. Alex sat at the picnic table's far end. From this perspective, it was easy to see how Alex's features had run like wax left in hot sunlight, weathered and wearied by crushed dreams and hard living. And now this illness.

Buddy glanced to where Jack, his second son, sat watching him from alongside the journalist. He could see Molly's face stamped there, her spiked features, her quiet watchfulness. Buddy felt immensely comforted by this gathering of family. Especially now. "Well, what would you like to know?"

"Do you mind if I record this?" The journalist's name was Chad, a sharp young man who spoke with only the slightest twinge of New York to his speech. His features were as crisp as his starched shirt. His hair was razor cut, his spectacles round tortoiseshell. His tie probably cost as much as Buddy's suit. He looked like every young New Yorker on the move Buddy had ever met.

Chad set the recorder on the table between them, checked to make sure it was running, and asked, "Could you tell me a little about what was behind your talk last night, Mr. Korda?"

"You follow the stock market trends more closely than I do. I'm sure you've heard anything I can tell you a dozen times before."

"Sure," Chad agreed. "But I was led to believe that there was something more behind your performance."

"It wasn't a performance," Buddy countered. "I simply shared with a group of businessmen my concerns over the future."

"That's not what I heard. From what I was told, you knocked them off their feet. Literally."

It felt to Buddy as though the family members were granting him their strength, giving him the capacity to say, "Are you a believer, Chad?"

"Am I a . . . ?" He adjusted his spectacles. "I'm paid to be objective, Mr. Korda."

"There is no such thing." Buddy felt the autumn sunlight beating down upon his shoulders. The warmth was magnified by the eyes on him. His two sons, his brother, all watching and helping in their silent way. "Objectivity is an excuse from those who prefer to keep life and faith at an emotional arm's distance. If you are not a believer, then claiming objectivity is a mask. If you are a believer, it will color every action, every thought, every feeling."

"Let's get this back on track." Chad leaned across the table. "We were talking about your speech last night. A couple of the people I interviewed were calling you a prophet."

"Then you'll have to talk to them about that." Strange that he was not the least bit troubled about all this. Chad's confrontational attitude rolled off him like rain on his car's windshield. "The Bible says that prophecy is for believers, not unbelievers. So unless you can speak to me openly as a believer, we will need to hold our discussion to market trends."

"Then let's just say I am a believer, for the sake of argument."

"There should never be arguments between believers," Buddy replied, not even needing to think it out.

"Okay, for discussion's sake, then." A trace of anger glinted through the spectacles.

"Then I would invite you to lead us in a word of prayer and ask the Lord to direct us forward," Buddy responded.

Chad watched him for a silent moment, his features tight. Finally he conceded, "You wanted to tell me something about trends?"

"Certainly. Anyone in banking is aware of current dangers. Or they should be. During the past five years, increases in stock values have added almost four trillion dollars to household savings. And this is extremely widespread, with more than half of all U.S. households owning stocks and mutual funds." Buddy had been watching these trends for years, and worrying for just as long. "The problem is, this is not *confirmed* wealth. This is *theoretical* wealth."

"If stock prices have risen and people own the stocks, then I don't see how this could be considered theoretical," the journalist countered sharply, still angered by his inability to steer the discussion as he would have preferred.

"It remains theoretical so long as people have not cashed in," Buddy answered. "They see the figures on their monthly statements, they watch how the values rise, and this affects their planning. But because they see how fast the stock values are rising, they *don't* cash in. Instead, they *increase their debt*. They borrow money to spend in the moment, expecting to be able to cash their stock holdings sometime in the future."

"That should make a banker like yourself very pleased."

"I can't be pleased when I see this debt based on false expectations," Buddy contradicted. "In this same period, household debt has jumped more than fifty percent, and today totals over *six* trillion dollars. This means if you measure the increase in stock prices versus the increase in debt, the net result is a *decline* in personal net worth of over two trillion dollars. This is an incredible shift, especially since it has happened so swiftly—in just five short years. Do you see where this is headed?"

"Suppose you tell me."

"People are not just increasing their debt to match the rise in their investment's current values. They are increasing their debt to match their *future expectations.* They are saying, the value of my investments increased by twenty percent last year, so it must do the same this year. I can afford this big new house or the brand new car."

Buddy shook his head, feeling the weight of this tragedy beating down with the sun. He was insulated from Chad and his petty anger, but not from the unfolding cataclysm. Not at all. "This is a horrific risk. Most households hold investments they can't easily use—life insurance policies, pensions, home equity, IRA accounts. This means that if there is an economic downturn, not only would they have difficulty meeting their debt payments, they could not pull out of these investments to cover their needs. They could lose their homes, their cars, everything. It is a recipe for disaster."

"But the market is in excellent shape," the journalist argued, clearly unaffected by Buddy's worry. In fact, he sounded almost bored. "The leading pundits predict another eighteen months of share price rises, minimum."

This was leading nowhere. Buddy rose to his feet and offered the young man his hand. "Then let's hope they are right. For all our sakes."

□

Alex remained behind as the two boys saw the journalist to his car. He waited until the backyard was theirs before announcing, "That kid doesn't have the sense it takes to pound sand down a mousehole."

"No, that's not it." Now that it was over, Buddy felt drained. "He is an extremely intelligent product of our culture."

Alex started to object, then changed the subject. "Agatha Richards came by again. She wants to work with me. After today I think maybe I'll need the help."

"What happened today?"

"I got maybe two dozen phone calls from Lionel Peters alone. He's set you up with speeches from one end of the state to the other, including one later on tonight. I tell you, that man's on fire."

Buddy nodded, wondering why he was not more surprised than he was. "Any others?"

"Are you kidding? By five o'clock this afternoon when Chad arrived, I'd fielded thirty-seven requests for you to talk. Thirty-seven, Buddy. In one day. And the later it got, the farther away the calls came from. The word's beginning to get out. When I closed up, the phone was still ringing like mad. I just got tired of answering it."

Buddy turned back to look at his house. He could hear faint cries of childish laughter through the open door. "I guess it's started, then."

"I'll say it's started." Alex leaned forward, making the table creak under his weight. "Listen, Buddy. Agatha wants me to move downtown. She owns some big office building. Said she'd give me a whole floor. Secretaries, banks of telephones, the works."

"That sounds like Agatha."

"I don't want to move downtown, Buddy. I like it where I am. I know where things are. I know where I stand. Downtown, well, I'm afraid I'd let things get on top of me."

Buddy turned from the house, saw the fear and the appeal in his brother's eyes. "You don't have to do a single thing you don't want to do, Alex."

"I don't?"

"You're in charge of this. You handle it exactly the way you want."

"I don't have to do what Agatha says?"

"You don't have to do what anybody says. Most especially Agatha."

Alex leaned back, surprised by his brother's unqualified reaction. "Well, then."

"A project can't have two heads, Alex. You talk with Molly, you talk with me, then set this up however you see fit." Buddy could not say why it felt so right to speak as he did. But there was no room for questioning. Despite his fatigue, the peace that had stayed with him through the interview still lingered. "Just try to set it up so we're not crisscrossing the state. Make the meetings fit together as close as you can."

"You got it." Alex picked a splinter from the end of the table and then said quietly, "You know, while you were talking with that Chad fellow, I had the strangest feeling."

"I did too."

"The longer he talked, it seemed like the smaller and smaller he got. Didn't matter that he was from Wall Street. Didn't matter that he thought we were all packing just half a load. It seemed as though we were protected somehow."

"I felt the same thing."

"Last night during your speech," Alex started, then stopped to squint up at the sky. "Last night, I watched that thing happen. I saw Agatha get all worked up sitting right there beside me. And I didn't feel much of anything. Oh, a twitch I suppose, but not much more."

"I didn't feel it either, Alex. It doesn't mean anything. Faith is not about having rapturous experiences. It's about following Jesus."

"Maybe it didn't mean anything to you. But sure as chickens wear feathers, it meant something to me. It meant I wasn't doing what you said." His examination of the table became more tightly focused. "All my life, I haven't followed anybody but the wind. And every time the wind changes directions, so do I."

Buddy watched his brother, scarcely daring to breathe.

Alex looked up. "I don't want to follow the wind anymore, Buddy."

"You don't know how long I've dreamed of hearing you say those words."

"I'm gonna take these first steps slow and easy. That's just my nature. I need to understand where it is I'm headed." Alex exhaled a breath that sounded as though he had been holding it for years. "But it's time to start."

Molly appeared on the back porch. "Buddy, are you two going to be much longer? The girls are starving."

"You go ahead and start without us. We'll be a few minutes yet," he said, and turned back to Alex. "My brother and I need to have a little talk about prayer."

⊣| SIXTEEN |⊢

Thirty-Four Days . . .

☐ Wednesday morning Nathan Jones Turner leaned back in his padded chair, and stared out the window overlooking his estate as he waited for Larry Fleiss to come on the line. As soon as Fleiss answered, Turner demanded, "Found my sure things yet?"

"I'm working on it."

"Do more than work," Nathan Jones Turner barked. "I want results, and I want them fast."

"Things like this take time. I'll need a week at least."

"Do you have any idea what would happen if the Securities and Exchange Commission caught wind of what I've done with the pension-fund accounts?"

"It gives me nightmares." Fleiss paused for a sip from his ever-present mug. "There's one more thing. Small, but we need to discuss it. You seen today's *Journal*?"

"It's here in front of me."

"Take a look at page two."

Turner flipped open the paper and scanned the story about a Valenti assistant branch manager predicting a serious economic downturn. The reporter concluded with the effect Buddy Korda's words had had on derailing the Chemtel deal. Turner snorted his impatience. "So?"

"Doesn't look like much on the surface, I admit. But I've been worrying about it ever since I heard they were gonna run it."

"You knew about this yesterday?"

"Pal over on the *Journal* staff, he called me last night. Said the journalist who covered it was really shook up. The editors all thought it sounded a little wacko, but they had the space and decided to go with it."

"Quite frankly, I can't see any reason for the clamor." Nathan Jones Turner waved an impatient hand toward the strengthening sunlight. "An assistant branch manager finally realizes that he is going nowhere, that nothing in his worthless little life will be remembered ten minutes after he is gone. So he sets out to make a final hurrah."

"My brain is telling me the same thing," Fleiss agreed. "But my gut . . ."

Nathan Jones Turner had ample experience with Larry Fleiss's gut feelings. Fleiss seldom made mistakes, which made this last trade—the first Turner had ever taken a significant personal loss on—so galling. "What would happen if someone started pronouncing that the market was headed for a major correction. No, strike that. More than a correction. A significant downturn."

"You mean," Fleiss said, "someone the market really trusted."

"Exactly. Someone with a voice that people began to pay attention to."

"One word. Disaster." The only change was a tightening to the metallic edge. "It would be a case of wish fulfillment. People believe it, so it happens. We'd take a bath that'd cost us a billion. More."

"If what you say is true, this peon has to be stopped before he can wreak any real damage."

"You said it, not me."

"Do you know people who handle that sort of thing?"

"You mean, find some sort of leverage, force the guy to shut up?"

"I mean," Turner replied grimly, "whatever it takes."

⊣∥ SEVENTEEN ∥⊢

☐ Wednesday morning Buddy drove to his brother's car lot. The evening before he had delivered another speech in a nearby town, one of the events prepared by Lionel Peters. Buddy had then spent a restless night reliving the sight of another crowd coming alive while he felt nothing at all.

He and Molly were scheduled to begin their first longer journey that very afternoon, overnighting twice in hotels before returning home. The thought of taking to the road so disturbed him that he was pulling into the entrance before he noticed the difference in Alex's lot.

The multicolored flags still fluttered in the morning breeze, but their shadows fell upon an almost-empty lot. Buddy climbed from the car and looked around. A smiling Alex appeared at the office door. Perhaps it was just his imagination, now that he was looking for such things, but Alex looked a little paler than normal to Buddy. Yet his shirtsleeves were rolled up, and his grin was firmly in place. "Well, if it ain't the man of the hour!"

"Alex, what's going on here?"

"I did what the competition have been after me to do for years. I sold out to the highest bidder."

"You're going to work for the dealership?"

"Probably. We'll see about that later." He waved him over. "Come on inside. Who'd believe it could be this hot in September?"

When Buddy stepped into the trailer's air-conditioned cool, Alex went on, "Last night I decided I'd give myself full time to this. Yesterday was enough to show it's going to take all I've got to give and more. The Chrysler dealership called to buy me out, and this time I said yes. Shocked the guy right out of his skin."

Buddy was astonished at how easily Alex spoke about the empty lot. "I can imagine."

"My two salesmen are already over there. Taking them on was part of the deal. And my cars. They'll be over to pick up the rest this afternoon. I've got three months before they expect me to start. Figure that'll be enough time."

Alex caught Buddy's look, and hastily added, "Don't worry. I didn't tell them about my illness, but I was straight about everything else. They only pay for my inventory now, and I gave them more than a fair price. They're happy to do away with the competition. They've done well by it, no matter what happens."

"I'm glad you handled it the way you did," Buddy said, feeling a twinge of pain just the same. "Very glad."

"I've got to try to play it straight if I'm gonna do this for God." Alex's grand smile reappeared. "Who in the world would've ever thought I'd say those words?"

Agatha Richards appeared in the doorway and announced primly, "Certainly not me."

Even Agatha's big-boned frame and overly erect posture looked petite alongside Alex. He grinned at her. "Sure does dress up the old place though, doesn't she?"

"I'll say," Buddy agreed. Agatha wore a quilted jacket with gold buttons, a long navy skirt of rich velvet, and a double strand of pearls. Every hair on her graying head was set precisely in place, every gem on her fingers and in her earrings sparkled in the morning sunlight. "How are you, Agatha?"

"Busy." She glanced through her thick lenses at Alex. "I certainly could use some help."

Alex asked him, "Are you on your way out of town?"

"Molly's just finishing her packing." Seeing the sadness on his wife's features was what had driven Buddy from the house. "The speech still on for this afternoon?"

"And tonight. And tomorrow lunchtime." Alex grinned. "After that, things get sorta interesting."

"What do you mean?"

"I'll let the lady tell you herself." He gave her a mock little bow, and said, "It's your show, duchess."

Such a remark would normally have been enough to entangle the speaker with the sharp side of Agatha's tongue. But today all she did was adjust her spectacles and say quietly, "If you'll step this way."

She led them down the trailer's narrow hallway. The back room had been transformed. Alex's desk was pushed over to one corner. The little conference table occupied the middle of the room. The framed letters were stacked beside the desk. The walls were now covered with seven state maps.

Buddy did a slow circle. There was no need for anyone to tell him why all the little colored pins were stuck in the maps. Most of the pins were reserved for their home state of Delaware. But a few appeared as far away as Illinois. "Oh, my!"

"Calls are coming in from farther and farther away," Alex proclaimed.

"Word is spreading," Agatha agreed, her precise voice unnaturally quiet. "Buddy, I've had to make some changes."

"I agree with her, for what it's worth," Alex said. He could not have sounded prouder if he had invented Agatha himself.

"There's not enough time for you to accept just any invitation that comes in. And currently there is far too much backtracking." Another quick adjustment of her spectacles. "I have started calling the organizations back and asking them to come together into one large meeting."

"I'll bet that went over like a lead balloon."

"Don't. You'd lose your bet," Alex happily replied.

"Up to now, all have agreed. There are a few scheduling difficulties, but not many. The response has been, well . . ."

"Miraculous," Alex offered. His grin threatened to split his face. "No other word for it."

"One meeting per city," Agatha said firmly. "And the timing set up so your driving is kept to a minimum."

Alex said, "Now tell him the good part."

"Lionel and Clarke met yesterday afternoon with the coordinators for a series of nationwide revivals, where they bring in big music groups and a number of big-name speakers and lay it on all day long."

Buddy felt his legs go weak. "The ones where they rent a whole stadium?"

"We're talking forty thousand people," Alex cried. "Can you get your mind around that?"

"No." Buddy made his feeble way to the nearest chair and plopped down. "No, I can't."

The pair stared at him. Alex said, "I thought you'd be pleased."

"Well, I'm not."

"Your word is getting out," Agatha said. "This is a big opportunity."

"This is terrifying, is what it is," Buddy replied.

Alex and Agatha exchanged a glance. "Look," Buddy told them. "We've got to get one thing clear right up front. What is absolutely necessary among us is total honesty. Nothing else is permitted in this little circle. Is that understood?"

His sharp tone sobered them both. Agatha answered, "Yes, Buddy."

"Total honesty," he repeated. "Utter openness. We can tell one another everything, and do so with the assurance that our words will be met with love and support. This is far more important than any planning we might do, or any meeting you set up for me. Out there is a world of woe and discord. In here, among us, we need to be able to retreat and cast off the masks, and show one another exactly who we are."

Alex nodded somberly. "A team."

"Precisely. And I'll tell you with all the honesty I have that I do not want to do this. I don't want to travel. I don't want to sleep in strange beds. I don't want to eat packaged food. I don't want to shake the hands of people who will look at me like I've fallen out of the sky. I don't want people to think I wear wings and a crown." He felt the events-to-come crowding in on him until he drew short of breath. He grabbed his chest, willing himself to relax. "And I do *not* like the idea of standing up in front of forty thousand people. *Forty* strangers are enough to give me the shakes."

"Take it easy, Brother," Alex said.

Agatha asked, "Can I get you something?"

"No. What you can do for me is pray. And let me come in here and unload. And give me absolute honesty in return. Will you do that for me?"

"Anything," Agatha replied.

"You just name it," Alex agreed.

Buddy's shoulders slumped. Forty thousand people. The number was too big to comprehend. "Sometimes I feel that it's all just a dream. That I'll wake up tomorrow and it'll all be over, that I can go back to just being Buddy Korda. Comfortable and happy with my little life in my little town."

"You know what Pop used to say. 'God comes to comfort the troubled and trouble the comfortable.'"

"Do you know, I had forgotten that." Buddy found it nice to have a reason to smile. "Pop would be proud of you, Alex."

His brother's features slipped into hollow sadness. "Shame I had to wait until it was too late."

"It's never too late." Buddy glanced at his watch and rose slowly to his feet. He walked over and took his brother's bulky form in a firm embrace. "Never too late."

He released Alex and turned to the stiffly erect woman. It seemed so natural, so correct to sweep her up as well, and enfold her in his arms and say, "I owe you more than I could ever say, Agatha."

Her rigid form relaxed enough to hold him fiercely. "You don't owe me a thing. I'm not doing this for you at all."

He released her, smiled, and said, "Good."

□

It was fitting that a daughter-in-law and two of their grand-daughters would be there to see them off that afternoon. Sad, but fitting. Anne stood with Molly by the car, while two little blond girls scampered around the big front lawn. Meredith was five and wise enough to let her younger sister catch her from time to time. Macon was four, and her progress was slowed because she insisted on running about while holding on to her floppy-eared bunny.

Buddy walked over, saw how the open trunk was full of suit-cases and bags, and had to turn away. He watched the girls. "I don't believe I've ever seen a bunny as dirty as that one."

"It used to be pink," Anne agreed. "But that was six hun-dred washes ago."

Molly leaned over and allowed the little one to run squeal-ing into her embrace. "That's all right, my darling. Your bunny likes to play in the dirt with you, doesn't he?"

Macon shrieked as though the hug tickled and then wiggled until Molly released her. Sunlight fell between the two grand elms and turned Macon's hair to sparkling platinum. Anne said, "I've told her that four years old is too big to be sucking her thumb anymore. Now I go in at night and find she's stuck one of those bunny ears in her mouth."

Buddy protested, "Look how the ears drag on the ground like that."

"I've given up worrying about where that bunny has been," Anne said.

Molly told her, "Your husband used to want to touch everything with his tongue. Learning to walk meant being able to get more to his mouth, and get it there faster."

"I remember that," Buddy said.

"Bugs, snakes, lizards, anthills, turtles, every puppy on the block, even the tires on Buddy's car. It went on for years."

"That man will never kiss me again," Anne declared seriously.

"They're little angels on the outside, but the dear Lord gives all children tummies of tungsten carbide." Molly wore a stiff blouse of dark ivory, with a lace collar that almost touched her chin. Her grandmother's cameo closed the neck, and from her pocket dangled her old-fashioned watch-pin. She lifted it to inspect the time and said to Buddy, "It's less than two hours to your talk."

Anne called out, "Come give Gram and Grandpa hugs."

The two little ones ran over, accepted the embraces with squeals and giggles, and then raced off to chase the sun. Buddy rose and saw the solemn light in Anne's eyes. His daughter-in-law said, "Paul told me to tell you that we're all proud of you, and that we'll be praying you through this, every step of the way."

Buddy started, "I wish—"

"Give everyone our love," Molly said, breaking him off. "We'll call once we get to the hotel tonight."

"Okay, Mama Korda." Anne hugged them and watched them climb into the car. When they started backing out of the drive, the two little ones waved and called and danced. Sunbeams and sorrow mixed in Buddy's eyes until he could not tell where the girls ended and the light began.

⊣| EIGHTEEN |⊢

☐ "Mr. Dorsett? This is Larry Fleiss."

Thad sat up straighter. "You're kidding."

"You've heard of me, then."

"Who hasn't." Larry Fleiss was a legend in his own time. A self-made trader, rising out of nowhere as all top traders did, going from strength to strength. "Is this really Fleiss?"

"The one and only. Have you seen today's *Journal*?"

"Afraid so." Thad gave a silent sigh. To be called by Larry Fleiss because of Buddy was the worst kind of insult. "Mind telling me why you're interested in Korda?"

"It's not the man, it's the article. If this talk of his is a fluke, it's a passing curiosity. But if it continues . . ."

"He could affect the bank's standing," Thad finished, loathing Buddy Korda anew. "If we can't control the ravings of one of our own, how can we be trusted to handle money on the Street?"

"I see we think alike." The voice sounded like a string plucked and sent buzzing over a tin plate. Of course. It had to be Larry Fleiss. His voice was as much a trademark as the man's ability in the markets. The metallic drone was a product of ten thousand market forays, putting hundreds of millions on the line and then watching the market spin. An adrenaline junkie. Fleiss went on, "I've heard some good things about you."

"You have?" Fleiss was one of the reasons Thad had joined Valenti. Here was a trader who was both fund manager and chief aide to the chairman of the board. Fleiss was the clearest possible signal that the sky was the limit. And the man had heard about *him*. "Heard what?"

"You're a trader with moxie. And you've got what it takes to rise to the top."

"Like you." Keeping his voice level, fighting down the excitement.

"Sure. What's your attitude toward this assistant manager of yours?"

"More fruit fly than manager. A wimp who's found his place in life." Thad cataloged the small-time habits, going through the recent conflicts and ending with the letter to the bank's top clients about refusing to accept new bank policies.

Fleiss's asthmatic breathing continued when Thad was finished. Then, "Sounds like somebody living in the past."

"The man is a throwback to horse-and-buggy days," Thad agreed.

"What do you suggest we do?"

"Strike directly." Thad did not need to think that one out. "Give Korda an ultimatum. Shape up or else. And if he doesn't drop this, we drop him. Chop him off at the ankles."

"I like your attitude, Dorsett. Think you can pass on the message from the front office?"

"With pleasure," Thad said with savage glee. "You can count on me."

⊣| NINETEEN |⊢

☐ Buddy drove up and over the hills west of
Aiden. The change in altitude was just enough for the first hints
of autumn to touch a few trees. They shone out from among
their brethren, hinting at changes to come. Buddy took the drive
slow and easy, trying to get used to the way things were. Hoping to find some breath of rightness to the new beginning.

Molly allowed him space and silence until they started down
the slope's other side. "How do you feel?"

"Do you remember what your mother used to say when
something riled her? She said she felt put upon." He took a steep
curve. "That pretty much sums it up for me too. I feel put upon."

"It's funny," Molly said. "I was just thinking about Momma
too."

He glanced over. Her face was tilted slightly, so that she could look out both the front and side windows. The scar that ran from her left ear downward was displayed in all its angry fullness. Molly went on, "I was thinking about the accident."

"Oh, Molly." This had to be a very bad day for her. Molly had not spoken about the accident in thirty years, not since the year before they were married.

"I was five, the same age as Jennifer and Meredith," Molly said, repeating the story he had heard just once before. "Momma was boiling bones on the stove to make marrow soup. The pot was boiling over. It was making such a mess. I had no idea how heavy it was until I tried to lift it off. It spilled all over me. Down the side of my face, down my neck and shoulder."

"I'm so sorry," he murmured, hurting anew for her. And not just because of the accident. Buddy ached over how the journey was already causing her such grief that she relived the worst time of her life. He was inundated with a desire to turn around and go home. Let the whole thing pass them by. Take the days left to them and just enjoy what was theirs. The temptation was so strong he felt little tremors run down his fingers and through the steering wheel.

"Momma was such a proper woman," Molly said in her own soft way. "She was a good person and a good Christian. But she was too concerned with what the world saw."

As suddenly as the tremors came, they passed. Buddy glanced over once more. This was something new. He had often thought the same things about Molly's mother, but had never spoken them out loud.

"Momma was devastated by what I had done. And so angry. I knew she was trying to hide her anger from me. But I knew.

She was *furious*. She shouldn't have been, and it didn't make any sense, so she refused to even see it herself. But she was so very angry."

One finger reached up and touched the scar. Buddy slowed so he could keep his gaze on her. Molly never touched her scar, except to powder it in the mornings. Watching her trace one finger lightly down the edge where healthy skin met the red-tinted scar tissue brought a lump to his throat.

"Momma stayed angry for such a long time. Probably not being able to admit she was furious even to herself made it last longer. At the time, all I knew was that I had done something terrible. And in my own way I understood better than she did. Momma was a *proper* lady. She was so concerned that the world thought good of her. And now her daughter had a scar that told everyone who looked at her that Momma was not a good mother, that she didn't look after her own daughter."

"You don't know that, Molly."

"I know the way she taught me to use makeup, long before other girls even knew what face powder was. I watched her take all my blouses and sew in embroidered collars that almost reached my ears. I learned from her how to set my hair so it would gather and spill over my left shoulder and hold it in place with bright ribbons, so attention would be taken away from my scar."

Molly dropped her hand, gathered it with the other in her lap. "I was so ashamed. I had disgraced my mother."

Buddy put on his blinker and pulled over to the side of the road. "You haven't disgraced anyone. Not then, not ever."

"But I did, you know." Her eyes were pools of grief. Deep inside, a little girl was still crying tears the woman no longer shed. "I saw it every time she looked at me. I was a scandal."

"Stop it, Molly, please." He reached over for her hands. "Look, there's still time if we hurry. I'll drive you back home. I can do this alone. There's no need—"

"That's not why I'm telling you this." One hand slid out to cover his. "I've let my mother's shame be a barrier for too long, Buddy. Coming to terms with this journey has brought up all the reasons why I've spent my whole life hiding. Oh, I know I'm shy by nature. But more than that is at work here."

Buddy leaned back but kept his hand in hers. He had no idea where she was going with this.

Molly looked out the light-streaked windshield. "For several years now I've been wanting to do something more. Something outside the church. I couldn't understand what it was or why I felt that way, but I do now. I wanted to grow beyond the barriers that I've let restrict all my life. I want to *grow*."

A flood of shame swept through him. He sat beside his wife of twenty-nine years feeling about two inches tall. Here he was, called in terms so vivid he felt as though his heart had been remolded in the process. And yet he was still looking for excuses to return to his comfort and his routines.

But his wife, who had a lifetime of quiet constraint to overcome, was willing to challenge her limitations for no more reason than a hunger to develop and the knowledge that he needed her. Buddy reached over and stroked a strand of wayward hair. "I'm so proud of you, Molly."

The words brought her back to earth and her quietly prim ways. "I didn't do anything."

"Oh, yes, you did." He stroked her cheek, let his fingertips run lightly over her scar. His wonderful, wounded little bird. "So much."

⊣‖ TWENTY ‖⊢

☐ Langston, Delaware, was a mill town. A forest of smokestacks lined the road, with high-tension wires for branches and billowing smoke for leaves. There was white smoke and black smoke and gray and brown and even one foul-smelling chemical factory with spumes of angry yellow. Molly covered her mouth with her handkerchief as they passed that one. The car's air conditioner couldn't begin to filter out the stench.

The church was in the border country between low-slung houses and the nearest factories. The exterior was red-brick dyed a dull gray by the soot. As they pulled up and stopped, they were surprised to see Clarke Owen wave and walk toward them. Buddy got out of the car, and Clarke called over, "How was your drive?"

"Fine." Buddy went around the car to meet him. "What are you doing here?"

"I'm your advance team. Hello, Molly. How are you today?"

"Just fine, Clarke. It's nice to see you."

Buddy demanded, "My what?"

"Somebody needs to travel ahead, make sure everything is up and running. Which reminds me. Three quick things." Clarke reached into his jacket pocket and came up with a palm-size mobile phone. "You need to carry this. The number is taped to the back, in case you want to tell somebody how to reach you. Be sure and remember to switch it off before you stand at a podium."

Molly stopped him from objecting by stretching out her hand and saying, "I'll take that."

"Number two. There's been a change tonight. We've been moved to a high-school auditorium. Seems there are more people wanting to hear you than the church could handle." He pulled papers from his inner pocket. "This is a contact number and address. This map shows both the auditorium and your hotel. Figured you'd like to stop by and freshen up after your talk here."

Before Buddy could form his objections, Molly said, "It looks like you've thought of everything, Clarke."

The assistant pastor gave a proud smile. "Trying, Molly. Trying hard."

"Clarke, I—"

Molly rounded on him and gave Buddy the same hard look she had used on her two sons. She said quietly, "Don't."

Buddy gathered himself. Molly rarely used that tone with him, but when she did, he knew to watch out. He clamped down on all he had to say.

Clarke glanced from one face to the other, then looked beyond them and waved over two people. "This is the couple responsible for the meeting here, Harvey and Gloria Rand."

The man was short and as florid-faced as his tie. "Saw you over in Wilmington the other night."

"We don't have a Bible Fellowship here in Langston," his wife interjected, showing more teeth than Buddy thought one mouth could hold.

"We like to get over there for the dinners," the man said. "Work business around those monthly meetings. Sure glad we didn't miss that one."

"It was positively thrilling," his wife agreed.

"We asked to hold the meeting here today because it's close to the factories. You're catching a lot of these folks between shifts." He waved an arm in the direction of the crowd that was streaming toward the church entrance. "You've got all kinds here, from secretaries to machine operators to vice presidents."

"The mayor said he'd try to make it," his wife added. "He goes to our church. I called him personally."

"Gloria has plastered notices all over town. She even tried to glue one on my forehead when I sat still too long." His grin turned a little nervous. "Are you gonna put on the same kind of show we saw in Wilmington?"

Buddy started to react to the nerves and the pressure with a sharp retort, something like, it wasn't a show. But again Molly's quiet voice was there first. "He most certainly is."

"Great, just great. Say, I don't believe we've met. Harvey Rand."

"I'm Molly Korda, Buddy's wife."

"Sure am glad you folks could make it today. Well, let's get on inside."

Buddy felt Molly's pressure on his arm and hung back. That look was back in her eyes. "Don't fight this, Buddy."

"I don't know what you're talking about."

"Yes, you do. All these people helping and making a big fuss over you. It's perfectly natural. And you need Clarke. What would have happened if you had gotten to Dover tonight and didn't know about the change of location?"

As if on cue, Clarke drifted back. "I almost forgot the third thing. Agatha Richards was supposed to tell you herself, but she couldn't work up the nerve. She is footing the bill."

Buddy felt like he was running just to stay up with the man. "What bill?"

"All of them." A merry smile slipped into view. "Every last one." He patted Buddy's arm. "I'm not going to hang around, much as I would like. I've got to get over to Dover and make sure things are set up for tonight."

□

It was the noisiest crowd by far.

Halfway through the talk Buddy stood at the podium, feeling utterly empty of any sensation whatsoever. He waited through the shouting and the clapping and the talking and the weeping. He listened to one person after another call out an affirmation of what he had come to say. He watched the hands waving and listened to all the amens. Yet he could not have felt more isolated from the experience if he had been standing across the road.

And yet, despite his sense of disconnection, he also felt a rightness. He could not explain why, but he did. So he remained content to stand there and wait them out, because he certainly couldn't complete his message with all this noise.

As he waited, he observed. He saw the tiredness of day-in, day-out hard work etched into most of the features. He saw the scars and even some tattoos, evidence of life before Jesus. He saw the patched clothes and the tough, seamed faces. He saw stains beneath most eyes, as though the factory smoke had engraved shadows into their features. And he found himself feeling for them.

This was strange as well, for Buddy had nothing whatsoever in common with them. He had always had difficulty communicating with people like this. Even inside the bank, he had found it hard to talk things out, as though he was trying to translate his thoughts into a language he did not really know. The people would sit there, numbed by the strangeness and the feeling that things were out of their control.

Buddy had often recognized the helplessness in their faces as they sat there on the other side of his desk. Try as he might to make them understand he was on their side, he never really felt as though he was getting through. Yet they kept coming back to him and sending their neighbors. They came to him with their debts and their mortgages and their questions, and after every such meeting, he would sit back drained and feeling like he had failed once more.

When they were ready to look his way again, Buddy raised his arms and asked for quiet. Many chose not to return to their seats, but they did become silent. "I have more to say to you, and I ask that you pay very close attention." He was talking to them as he would if he was trying to explain a second lien. "This is going to sound complicated, but it's only because you don't know the words. I imagine if you took me into your place of work and tried to tell me about one of your machines, I'd be lost in fifteen seconds. You'd say things like flange and CNC panel, and I'd want to turn and run away."

"Me too, boss," called a deep voice from the back. "Me too."

He smiled with the laughter. "All right. You've heard me say there is a difficult time coming. And now I need to tell you the second part of the message. The part about how to prepare. Mind you, I'm not telling you what to do. I'm telling you what the message was. And I'm asking you to go home and pray about this. Pray hard. Then go and do what you feel called to do."

Then it hit him. Hard.

Perhaps because it was so unexpected, the power almost overwhelmed him. Suddenly he was not looking out over a group of strangers with whom he had nothing in common. He was *with* them. And they were *family*. And in their quietly intent faces he saw a need, a desperate appeal, an appeal to which his heart reached out in love and mercy, a feeling so mighty it felt as though a fist had clenched his throat shut.

Their lives were threatened by so many things beyond their control. And here he had come, to tell them of dreams and portents that threatened calamity. Buddy felt his entire being humming with an urgency to prepare against the coming storm. Not for himself. For everyone.

He did not know how long he stood there. They stood or sat and watched him, and they did not seem to be concerned about the silence. Buddy wondered if they could feel the vibrating energy, the sense of standing and hearing the clarion trumpet of heaven. He cleared the tightness from his throat and forced himself to speak. "The message is this: Take every cent you can spare. Go to a stockbroker you can trust."

He took great comfort from the calmness in his voice. To his own ears it sounded as if someone else was doing the speaking. "Is there a stockbroker in the audience?"

"Right here, sir." A man stood and waved. "I'm a broker."

"Are you a Christian?"

"I am." No hesitancy, no doubt. "Praise God, I am."

"Do you accept the message of today?"

"I've been feeling it in my bones for months."

Buddy nodded and pointed at the broker. "Here is one person you can work with. I'm not telling you to do it with this particular gentleman. What I *am* saying is that, if you feel led by my message, you need to work with someone who will accept your instructions and not talk you out of what you feel called to do. Because what I'm here to tell you would be considered very risky by a lot of people. As a matter of fact, some brokers would refuse to work with you at all. They would say that people who deal in options need to have a lot of extra capital. In other words, they need to be rich enough to be able to lose it all. Which you are not."

Buddy looked at the broker, waiting for him to object. But the man met his eye and nodded. Once.

Buddy turned back to the audience and went on, "There is a certain kind of stock transaction called a *put option*. It means you are predicting that the price of the stock will fall. It also means that you put as little as five percent down on the purchase. It is tremendously risky. But the gains are potentially very great.

"The intention here is to take whatever you can scrape together and make enough to see you and your families through the coming famine. The message is this: Take all you can and invest in *put options*. The options should be for shares in any of the nation's top twenty banks. The options should come due in three to five months.

"But you are not to wait five months. In exactly thirty-four days, you are to sell them all. No matter what the market may be doing, no matter what your broker may tell you. Sell them all.

"Half of all profit from your investment in put options should be given to your church," he concluded. "These funds are intended to help see the church family through this crisis. A group from the elders and deacons must be chosen to oversee the fund for as long as the famine lasts."

When he finished his talk, Buddy looked out over the crowded hall. The silence lasted a long time. Whether it was because the people were frightened by his announcement, or because they were caught up in the same quivering energy that he was feeling, Buddy could not tell. Finally the broker rose to his feet once more and proclaimed, "I feel the rightness of what my brother is saying."

"So do I," said a woman's voice from the back. "Right as rain."

Buddy could sense the audience's sudden restlessness, felt the power fading away, knew it was time to end this and move away. "Let us close with a moment of prayer."

⊣| TWENTY-ONE |⊢

☐ Molly drove all the way to Dover, Delaware, granting Buddy space and silence and an occasional comforting touch. Buddy sat in the passenger seat, watching the countryside and the busy road and the sunlight flickering down through the trees. Thinking was too much of an effort. Little flashes of thought or memory came and went but did not catch hold, like bubbles rising to the surface of water.

When she saw the exit sign, she asked, "Is it the first or second exit we're supposed to take?"

Buddy pulled the papers from his pocket and checked the map. "First."

She made the turn and asked, "How do you feel?"

"Fine. Drained, but fine."

"Will you be all right for another talk tonight?"

"I think so." What had happened in that church flashed clearly before his eyes. "It really felt right back there."

"It's nice to hear you talk like that. I want you to feel confident about what you are doing." She stopped at the intersection. "Which way?"

"Right, and then right again at the first light. The hotel should be on our left."

She checked both ways and pulled into the right lane. "You are God's messenger. You need to grow in confidence in your work and your message."

Buddy felt a trace of the same resonance he had sensed while up at the podium. *Grow into it.*

"You spoke with such authority up there. And I'm not just saying that because I'm your wife."

"I know you're not. I felt it too."

"It's time you accepted the importance of what you're doing and give yourself to it. Fully and without reservation."

Buddy waited until she had made the turn and pulled into the hotel's front parking area to say, "I'm glad you're here with me, Molly. So very glad."

□

There was a message waiting for him to call Alex. He used the mobile phone for the first time as Molly checked them in. The little buttons were unfamiliar and left his fingers seeming too big and clumsy. When Alex answered, Buddy turned his back to the hotel lobby as he raised the phone to his ear. He felt very foolish. "I got your message."

"The bank called. Some guy by the name of Thaddeus Dorsett. One of those real smarmy voices, fake as white margarine." Alex snorted. "Sounded like somebody you'd like to shoot on sight."

"No, Alex."

"How about we just watch him trip on the rug as he enters the room. Bring him down a few notches."

"That is not a worthy thought."

"Well, he said it was urgent. Real urgent. Gave me his home phone, asked you to call as soon as you could." Alex read off the number, then asked, "Did Clarke tell you about the change of venue for tonight?"

"Yes. Alex, what is this about Agatha paying our bills?"

"Hang on a sec." The phone was laid down, and Buddy heard the sound of a door being closed. Alex picked up the phone and said, "Okay, now we can talk. It was her idea, Buddy. She came up with it all on her own."

Molly chose that moment to walk over and say, "The bill's already been taken care of. Do you want to go on to the room?"

Buddy nodded and followed her through the lobby as he said into the phone, "I can't accept this." Then he had to hit the brakes hard, for Molly turned and gave him a warning look.

"I told her you probably wouldn't like it. She didn't put up the fuss you'd have expected. More like a real wistful hoping."

Molly asked him, "Is that Alex? Are you talking about Agatha?"

He nodded. Alex continued, "She really wants to do this, Buddy. She said that she'd only be giving the money to God in some other way, that you have a divine message, and that she wants to do as much as she can to help out. A lot of stuff like that. I didn't have the heart to say no. I could have argued with her if she had gotten on her high horse, but not when she is like this. Sounded like she was pleading with me."

Molly told him, the warning still in her eyes, "Remember what we talked about in front of the church this afternoon? Let people help you, Buddy."

"It's fine, Alex."

Alex said, "It is?"

Molly continued, "You're not a banker here. You're not signing papers for other people's time and money. The only debts you have are with God, and those you'll never be able to repay, so you don't need to try."

He could not resist the desire. Buddy reached over with his free hand and hugged Molly close. He didn't care how silly he looked walking through the hotel lobby talking on the phone and hugging his wife. He said, "Alex, please thank her for me the very best you can."

□

"Thad, this is Buddy Korda."

"Where are you?" The voice was tight, clipped.

"We've just checked into our hotel."

"We?"

"My wife and I. I'm on my vacation, as you may recall."

"No, you're not. I know all about your little escapades. So does the home office."

Molly's antennae must have been up and working, because she turned from her unpacking to walk over and stand by his chair. Buddy glanced her way as he said to the phone, "I see."

"No, that's your problem, Korda. You don't see at all. This is not some stunt you're going to be able to walk away from and forget. It has seriously damaged your career."

Buddy could see the manager's face there before him, the yellow eyes, the feral snarl unveiled. "My career?"

"What's left of it. If you want to have any job at all, you'll pack up and head straight home. Do not pass go, do not collect your two hundred dollars for the little talk you *won't* be giving tonight." The tone hardened to a surly growl. "Not if you want to have a job tomorrow."

Buddy felt the voice battering him, or at least trying to. Which was a surprise, because he positively loathed confrontation. Yet in this confrontation, which threatened the position he had given his life to, he was able to hold to his calm. "I see."

"You'd better. That is, if you're the *least* bit interested in holding on to your pension." A pause, and when Buddy said nothing, Thad continued, "That's right, Korda. There's more than just your own little job at stake here. Think about what you're doing to your family. And your own future security."

Buddy found himself searching for some sign of panic. His own lack of internal reaction was as bizarre as this conversation. "Well, thank you for calling, Thad."

His reaction threw off the bank manager. "This is the only warning you're going to get," Thad said, but the cutting edge had been dulled. "And frankly, if it had been left up to me, I wouldn't have given you this one. If you give your little talk tonight, don't even bother to come back to clean out your desk."

Buddy cut the connection and said to Molly, "The bank is going to fire me if I keep this up."

Molly's face was wreathed in concern. "How do you feel about it?"

"To be perfectly honest, I don't feel much of anything right now." He gave his heart another mental check and said doubtfully, "Maybe I'm just in shock."

"I don't think so." Molly sank to the edge of the bed closest to Buddy's chair. "Honey, have you been listening to your own messages at all?"

"Of course I have."

"I'm not so sure about that. Buddy, if what you're telling the world is true, five weeks from now, what shape is your bank going to be in?"

The thought pushed him back in his chair. The bank was going to collapse. It took a moment before Buddy realized he had not spoken out loud. The bank was going to go under.

His bank. That was the way he thought about it. He had given his adult life to making the bank's balance sheet and profit statement as sound as he could. He had served his community through his bank. It was as much a part of him as his eyes or his feet. And it was going to collapse.

"While we're on this," Molly went on, "have you thought about doing with our savings what you're telling others to do?"

"No," he replied slowly, his mind still caught by the earlier thought. It had been shown clearly, even made a part of his dream. But he had refused to see. His bank was going under. "The money for the ridgeline has been deposited into our account, I checked that before we left. Easiest transaction I've ever made. But I didn't do a thing with it. I guess I've missed that too."

"Well, you can worry about it tomorrow." She patted his knee. "Right now I want you to lie down and have a rest. You look exhausted."

□

Molly let him sleep so long he had to button his shirtsleeves and knot his tie in the car. It had been a curious slumber, leaving him more tired and woozy than before he had lain down, as though all he had done was give his body and mind a chance to reveal some of the stored-up tension. He had dozed in fitful bursts, tensing and jerking awake every few minutes. The same thought continued to course through him even when he was asleep. His bank was going under.

When they pulled up in front of the auditorium, Molly stopped him from opening his door by reaching over and touching his arm. "Are you all right?"

"It's a hard thing to accept, Molly. My bank is not going to make it. I can feel it in my bones."

"Would you listen to yourself?" she said softly. "Going out to pass on a message about turmoil afflicting the whole nation. You've just received word you're going to be fired for your troubles. And what are you worried about? The bank."

"A lot of people rely on us," he said feebly.

"Of course they do. Here." She reached into the purse beside her and pulled out a little note card. "I want you to have this."

"What is it?"

"A passage I thought of while you were sleeping."

Buddy turned on the interior light and held up the card. He read: "*A man can receive nothing unless it has been given to him from heaven.*" *John 3:27*

"I just wanted to remind you of what you already know," Molly told him.

"This is perfect." He reread the passage, looked up. "Thank you, Molly."

She turned shy. "I could do this every day if you like. Find a passage for you to take with you into your talk."

"I would like that," he replied, "more than I can say."

□

Clarke met them halfway to the auditorium. "I was just about ready to get worried."

"He needed to rest," Molly said firmly.

Buddy accepted the outstretched hand. "What are you doing about your duties in the church?"

"I asked for a leave of absence. The elders agreed unanimously. Even the ones who had not heard you speak that night said I should come help you." Clarke extended his smile to include Molly. "Maybe that's an indication of how vital they think my work is around the place."

"Don't you think that," Molly scolded. "Not for an instant."

Clarke said to Buddy, "Before we get started here, there's one thing. We've had some journalists show up tonight. I know who they are, at least I think I do. Should I let them stay?"

Buddy reflected a moment and could only come up with, "We don't try to keep anyone else out. I suppose we shouldn't start with them."

"I agree," Molly said. "Who knows? Maybe they will feel the Spirit and come to their knees and their senses."

Both men looked her way. It was not like her to speak her mind in public. Buddy reached over and took her hand. It was a good change.

Clarke went on, "A lot of them wanted interviews. I figured you'd be too tired to do it tonight. So I said anyone who wanted could show up tomorrow after breakfast. The television folk have been after Alex all day. They wanted to have you all to themselves, one at a time."

"No." Buddy did not need to think that one over.

"My sentiments exactly." Clarke motioned to his right. "Here comes the lady responsible for tonight. Mrs. Sandown, can I introduce Buddy and Molly Korda?"

"Such a pleasure, I just can't tell you." She was nervous and excited and dressed in a sharp businesslike outfit of navy serge. "My husband and I heard you speak at the Bible Fellowship dinner over in Wilmington. Well, more than heard. He's had to go to Boston for a sales meeting, but he helped me set this up. It's been amazing how willing the churches have been to get the word out. Nothing at all like what I might have expected."

The words no longer held the power of surprise for him. "I'm grateful for all the work you've put in."

"You have something important to say, Mr. Korda. I feel that everybody needs to hear it." She gave a nervous glance at the doors leading to the high school gym. "The reason why we needed to change venues is that we've had a surprising response from several African-American and Roman Catholic churches." She exhaled what seemed to be a breath she had been holding all afternoon. "And someone wants to video your talk. Not the press, we've already had it out with them. This isn't a circus. A member of my church works for the local television station, and I know he'll do a good job." Again the anxious waiting.

Buddy thought it over and decided. "I think that would be a good idea."

"There isn't that much time to get the word out," Clarke agreed.

"We'll ask that it be distributed only to churches, but you know how these things are." She twisted her hands together. "Do you think the Spirit will be with us like it was the other day?"

"I hope so," Buddy fervently replied. The people headed for the entrance doors in a solid stream. "I surely do."

□

Perhaps it was because of the sound that bounced off the hardwood floor and the distant ceiling. Perhaps it was because of the bleacher seating, or because of the size of the audience. Or perhaps it was simply because Buddy was so tired. Whatever the reason, it seemed as though the meeting would never end. Time after time he had to stop and wait for the noise to abate before he could continue. But he did not feel a thing. Not when people started crying and shouting and moving down the steps to stand in the middle of the gym and wave their hands in the air. Not when he reached the message's second portion and waited for the sense of authority to confirm his work. Nothing.

Whenever the noise forced him to halt, Buddy found his thoughts returning to the realization of that afternoon. His bank was going under. It was so strange that he had not really accepted this before. He had only thought of it in passing, like a stone skipping over the surface of a lake, not taking it in deep, not seeing what this meant.

He arrived at the final portion of his talk feeling that the evening had worked on him like a crowbar. His lack of vivid spiritual experience seemed to leave him not only empty, but exposed.

After it was over and Molly was driving them home, she asked, "Where do you feel like eating tonight?"

"I'm not hungry," he said dully, which was only part of the truth. He was tired, yes, but he was more bothered than tired.

She gave him a worried glance. "You need to have something, honey."

"I'll get a soft drink and crackers from the machines at the hotel. You can order room service." Buddy leaned back on the headrest. He did not even feel angry. Just grumpy.

He could understand what was happening. He had felt a glimmer of this in his prayer for Alex's health, then again in front of the church. He was being instructed to look beyond himself and his own concerns. But he didn't want to. Not the least little bit. If truth be known, the prospect was appalling. The sorrows and burdens of countless believers loomed before him like a great gaping maw. Ready to take him in and swallow him whole.

He felt Molly's eyes on him, and so he said what was there in front of him. The safe and selfish complaint, "I didn't feel a thing again. Not one thing. I felt like I was up there all by myself the whole time."

"Didn't you see the crowd?"

"Sure. They were there, and I was a thousand miles away." He sighed to the window. "When I'm up there and God is silent, it rattles me. I wish I had thought to ask for that as a sign. One that would continue for as long as this work does."

"Maybe God is keeping that back because it needs to be used sparingly."

"Why, Molly? Can you tell me that?"

"No, I can't. It was just an idea. Maybe we grow stronger through the silence."

"I don't feel strong. I feel drained." More than that. Buddy felt the burden of this new calling. The *challenge*. His horizons were being reshaped. And he didn't like it. Not one bit.

Molly drove into the hotel parking lot. She cut off the engine and turned to him. Buddy took that as a signal to go on. "I found myself growing jealous standing up there, watching my audience struck by the Spirit. Jealous and isolated."

"They're not your audience," Molly said quietly.

Buddy stared at his wife. "How do you have this ability of shaming me so quickly?"

Instead of responding, Molly opened her door and got out of the car. When Buddy was out, she said, "I admire you for asking these questions. I've never even thought of them. I never even thought I was good enough to deserve God speaking to me at all."

"You mean, you don't feel anything in these talks I'm giving?"

"Not a single, solitary thing." When they had walked to their room, she unlocked their door and turned on the light. After Buddy had shut out the night, she went on. "I've always simply accepted God's silence. The way others go on sometimes, well, I've assumed that's because He has something to say to them. But He doesn't need to say anything to me."

Buddy stood by the door. He felt slapped by the impact of Molly's words. Spanked for being a naughty child. That was exactly how he felt. Childish.

She looked at him. "Maybe what I need is to ask Him to speak with me. But I don't know how. Would you ask Him for me?"

"Of course I would." Hiding his shame over being so demanding. Having felt so much, received so much, his wife had never felt anything at all. "Why don't you sit in the chair?"

Buddy waited until she got settled and then walked over and placed both hands on her shoulders. He said aloud, "Heavenly Father, when I hear my wife speak, I hear the wisdom of one who would probably make a better messenger than me. Yet she has never felt the gift of Your presence move through her. And that is what I am asking for now. Breathe upon her, holy Lord. Make Your gentle Spirit move within her."

He stopped speaking. But the prayer continued within the depths of his soul. *Over and over I come to this place, Father,* he prayed. *All my life I have missed the mark. And I'm doing it again right now. I'm being selfish and demanding. I'm weak and afraid and unwilling to trust that You will be strong for me. I'm sorry to have failed You, Lord. Again. Shape me anew. Make me a servant who lives for You. Grant me the gift of selflessness. Do with me as You will, and show me how to obey.*

Buddy spoke aloud the final words, "In Jesus' precious name do I pray. Amen."

He felt the faintest breath across his face. A trace of motion, an angel's wing so soft that he could have easily ignored it and pretended it did not exist, save for the glory that infused his soul. He felt Molly's hands come up to rest upon his own. Warm peace flowed back and forth between them.

Standing over his wife of twenty-nine years, sensing with a wisdom that was not his own, again the unspoken lesson was made clear. How the time and the experiences and the love and the shared prayers had united them. They were one person, living out a single life in two bodies. Joined by the same gentle Lord whose power was so great it did not even need to be noticed. Whose presence was always there, always working, always loving, if only he would step beyond his own selfish barriers and allow himself to be lifted up upon the wings of heaven.

⊣┃ TWENTY-TWO ┃⊢

☐ Thad Dorsett drove through Aiden's darkened streets, impatient with everything about this town, even the night. For the thousandth time since being posted in this backwater, he wondered if he had made the right decision by staying with the Valenti Bank at all.

Most banks treated traders like tigers on a chain. They were tightly controlled and never given the chance to roam the jungle unleashed. Which was why Thad had leaped at the chance to join the ranks of upper management. Rumor had it that Nathan Jones Turner, Valenti's new owner, was planning to raise a few traders to board level and grant the profit makers real power. This was the only reason he continued to hold on to his impatience and make it through the horror of living in Aiden, Delaware. Thad felt as though he had been holding his breath for months.

When a stockbroker received an order from anywhere in the nation, he did not himself make the buy. He passed on the order to a person who handled thousands upon thousands of such transactions each day. The same was true for fund managers. Their buying and selling went through *traders*. Some operated from the floors of exchanges, such as the Chicago Mercantile where Thad had cut his teeth. Others worked from trading floors within large banks and fund groups. Traders sometimes operated on their own, working sums granted to them by people who trusted their savvy and knew that the time spent discussing a possible buy was time lost from the trade. These were known as *indies*. Most indies came and went like moths chasing flames.

Some people along the Street thought Nathan Jones Turner was insane to even consider offering traders the keys to the kingdom. But Thad knew better. Executive status meant faster access to capital. Speed was everything. Every day trades accelerated and rose in size. Going through various levels to gain permission meant losing out to the guy who could do it faster. Thad had lost out too often because his cap was set too low; his cap being how large a buy-sell order he could make without authorization from higher up the food chain. Thad wanted direct access to major funds. He wanted his name on the line and his deals to shake the Street. Gaining that clout was worth any price. Even enduring the straitjacket life of Aiden. For a while.

Thad Dorsett had come out of nowhere. That was how Thad described growing up in a suburb of Gary, Indiana. Son of a pastor and a doting mother, he had been trouble since before he could talk. He had more savvy than both parents combined. He understood things they would never grasp and tried hard to ignore. These days, the strongest emotion he felt for his family was impatience.

But he seldom thought of his family. It was a trait common to the trader breed. Whenever someone in the bank asked where he was from, Thad instantly knew he or she didn't trade. For a trader, the only personal history that mattered was the guy's last deal.

His parents would have loved Aiden, though. It had all the charm of a church picnic and about as much excitement. People around here lived life at one-quarter speed. He was being driven nuts on a daily basis.

Which was why he did not mind this present assignment. Not in the least.

At a quarter to one in the morning, Aiden's streets were as dead as yesterday's trade. Thad passed a patrol car and saw the cop's head propped on the backrest. Thad imagined he could even hear the snores. No question, this job would be a snooze.

Finding the doctor's address had proved harder than Thad had expected. Buddy's secretary had been no help at all, giving him a hard stare and demanding to know why Thad was asking for the doctor's name. Because, he had said, trying for nice, I need to complete records for the home office. Lorraine had looked at him standing there and said in a cold voice, "Then you'll just have to wait until he's back, won't you?" She had even taken her organizer home with her that evening. No question, Thad thought to himself as he scouted the empty night, she was definitely another on the way out.

Because of Lorraine's suspicions, Thad had been forced to spend the afternoon calling all the town's doctors. He had repeated a dozen times or so how he needed to make a follow-up appointment for Buddy Korda. He had known of the doctor's visit the morning of their argument and had seen Buddy clutching his chest for a couple of weeks up to the start of this latest mess. Which was why he was going to all this trouble. He had a hunch, nothing more. But traders learned to follow hunches. Good traders were known for the quality of their gut feelings.

Thad pulled into the parking lot and resisted the urge to blow the horn to see if he could maybe add a little risk to the exercise. He pulled his tools from the trunk and sauntered across the lot, feeling like the real Thad Dorsett was being released. The tiger unchained. He knew what he wanted for this. He could even see himself making the request. No, not a request. A payback.

The outer door gave the instant he slid his credit card through the crack and pressed down. Not even a dead bolt. Why bother, when people didn't break in? He smiled as he crossed the lobby, thinking of an ad he should place in the New York papers: *Take a thieves' holiday in Aiden, Delaware. Friendly people, sleepy cops, no alarms, special rates, package tours.*

The doctor's office was a little tougher, but not much. The plywood frame gave with the first tug on his long-handle screwdriver. He intentionally left signs of his entry. That was part of the plan.

He scouted the lobby, slid into the reception booth, checked all four walls, popped open the closet. He could not keep his grin from spreading. Incredible. A doctor's office without an alarm, in this day and age. Well, let this be a lesson to them.

He knew he should be hurrying. There was still the risk of a silent alarm. But something about the empty streets and the slumbering cop and the lack of a dead bolt downstairs left him feeling as if he could browse.

Thad felt the years slip away, sliding back into the nights of being a teenage juvenile delinquent again. He recalled how his parents had thrown up their hands in despair, especially after the police station started calling to ask if the reverend's son was home and in bed every time some young perpetrator disturbed the night. Those had been the days. Carefree and wild, leading a pack of wolves through darkened streets, nothing but fun and easy money, easy women, easy highs.

Seminary had been his own idea. Knowing he could not handle it for more than a semester, he nonetheless needed something on paper to balance out the rap sheet. Thankfully his dad's position had kept him from being arrested for anything serious. Still, there had been a list of misdemeanors stretching from joyriding to underage drinking to destruction of property. A semester of seminary was his way of whitewashing the whole deal, claiming to have turned over a new leaf. His parents' distrust of his motives had not bothered him at all.

Thad focused on the doctor's filing cabinet, which was solid steel with a security bar running down one side. But he knew how to ply the crowbar to spring the entire side. A lot of the old-style mom-and-pop shops used these places to hide their cash boxes during the week, and he had gotten to where he could jimmy a door, slide in, and spring a cabinet in thirty seconds flat. He ignored the clatter as the metal siding fell to one side. He pushed the files back, fiddled with the internal catch, and slid the security rod up and away. Good to know he hadn't lost the touch.

He tugged the cord controlling the blinds until enough streetlight fell inside for him to read. He riffled the files, quickly finding the one for Korda. Had to smile again. The guy's first name was Broderick. What a hoot.

Then as Thad read the last typed entry, he laughed aloud. He could not have come up with something more perfect if they had let him write it himself.

□

The call for which Thad Dorsett had arrived early at work finally came through a few minutes past eight the next morning. The metallic whisper gave no greeting, did not even bother to identify himself. "So did you get through to your man?"

"He's not my anything, Mr. Fleiss. But yes, I spoke with Korda yesterday afternoon."

"And?"

"And I did just like we said. Laid it on the line. Either straighten up or watch his job and his pension and his reputation disappear." Thad found it easier to discuss this on his feet. He pulled the phone cord free and began pacing. "Only I'm not so sure it did any good."

"He hung up on you?"

"No, he heard me out all right. But he just didn't seem to care. And since then I've learned that he went ahead with his talk." Thad gripped the phone hard enough to wring it dry, wishing it was Korda's neck. "Believe me, Mr. Fleiss, I was tough as possible. I did everything but crawl through the line."

"I believe you. And the name's Larry."

"Right. Thanks." Suddenly his hands were wet with relief. "You don't sound surprised."

"I'm not. Guys like that don't scare easily."

"Guys like what?"

"On a mission. You get them on the Street now and then. Fund managers and analysts who decide they've got the answer to all the world's worries. Usually it's a theory they've spent their lives perfecting. Every one I've ever heard of has had more holes than cheese from the land of snowcapped peaks. But this one beats them all." There came the sound of a noisy sip. "So what do you suggest we do?"

Thad liked the sound of that. What do *we* do. "I've already started nosing around."

"That's what I like to hear. Find anything we can use?"

"A lot." He felt like a bird riding high currents and catching the first sight of his prey. He was barely able to reign in his excitement. "His organization consists of an alcoholic brother working from a semibankrupt used-car lot."

"You've got to be kidding."

"Nope. Alex Korda, that's the guy. Oh, and a rich local widow as his part-timer. I drove by the place yesterday. He's got maybe ten derelict heaps sitting out front; he couldn't get fifty bucks for the lot."

"If this wasn't so worrisome, it'd be a hoot."

"Wait, it gets better." He took a breath. "Buddy was complaining of chest pains for a couple of weeks before all this started. So I managed to get inside the doctor's office last night. Took a look at his medical records."

"You don't say."

"Got them right here in front of me." Thad found breath hard to come by. As hoped, Larry said nothing about a doctor's records being strictly confidential or that it was illegal to read them. He struggled to keep his tone easy as he said, "You're not gonna believe what it says."

⊣| TWENTY-THREE |⊢

Thirty-Three Days . . .

☐ Buddy was halfway through his Bible reading and a second cup of coffee when he heard a little chiming. "Do you hear that?"

"It's your phone," Molly called from the bathroom. "Top of my purse."

He fumbled about, flicked it open, and said, "I'm not sure I like this thing one bit."

"You will." Alex sounded far too awake for this time of morning. "It'll grow on you like a third ear."

"Are you already at the office?"

"Been here for hours. Got so much going on I could start my own whirlwind." A chuckle. "Agatha beat me by an hour. Made the mistake of giving that woman her own key."

Buddy heard his brother's hoarse breathing and had to ask, "How are you feeling?"

"I'm fine."

"You've got to take care of yourself. Don't work so much—"

"Now look here." The voice turned flat. "You're not going to be pestering me about my health, Buddy."

"I'm worried about you."

"Well, you shouldn't be. You've got enough in your head already."

"Promise me you'll take care, Alex."

"I promise you I'll do everything the doctors tell me. There, how's that?"

"All right, I suppose."

"You're worse than Agatha for fussing." The tone lightened perceptibly. "That's some woman. She's been a big help, let me tell you. But my, she sure can talk. Got me agreeing to go to church with her some Sunday."

That brightened Buddy's day considerably. "This is good news."

"Can't hardly believe it myself. After you and Molly asking me year in and year out, here she just up and invites me, and I up and say, fine." There was the sound of pages rustling. "And now to business. I'm about ready to fax your itinerary to the front desk. You're gonna be one busy fellow."

"Are you leaving me time to breathe?"

"Wait, I think I've got that down here somewhere. Yeah, here it is. Thirty seconds for drawing breath, one week from next Tuesday."

"I can't thank you enough for all your help."

"And Agatha."

"Agatha too." He could still not get over that particular pairing. Agatha and Alex. It was like mixing oil and water and ending up with perfume.

"Take care, now. Agatha says to tell you she'll be praying for you through this interview."

Buddy cut off the phone and sat staring at nothing until Molly opened the bathroom door. She stood there in her robe, saw his expression, and asked, "What's the matter?"

"Nothing." A long sigh. "I was just missing my brother."

"He's not gone anywhere yet."

"That's pretty much what he told me. He said I shouldn't worry."

"Alex is right." She walked over and sat beside him. "I want to thank you for praying over me last night."

"I didn't do a thing."

"Well, you did and you didn't." She leaned over and kissed him. "You are a good man, Buddy Korda. I knew it the first moment I set eyes on you. I know it now."

They sat there sharing the moment until Buddy caught sight of the time. "I'm going to be late for the interview."

"You go ahead, I'm not coming. You can handle those press people without me. I need some quiet time with my Lord." She reached to the bedside table and peeled the first page from the hotel pad. "Here. I found this one for you."

Buddy accepted the page and read it aloud: "'Therefore gird up the loins of your mind.' 1 Peter 1:13." He looked up. "Just what I needed to hear. As always."

She reached around and gave him a squeeze. "Now go and serve Him well, my husband."

☐

Buddy hesitated halfway across the hotel lobby. From where he stood he could see that the hotel's conference room was already full of lights set on metal stalks, cameras on tripods, cables, and people. He forced his legs to carry him forward.

Just inside the double doors, Clarke Owen was talking to a nervous man in a bright red hotel blazer. When Clarke spotted Buddy and waved hello, the man turned and stared, showing confusion when he did not recognize Buddy.

The room held a circular table with maybe two dozen chairs around it. Every seat was taken. At his appearance, the buzz of conversation continued. A couple of people watched Buddy's progress toward the front of the room. The others ignored him entirely as he squeezed past. He decided it was best not to hesitate or his nerves might freeze him solid.

"Good morning," he said loudly when he reached the podium, and there was a sudden flurry of activity.

"Wait a sec," called a voice from the back. Klieg lights flashed on, momentarily blinding him. "Okay, could we check your sound level?"

"My name is Buddy Korda," he said, speaking into microphones taped together like a bunch of metal asparagus. "Are we ready to go?"

"Okay on sound," the voice from the back said.

"Rolling," confirmed another.

"Go ahead, Mr. Korda."

Buddy touched the knot on his tie and wondered why he had agreed to this at all. It was far more intimidating than his talks.

At least there he had felt a sense of shared conviction. Here he felt nothing except apprehension.

And yet he knew what he needed to say. There was no question. All of the worries he had felt over the past several years suddenly solidified into a cohesive pattern.

He began without preamble, "Between nineteen twenty-five and twenty-nine, share prices roared up over four hundred percent. It was rank speculation. Yet newspapers around the nation proclaimed that an era of national growth and wealth had arrived. There was going to be a chicken in every pot. Everybody was going to own two automobiles. As long as a person had personal drive and ambition, the sky was the limit.

"Then, on the morning of October 29, 1929, the impossible happened. In a flash, the orders pouring into Wall Street made a one hundred eighty degree turn. Everywhere the only order was to sell, sell. It was the greatest market crash in history. Investors who had once counted rising paper profits were abruptly sent spiraling into very real debt."

Buddy caught several journalists exchanging weary glances. He noticed that no one was writing anything down. A couple of people standing by the back wall crossed their arms and leaned back, their faces falling into the shadows cast by the television lights.

Buddy plowed on, "For those who had money, the twenties was a time to get rich quick. Over a million Americans had money in the stock exchange, more than ever before. But most people didn't recognize it as such a good time. I'm not talking about the people who hit it big, the people living in uptown Manhattan with money to burn. I'm talking about the people living in small-town America. They had no idea this was such a grand time.

"I can remember one old-timer telling me he could hardly believe the news that America was on a roll, because his own family almost starved during the recession of nineteen twenty-three. But all the records show there was enormous growth in industrial production and personal wealth. But these are records, mind. After the fact."

He paused and then added, "Just like after this current period has ended, people may look back and say, oh yes, the nineties, they were *the good years*.

"Let me remind you of a few statistics about these current good years. While the number of millionaires has tripled in the nineties, the number of households without a job for more than a year has increased sevenfold. The annual rate of personal bankruptcies is *eleven times* higher than during the late eighties. The disparity between the nation's richest ten percent and the poorest twenty percent has more than doubled in the past decade. And most important of all, the income of middle America, the sixty percent just trying to make ends meet, has actually declined."

A laconic hand was raised. "Excuse me, Mr. . . ."

"Korda."

"Right. Are you telling me we're in for another Great Depression?"

"I know you've all heard the depression stories before," Buddy replied. "And that's become the problem. People aren't listening anymore. I'm simply telling you that it *could* happen."

A bored voice from the table's other side demanded, "But aren't you supposed here to proclaim some prophecy of gloom and doom?"

"I'm simply telling you that a serious downturn could very well occur. One that might even be worse than the crash of twenty-nine." He was not getting through. Every notebook around the table remained as closed as their faces. "There are dozens of points I could make. But since we're talking about the stock market, I'll stay with that. Just as happened in the twenties, through the nineties we have seen an unprecedented number of small investors enter the stock market, either directly or through mutual funds. This has pushed the market higher than it has ever been before. Even higher than in the twenties, in terms of profit-to-price ratios.

"The market senses this imbalance. These days, share prices react hysterically to the smallest bit of news—a quarter percent rise in inflation, the smallest change in unemployment figures, the tiniest drop in quarterly profits. Factors that have no real effect on the economy are blasting the market like well-placed grenades."

A bored voice pressed, "Could we talk about your prophecy, Mr. Korda?"

"Let me just finish this point," he said, feeling sorrowful panic that he could not get them to sense the warning. "This nervousness is most dangerous because it could herald an extreme response to bad news. At that point, other factors may well begin an uncontrollable downward spiral.

"For example, most stock transactions are now controlled by computer. Price levels are electronically set to trigger a sell order. This is fine, so long as we are talking about a million small shareholders setting their own orders. But that is not the situation. We have enormous mutual funds now controlling sums that even ten years ago would have been unthinkable. In the early eighties, a hundred-million-dollar fund was enormous. Nowadays, that is less than what the top twenty funds buy and sell *each* day.

"So now we have these huge funds with gigantic share holdings. Their computers are flagged to issue a sell order *instantaneously*. They have to do this. Shares are traded twenty-four hours a day now, with the market in Tokyo opening just as Wall Street is closing. Markets in London and Hong Kong and Sao Paulo all trade in American stocks. All of them. There are limits now in place, which supposedly hold the amount of decline possible in these sell-offs. But they are limits placed *by each individual market.*

"So let us build a scenario, one which could all too readily occur. Bad news arrives. A sell order is launched, one so big it tilts other shares. This we know happens; it is well documented. One share price falling affects all others in that industry, which in turn drives down the Dow average. Other computer flags are raised at the Dow's overall drop. More sell orders are initiated. Other industries are affected, one after the other. The Dow drops like a stone, hitting the artificial limit set for that day. Then a mutual-fund manager, with four or five billion dollars at his disposal, decides now is the time to get out of the market entirely. He dumps their holdings. This is still possible. How? By transferring their sell orders to Tokyo, and then London, and then Frankfurt. Because all of these markets also trade in American shares. And each of these markets' daily floor levels are independent. So the funds continue to chase around the globe, with the panic growing each time their sell orders are halted by another artificial floor."

They were watching him now. Not taking notes, but at least listening carefully. And the cameras continued to roll. Perhaps some word of this might get out. Buddy looked at one face after another, willing them to listen, understand, and write of a need for caution. "The result, I fear, is that our market structure would collapse like a house built on sand and caught in a hurricane.

"I urge you to warn your audience. Get out of the market now. Get out of debt now. Be as ready as you can for a severe economic downturn." He waited then, steeling himself for questions that would drive attention away from his message. But before the reporters could gather themselves, he was struck by a silent urging, one he accepted with relief. "Thank you all for coming."

Reporters sprang to their feet. "Mr. Korda—"

"Wait, please, I want to ask—"

"That is all I have to say at this time," he said, thankfully reaching the door.

TWENTY-FOUR

Thirty-One Days . . .

☐ Saturday morning found them in a hotel in Williamsport, Pennsylvania, where Buddy was struck by three body blows in the space of twenty minutes.

First came the call from his doctor. As soon as Jasmine Hopper had introduced herself, Buddy started in on his apology. "I've been busier than a one-legged man in a polka contest."

"That's not why I'm calling. There's—"

"I'm feeling fine, Jasmine. Really. I'm sorry I didn't make another appointment. I've been so busy I forgot to call."

"Buddy, I'm not calling to ask about your health or your missed appointment."

"You're not?" At the sound of knocking, he carried his cellular phone over to open the door. Clarke Owen stood holding a bunch of newspapers. "Is something the matter with our children?"

Molly opened the bathroom door, her makeup powder in one hand and the pad in the other. Buddy looked at her as Jasmine said, "No, Trish has come down with what I suspect is a strep infection, but otherwise your family is healthy as far as I know."

Buddy swiveled the mouthpiece away and said to Molly, "Trish has strep throat, but otherwise everybody's fine."

"Is that Jasmine?"

"Yes." To the phone, "Why are you calling?"

"I got your number from Alex." She sounded extremely worried. "Buddy, there's been a break-in at my office."

"Jasmine, I'm so sorry." Scrunching up his forehead, he wondered why his doctor was calling to tell him about a burglary. They were friends, yes, but Jasmine Hopper was friends with half the town. "What can—"

"I wanted you to hear this from me first." She took a deep breath. "They were after my files, Buddy. *Your* file."

Buddy's gaze shifted from Molly to Clarke to Molly again. "My file."

"I've spent the past two days making sure it wasn't just misplaced." Another pause, then she went on worriedly, "Buddy, you were so tense at your last visit. And you were so insistent that everything was perfectly all right. These are classic symptoms of denial."

Everything fell into place. He took in Clarke's somber expression and the newspapers in his hands. Buddy said, "I understand."

"I wrote into your file that if the pains persisted, you would need to have a psychiatric examination." These words were spoken in an explosive rush, as though she wanted to get them out and over with. "I'm so terribly sorry, Buddy."

"You did what you thought was right."

"If these notes are passed to the press, we can prosecute."

Buddy decided there was no need to point out that the damage would still be done. Jasmine clearly felt bad enough already. "I have to get going, Jasmine. Everything is fine. Don't give it another thought. And thank you for calling."

Buddy cut the connection and said to Clarke, "Is it bad?"

"Bad enough."

Molly demanded, "What are you talking about?"

"*The New York Times* and *The Wall Street Journal* have both launched attacks at Buddy. Well, partly at Buddy." Clarke's expression became pained. "I'm so sorry."

"Alex," Buddy said. "They've gone after my brother."

"It's pretty rough. They talk about his alcoholism and his run-ins with the law, and they make his business out to be on its last legs."

Molly moved up to grasp Buddy's arm. "He must be beside himself."

Buddy lifted the cell phone and dialed his brother's number. When Alex came on the line, Buddy said, "Don't pay them any mind at all."

Alex's tone was edged by a new grimness. "If my ramblings have taught me anything, it's that I can't please everybody, but I sure can irritate the whole world at once."

"The more our message gets out, the more the financial establishment is going to attack us," Buddy said. "We've known that from the beginning."

"Seems to me you'd be better off if I was to retire and leave this work to better hands." There came a sound of hoarse breathing, of needing to take a moment to gather the energy to continue, "I'm not polished enough. I'm not a pro."

"If you quit, then I do too," Buddy said, gripping the phone so hard his hand shook. "And that's a promise."

"I'm carrying too much baggage to be much help to anybody." Alex sighed, weary at seven-thirty in the morning.

"That's not true, Alex. Not at all." Buddy found himself recalling something he had not thought of for years. The words had been repeated often by his favorite Sunday school teacher, the man who had brought Buddy to the Lord when he was fifteen years old. "Being the person God wants us to be is a victory over our past," Buddy recited from memory. "It means not just embracing His call, but also overcoming our limitations."

"God called you, Buddy. Not me."

"He's called us both. I know that in my heart of hearts."

There was a moment's silence, then, "You mean that, little brother?"

"We're in this together, Alex. And that's all there is to it." He reached into his jacket for Molly's card. "I want to read you something Molly found for me yesterday. It's from the twenty-seventh Psalm."

> When the wicked came against me
> To eat up my flesh,
> My enemies and foes,
> They stumbled and fell.
> Though an army may encamp against me,
> My heart shall not fear;
> Though war may rise against me,
> In this I will be confident.
> One thing I have desired of the LORD,
> That will I seek:

That I may dwell in the house of the LORD
All the days of my life.

When Alex had finally agreed to carry on and Buddy set down the phone, he tensed against well-meaning objections from Clarke. Instead he found himself facing a warm smile. Clarke told him, "That was a great thing you just did."

"It was beautiful what you told him," Molly agreed softly.

Clarke folded the two top papers he was carrying and dumped them in the trash can. "We sure don't need this mess."

"You two go on down to breakfast," Molly said. "I want to call and see how Trish is doing."

Buddy followed Clarke from the room and asked, "What are those papers you're still carrying?"

"One paper and one magazine." As they walked the hallway, Clarke showed him the cover of *Money* and said, "This came out today. Listen to what it says about you." He flipped to the page he had already turned down and read, "A mild-mannered, narrow-minded, small-town banker has hit the financial pond like a meteorite, and the tidal waves are still flowing outward. The question is, Whose boats are going to be swamped? If what Buddy Korda's increasingly convincing arguments say is true, it could very well be almost all of them."

Buddy accepted the magazine and slipped it under his arm unread. "If only there was some way for them to really listen."

Clarke glanced at him. "Time is pressing down on you, isn't it?"

Buddy nodded grimly. "More with every passing day."

□

Sunday they decided not to try and go home, much as both of them wanted to see the family and worship with their own church. But Sunday evening Buddy was scheduled to address a church gathering in Philadelphia, and the hours simply could not be found.

The following week, Buddy and Molly started early and traveled hard. On Monday they visited Camden and Trenton, New Jersey, before traveling Tuesday to meet groups in four different Connecticut towns. After overnighting in Bridgeport, they flew Wednesday to Providence, Rhode Island.

Like a stone dropped into a still and expectant pond, the ripples spread ever wider. People began approaching Buddy after his talks, introducing themselves, saying they had seen his video at a prayer meeting in Baltimore or a church luncheon in Chicago or a specially called gathering in Jacksonville, Florida. They told him how they had traveled six hundred, eight hundred, a thousand miles, just to hear what he had to say in person. Just to make sure the incredible power they had felt from the video or tape was really there. Just to shake his hand and thank him and say that without a doubt, he was a prophet called by God to warn the faithful.

Buddy endured these encounters because he had to. He masked his winces as best he could, especially when they looked at him with something like awe and wanted to hang on to his hand. He deeply loathed the sensation that they were trying to cling to him as though he were something holy. But he could not be rough with them. He could not turn and flee as he wanted. He had to accept and endure. It was the message that was important. He could do nothing that would take away from the power of the message. He could not.

⊣| TWENTY-FIVE |⊢

Twenty-Seven Days . . .

☐ Wednesday morning, Larry Fleiss refilled his cup from the coffeemaker built into the left wing of his desk before swinging his Swiss-made leather and titanium chair around and scanning the screens. No major change, little action for that time of week. The Fed was scheduled to release its quarterly review of interest rates in two days, and the market was still trying to figure out which way the central bank was going to jump. He sipped from the cup, his fifteenth of the day. He averaged twenty before lunch, another two dozen by market close, an even fifty by the time he left. He went through a pound of Costa's best every day. He had long since stopped tasting much of anything.

Fleiss could not help glancing at the phone. There were nineteen lines into his office, plus the mobile and the two faxes and the six direct satellite hookups to the major overseas markets. But the phone he could not help looking at was the one linked to Nathan Jones Turner's office at the estate. He had spent all morning waiting for that call. He was supposed to have checked in with Turner an hour ago, giving him the word on a sure win. Which he did not have. But Fleiss had a hunch he knew where to find one. His gut told him so.

Only, if he was going to pull it off, he could not place this call himself.

He turned his attention back to the file, the only bit of paper on the desk's broad central dais. Thaddeus Dorsett. What a name. Still, he liked the feel of this guy. He flipped through the pages, already having committed the information to his prodigious memory. This was not an ordinary employee file. One of the changes Turner had brought to Valenti was a deep-profile investigation for all top managers. Fleiss was one of only three people permitted to see the information.

Thad's earlier delinquencies indicated a reckless spirit. This was good. Fleiss was not looking for somebody who was frightened by risks. And the way he had broken into the doctor's office, taken the guy's private records, and left the other files poking out as a warning—all this was very strong. Fleiss had probed a little after Thad had delivered his report, wanting the details, glad the guy did not pussyfoot around, but simply told him in an almost bored manner how he had obtained the information. Thaddeus Dorsett lived for the thrill. He knew the borderlands beyond law and legality. All this was good. Very good. Fleiss needed somebody like this. He needed him desperately.

Turner's firing of his top analyst-trader had wounded Fleiss badly. Fleiss needed a pair of legs, somebody to implement and to hunt and to be the face the Street saw. Somebody Fleiss could trust to be his man and his alone. The trouble with taking someone from within the ranks of Valenti's trading arm was that Turner's spies were everywhere.

But finding the sure thing could not wait. Fleiss had spent the last week and a half hunting and worrying. But he had the entire bank's operations to cover as well. No. What was needed here was a number two who was not squeamish about where legalities ended and profits began.

Fleiss resumed his perusal of the file. He liked the feel of Thad Dorsett. It was one thing to trade for a year or so. Most could not take it longer than that. They burned up or burned out. But there was occasionally somebody who lived for the trade. Market junkies, modern-day privateers. Fleiss closed the file and tapped his fingers on the cover. Yes. He could very well imagine Thaddeus Dorsett was going crazy in that branch office.

When the phone finally rang, Fleiss had to stop himself from reaching out. One ring, two, then on the third he finally picked up the receiver and said, "Fleiss."

The querulous tone demanded, "Did I forget something? Was there a miscommunication somewhere? Weren't you supposed to be in touch already this morning?"

"Been busy watching the market."

"In case you have forgotten," Turner lashed out, "I do not like to be kept waiting. Not by anyone."

"You also don't like to be bothered." Fleiss was dancing on the razor's edge here. Since the exchange rate debacle, Turner had been viciously unpredictable. "I don't have a thing to report. If I don't have something to say, a call goes under the head of bothering."

"You're not paid to *report*. You're paid to find me a way out of this mess!"

"You told me to find you a sure thing. I'm still looking."

"Well, look faster!" Turner was breathing hard. Which was a warning in and of itself. The man was notorious for losing his cool in spectacular fashion. "Every day we wait is another day we might be discovered."

"I'm on it."

"You'd better be. This had better dominate your every waking thought and shape your nightmares." A moment's heavy breathing, and then, "I can't understand what is taking you so long."

"Middle of next week," Fleiss promised. "Soon as we figure out which way the Fed is gonna jump, I'll have a better handle on how to—"

"Do you know, are you the least bit aware, that I have to make the second *cash payment* for the hotels at the *end* of next week? And if I *don't* make the payment, I lose the *fifty percent deposit* I've already made! Of course you're not aware! How could you be? If you knew, you wouldn't be hanging about! Because if you *did* know, you'd also know that *I don't have the cash!*"

"Middle of the week," Fleiss repeated, and decided now was the time to strike. "Listen, about the *Journal* article."

"What?" The anger switched to confusion. Turner was not a man used to having the conversation's direction dictated by anyone else. It threw him off balance. "I don't—"

"The article about one of the bank's employees. That Korda guy. There's been a follow-up. And some of the other news services are taking notice."

"I fail to see how you can be so fixated on this worm when we are faced with a total fiasco!"

"Like I said," Fleiss persisted. "There's a risk here. What if one of the pension funds decides they don't like how we're managing our people and we can't be trusted to manage their money."

"You're talking nonsense." But the old man's tone held a trace of uncertainty.

"Any move of a fund would expose our illegal borrowings," Fleiss pointed out.

"All the more reason for you to get moving," Turner snarled.

"You told me to handle it," Fleiss reminded him. "I've found a guy at the Aiden branch. He's one of the traders slated for top management who is putting in his time as a branch manager. He's sharp, and he doesn't like this Korda guy any more than I do."

"Doesn't like who?" Clearly Turner's mind was only partly held by this conversation.

"The assistant manager, the one who's causing all the ruckus. This manager, he has a plan to take care of Korda. But he wants out. He's going crazy there in the branch. He wants to move back into trading." Fleiss kept it casual, making it sound as though it was no big thing. "Wants his own portfolio, the works."

"Well, if he can handle this problem, do it." Turner was still too distracted to pay much attention. "But I want you to concentrate on what's important here."

"Will do."

"I want *answers*. I want *results*. Find me a way out of this mess. And find it *now*."

Fleiss hung up the direct line, thoroughly satisfied. He then picked up another phone and prepared to make urgent arrangements for Thaddeus Dorsett to travel up to the Big Apple.

─┃ TWENTY-SIX ┃─

Twenty-Six Days . . .

☐ Thursday morning, Nathan Jones Turner's personal helicopter attendant met Thaddeus Dorsett as he came off the private jet at Kennedy. Thad accepted the attention as though he had known it all his life.

The amenities were exactly what he had always thought a private chopper should have—soundproofing so thick the rotors' noise was cut to a barely audible whine, newspapers and magazines still in their wrappers held in a chrome-and-wood stand, crystal decanters and a refrigerator in one corner, a smiling hostess to keep him company, two pilots, three color-television sets, and big windows through which he could look down as the Big Apple swept into view, ripe for the plucking.

He had never before been to New York. It was not a confession Thad would have made to anyone. But early in his career, he had promised himself that there was only one way he would arrive in New York City, and that was in style. A winner. A big-time guy. A name.

He had made his mark in the Chicago dealing rooms, always hearing the extra edge that the New York guys held in their voices. They were top of the heap, and made sure that everyone understood this. The saying went, a trader never made it any-where until he made it in New York. Thad accepted the saying as fact. But he also knew that landing at the bottom in New York meant hitting hard and fighting mean. He had always figured he would battle his way out of the trenches where the competition was a little easier and the scars quicker to heal. Then he would arrive in New York with power and experience behind him and burn his emblem into the Street.

The pilot's voice sparked over the intercom. "That's the Turner Building to your right."

"I know."

"Oh," the stewardess said brightly. "Have you come in by air before?"

He did not respond. He did not want to share this moment with anyone. No, he had never come in by air, by road, or by any other way. But he had seen this picture before. Seen it and studied it so often it was burned into his heart, branded like all the desires that fueled his drive to get here.

The Turner Building was world famous. It was the area's sec-ond highest building and occupied the Street's most prestigious location. To its left was the Federal Building, where George Wash-ington had been sworn in as president. The Stock Exchange was a half block down Broad Street. The Federal Reserve Bank was a block in the other direction, just beyond the Chase Manhattan

Plaza. The Turner Building stood proud and imperious at the heart of financial power, surrounded by the biggest players in the world, fighting and scrapping for profit and position.

They used the chopper platform atop the Irving Trust Building, since the Turner's was crowned by an art-deco tower. Thad bid the chopper crew a distracted farewell and allowed himself to be led away by some Valenti lackey. He gave no response to the guy's oblique questions, knowing rumors would start flying as soon as the guy was back. How some young man from a branch in the middle of nowhere had been brought in on the old man's chopper and taken straight into Larry Fleiss's inner sanctum. Thad sighed with pleasure at the glances thrown his way as they entered the foyer, now dominated by Valenti Bank headquarters. This was better than he had ever imagined.

The Valenti Bank's trading operations, he knew, were spread over four floors, a total of 130,000 square feet. From this arena the bank generated almost 50 percent of its total operating profit.

Larry Fleiss's office was on the top trading floor, the sixtieth. Thad nodded as the guy held open the door to Fleiss's outer office. He smiled in response to the secretary's greeting and took a good look around.

The anteroom positively pulsed with luxury. Items scattered decorously about the room vied for his attention. The walls held two Degas watercolors and what appeared to be a Rembrandt sketch. The floor was rosewood, the carpet silk Esfahān. Side tables groaned under crowded burdens of crystal and silver. Thad found himself salivating over the thought of moving in.

Fleiss's interior office was refrigerated to within a degree or two of freezing. But Thad's involuntary shudder had little to do with the cold and everything to do with the man behind the desk.

Larry Fleiss looked like a human slug wearing a blond mustache and toupee. His skin was so white it looked blue, matching the milky paleness of his eyes.

Thad realized Fleiss was watching him, observing his reaction. So he kept hold of his poker face and said, "Great desk."

Fleiss gave a tiny lift to the edges of his mouth. His hand raised far enough to wave Thad into the seat. "Had it custom-made. I call it my powerboard." In person, the man's voice was even more eerie than on the phone, a metallic monotone barely above a whisper. "Forty-seven thou including all the toys. Even got a built-in sink."

"I want one." And he did. Thad wanted it all.

A single flicker of approval. Wanting another person's toys was definitely something Fleiss could identify with. And handle. "How are you doing in your branch, what's the name of that town?"

"Aiden." He did not need to think that one through. "Dying a slow death."

"I can imagine." The voice was utterly toneless, a single rasping note so emotionless that it sounded machine made. "I suppose you want out."

There it was. Finally. His ticket out of slumber land. But he was nothing if not a trader. And a trader never accepted the first offer. "No thanks."

Fleiss blinked his surprise. "What?"

"I want it all." Forcing his voice to remain bland. "The gold ring. A job in HQ. A book all my own." A book was a trader's personal trading capacity. The larger his book, the greater his clout in the market. "Two-fifty ceiling. Euromarkets and currencies included. Bonus linked directly to my own profits, not the bank's."

"Two hundred and fifty million ceiling. Interesting." Fleiss turned away. He ran a quick glance over the screens, automatically checking the market's frantic pulse.

Thad felt a sudden terror over the thought that he might be turned down. He fought down the desire to backpedal and accept less. Fleiss reached for his mug and glanced at him over the lip. He lowered the cup and hit a button with its edge. A lid on the desk's left-hand ledge slid back, and a gleaming coffee system rose into view. It was all there—a stainless steel sink and spigot, matching coffeemaker and grinder and utensils.

"Add a desk like yours to the list," Thad said approvingly.

A flicker of humor came and went. "Good to know we think alike."

The thrill was electric. "Does that mean yes?"

"I'm looking for a new number two. Are you interested in the job?"

"Answer directly to you?" Thad could scarcely believe his ears. "Are you kidding?"

"I never kid about trades."

"Then the answer is yes."

"Okay, but first you've got to pass the test." Fleiss spooned beans into the grinder, waited until the whine had ceased, and poured the black dust into the maker. The room was flooded with the perfume of fresh-ground coffee. "Find me three sure things."

That was a no-brainer. "Buy the next three Treasury issues."

"No can do. I want a minimum twenty-five percent instant return."

Thad laughed out loud. "There's no such animal."

"There'd better be, or you go back to hibernating in Aiden."

Thad watched the man rinse out the pot and fill the machine with water. "You're actually serious."

"I told you, I never joke about the market. Three sure things, Thaddeus Dorsett. Find them and the job is yours." He waved a hand toward the unseen trading floor. "Have somebody out there find you a desk. You've got forty-eight hours."

"Great." Unexpectedly, he did not feel dejected. Impossible simply meant it had not been done before.

"Wait a sec." Another button was hit, and another panel slid back. An upright filing tray rose into view. Fleiss flipped through the headers, pulled out a red-flagged file, and tossed it across the desk. "Have a look at this."

"What is it?"

"The last trade of the lady who had the job before you." Fleiss turned back to his screens. "I gave her the same assignment. She failed. Learn from her mistakes."

⊣╟ TWENTY-SEVEN ╟⊢

☐ Wall Street was all concrete and bustle and noise. Even on the brightest day, sunlight remained as out of place as a stranded tourist. Sunglasses were used in all weather, however, especially by traders. After sixteen hours spent in front of flickering trading screens, with fluorescent lamps spaced out over acres of trading floors, eyes found even the cloudiest of days to be outrageously bright.

The mountains of Wall Street were home to their own brand of trolls. Only here they were dressed by Valentino, driven by Porsche, fueled by liters of caffeine. They hoarded their gold and guarded it with bloodthirsty vengeance. They substituted hand-held faxes and satellite links for broadaxes, but they were trolls just the same. They even had their own language. Sunlight scared them. Fresh air was as alien as a moral code.

Thad waited in the window table of a deli across the street from the Turner Building until the lunchtime flood began. He closed the file he had been studying and crossed the street. He fought his way through the careless throng and rode an empty elevator back to the sixtieth floor. Instead of going right and entering Fleiss's outer office, he turned left, pushed through the double doors, and entered the war zone.

Even with half the traders at lunch, the scene was one of barely controlled bedlam. The floor was eighty yards square and home to four hundred electronically wrapped trading desks.

Traders roared and shouted and jostled and wrote and signaled. Paper fluttered like confetti. Sweating runners raced from the desks to the communication booths rimming the war zone. Each desk had four video monitors and six phones. Overhead were triple banks of more monitors showing the latest trading positions from dealer floors around the world. Above that flashed news service bulletins on lighted tracks that swept around all four walls.

Eight bored bicycle messengers stood in line at the receptionist's desk, waiting their turn and staring out over the pandemonium. Thad walked straight up to the harried receptionist and declared, "Larry Fleiss told me to find a desk."

"Yeah?" She did not even look up from signing the messenger's sheet. "Well, nobody's told me a thing."

"Take it up with Larry. In the meantime, where's your duty roster?" He spotted the clipboard and pulled it up.

"Hey! Get your hands—"

Thad stopped her with a look. The look where the frustration and the rage from six *months* imprisonment in Aiden all came through, leaving no need to raise his voice as he said, "I told you. Take it up with Larry." He shoved the roster back at her, stopping just before it jammed into her stomach. "Now, one more time. Where is the closest free desk to Larry's door?"

She gave him an uncertain glance, checked the page, and said dully, "Try one forty-two."

"Perfect."

"Hey!" This time without the edge. "You got a name?"

"Indeed I do," Thad said, moving away.

He found the desk without asking, which was good. He had no intention of talking with anybody. Let them come to him, and in their own good time. He dropped the file, managed to scout the room without seeming to, and spotted the table used as a dumping ground for the financial forecasts and business dailies. He walked over, scooped up a double-handful, and moved back to his desk. *His* desk. Just thinking the words gave him a rush.

Eyes tracked his every move. Totally normal. Anybody new was a threat. Thad opened the first forecast bulletin and scanned the crowd with overt glances. Even without looking directly, Thad could spot all the typical characters. Over there was the girl who brushed her hair continuously and stared at her reflection in the compact mirror taped beside her central screen, as she chattered on two phones. Farther down the aisle was the guy who chewed his way through three combs a day. Next to him was the cigar chomper, not allowed to light up, so he mangled a stogie or two per session. The man who used his tie like a noose, tightening and loosening it in constant jerks. The woman who balanced a tennis racket, or bounced it from knee to knee, pretending she could still run through six sets. The woman who scooted continually back and forth across the aisle on her wheeled office chair. The guy who chanted the news as it flashed along the overhead screen, not even hearing it himself. The pair who compared lies about women and big nights between trades. All the frayed nerves of veteran Street people.

By the time the lunch hour ended and the tension heightened into a full-throated roar, Thad was moving smoothly into the pattern and the patter. He sat like a stone idol before his own bank of screens, tracing the market's movements and listening as the other traders scurried.

He knew he was being inspected; he knew his first move would be watched by four hundred sets of eyes and tracked on screens here and in every other office of Valenti right around the globe. The mystery guy. New to the scene, vetted by Larry Fleiss himself. Not even a hello to the floor manager. Not even a nod to the other traders. The size of his first trade would inform the others of his authority. Thad was determined to make it a whopper. He sat and felt the rusty adrenaline faucets squeak slowly open again.

He perused the file of the last trade by Larry's former top trader and whistled at the size. Almost eight hundred million dollars in yen options spread over a ten-day period. He did not need to check the screens to know the bank took a hit on that one. A big hit. The yen had been dropping steadily, contrary to every pundit the length and breadth of the Street.

He then browsed the financial newsletters and the business dailies. Thad was not looking for answers. If these news sheets contained surefire wins there would be no losers. As it was, the Street was littered with the corpses of traders who had followed sage pundits down to their last bitter nickel. No. Thad was looking for *questions*. Where was the market's attention? What was hot? The biggest action would be focused on the fad of the moment.

Yen. The Japanese currency seemed to be on everybody's mind. Why did it keep falling? Some of the experts claimed it was interest rates, others the Tokyo market, still others the rising U.S. economic forecasts, more still the instability of the Japanese government. Taken together, the sages sounded like a group of New York taxi drivers discussing football.

Thad turned his attention back to the trading file to study the positions the bank had taken more closely. He was still at it when the red light at the top of his phone began blinking. Traditionally, this was the link between every trader and the floor manager or chief trader. Thad grabbed the handset and gave an overloud bark. "Dorsett."

"Hey, sport, tone it down." The rasp could belong to only one man. "What looks good?"

"Not a lot. Franc and mark Euros are bouncing all over the chart."

"Yeah, the market's had a bad case of the heebie-jeebies for weeks. How about the yen, it moving?"

Thad knew the overly casual question was a test, but he was ready; he had watched it ever since reading the file from Larry's former number one and the trade that ended her run. "There's some big money pushing yen all day. In and out. Two big players at least. Could be central bankers on the sly, trying to turn it around."

"What's your feeling?"

"It's too low," he said, knowing he was going out on a limb, especially since that was exactly the basis upon which the last fatal trade had been made. "Way too low."

"Come up with anything yet?"

In four hours? Who was Fleiss kidding? "Working on it."

"Deadline's been moved up. First thing tomorrow, in my office. Be ready." Larry hung up.

□

Thad Dorsett left the Turner Building in the breathless moment between evening and night. No need to stay any longer. He knew what he was going to tell Larry. Hanging around would only tempt him to give in to worries, which was death for a trader. Thad pushed through the outer doors and glanced up. The sun had set, light was fading, and the little strip of sky visible between the buildings was awash in rosy hues.

As he started across the plaza fronting the bank, a voice behind him called, "Mr. Dorsett?"

"Yes." Warily he backed away from the slender man in the dark uniform. He could never be too careful. Not here in New York.

"I'm Jimmy. Your driver."

"My what?"

"I've been assigned to be your driver, Mr. Dorsett." Taking no notice at Thad's surprise, he pointed at the suit bag Thad was carrying. "Is that all your luggage?"

"Yes." Reluctantly, Thad allowed the stranger to take his grip. He had only brought one change of clothes, not expecting to be here longer than a day. "Where are you taking me?"

"Wherever you want to go, Mr. Dorsett." The man started down the broad marble stairs toward the dark stretch limo parked in front of the bank. "But you've got a suite reserved at the Plaza. Maybe you'd like to stop off there first."

"You don't say." Thad allowed the driver to open his door, and he slipped into the backseat and smiled at the leather-lined space. When Jimmy was behind the wheel, he said, "Go down Broadway, will you?"

"Sure thing, Mr. Dorsett."

He sat back and enjoyed Broadway as it unwound about him. The garish carnival of night was gradually waking up. He felt as though it were all coming alive to welcome him.

This was the way to live in New York. No jamming into subways filled with a solid wall of flesh. No cringing over the dictates of a boss frightened for his own job. No struggling to live with impossible city prices on an impossibly tight budget. None of that. Thad sighed and settled himself deeper into the luxury. He was made to see life from the backseat of a limo. It was his destiny.

When he had just been starting out, he had heard somebody say that it was time to move to New York when one didn't need to ask the price of anything. Thad slid his hand over the limo's walnut paneling, and decided that the time had almost arrived.

TWENTY-EIGHT

Twenty-Five Days . . .

☐ The telephone's red light was blinking when Thad Dorsett arrived at his trading desk Friday morning. He did not bother to pick up the receiver; he just walked back through the doors and into Larry's office, feeling eyes follow him the whole way.

Larry greeted him by waving a hand at the seat opposite his desk and saying, "Okay, let's have it."

Though he had steeled himself for this moment, still his hands were suddenly slick with sweat. His chance to grab the ring and rise to the top depended on the gamble he was about to take. Larry had demanded three surefire trading deals. No limits, no defining boundaries. Just a guaranteed profit.

Thad took a breath and then began with, "We could make a major trade and arrange to front ride it." Then he stopped.

Fleiss blinked slowly, his only reaction.

Thad gave him enough time to object and then plowed on. "We've got control over large pension funds. Arrange for them to buy a block of stocks. Several stocks, because we couldn't make more than a quarter-point off each buy without alerting the SEC's watchdog group. We precede the fund's purchases by acquiring these stocks ourselves through dummy corporations. Ones far removed from the bank. Then we sell the shares on to the portfolios after tacking on a hit."

Thad watched Fleiss retreat behind his mug. Only the tiniest flicker of his eyes gave any indication of the intense thought being given to his suggestion. This in itself was a good sign. Very good, in fact, as it meant the idea was being taken seriously. Despite the fact that front loading a trade was highly illegal, Larry was earnestly considering the possibility.

Front loading a buy meant that the stocks bought for a customer actually were drawn from another account—an account controlled by the trader. This meant the trader could tack on an extra half-point or so per share and pocket the difference. On an actively traded stock, this much of a differential was found within every trading day. If questioned, the trader could simply claim to have caught the stock on the upswing. A 100-million-share purchase could result in a five million dollar instant profit. Front loading had been a favorite scam during the late twenties, when the market had heated up to the point where such frauds would rarely be detected. Pulling a trick from the history books might well work, at least once.

Thad allowed himself the first full breath of the morning and let his mind roam. Trading was the empire of the nineties. The futures market was transforming itself so rapidly that regulations and laws could not hope to keep up. Such trading was totally invisible to the common people, yet it was beginning to control their destinies like an economic puppet master. This was where Thad wanted to be, where he *belonged*, running a massive empire built on trading.

Financial trading knew neither borders nor loyalties. Patriotism was an outdated joke, as practical to a trader as a steam locomotive. Money circled the globe in an electronic sea, with tides and currents determined by the highest rate of return.

Windows of opportunity opened for seconds only. New information surged like geysers. Traders discounted companies before factories were built. They took their profits before the products hit market shelves.

They bundled Iowa mortgages and sold them to buyers in Paris or Calcutta or Baghdad. Computers were trained to fire off contracts as soon as enemy tactics were spotted. Millions were lost or gained in the blink of an eye. Cash was never touched. Zeros proliferated on daily balance sheets like goose eggs.

Larry shifted in his chair. "And the next alternative?"

"Door number two." The file remained unopened in Thad's lap. He had no need to review his notes. "We set a rumor in motion. You've got contacts at the *Journal* and other places."

Larry shrugged casual agreement. "So?"

"So at the next auction of U.S. treasury bonds, your connections report that the yen is so low and the Japanese banks are in such bad shape, they're not going to buy. Have the rumor start in London. Feed it through viable trading operations to your *Journal* friend so he's covered."

Thad waited. If his first suggestion was illegal, the second was totally outrageous. Being caught would stain the reputation of the entire financial community. Not to mention that it would result in felony charges and sky-high fines for all involved.

But all Fleiss said was, "How do we cover ourselves?"

Thad felt the band of tension around his chest tighten another notch. So close. "Both bond and stock markets will react, we go short in both. A one-time rake-off. Everybody knows the Japanese hold to the blue chips; we take short positions through other traders in different countries on the major utilities and federal treasury notes."

Again he waited while Larry mulled it over. Thad wondered if this was just an exercise or the real thing. What kind of pressure would push a major Street player to take such a risk? Thad could not imagine it, which was why he figured the exercise had primarily been to show one thing: that he was willing to go all the way and do whatever it took to succeed on the Street.

Another slow blink, a single nod. Then, "And the third?"

"The third." His breath quickened. "The third needs a little more work, so I can't talk about it yet. But it's good. And big. Bigger than the other two combined. And what's more, it's totally legit."

And more than that, it was too good to give up without being able to implement it himself. Thad had decided that in the sleepless hours of the previous night. He would give it up, but only in exchange for the gold ring. He readied himself for a battle over this and was determined not to give in.

But Larry did not object. "Okay. Good work." Larry gave another nod, then slid a folded newspaper across his desk. "Now take a look at this."

Thad picked up the paper and saw it was the business section of a Philadelphia paper. Then his eye spotted a name in the lead article, and he sank into the seat. "I don't believe it."

"Had it couriered up this morning by one of the branch managers. Seems your man Korda's got some of our local people running scared."

"Don't lay the goofball on me," Thad objected, reading swiftly. "Korda is not my anything."

The headline read, "Now Get Ready For A Real Bear." The lead paragraph began, "For months the market has been celebrating the longest running upturn in history and thumbing its nose at all those who predicted a downward correction of 10 percent or more. But Valenti banking official and economic pundit Buddy Korda insists otherwise. After addressing close to a thousand like-minded people at a standing-room only affair, Mr. Korda stated in an interview with this paper that . . ."

Thad slammed the paper back onto the desk. "They're calling him a pundit!"

"Keep it. Having that thing around gives me bile."

"Don't tell me you actually think there's something to what this wacko is saying."

Fleiss slid his cup around in a slow circle on the immaculate desktop. "You're a good trader, Dorsett. But you haven't been around the market as long as I have. The Street is as nervous as I've ever seen it. They're a wolf pack and have a pack mentality. The secret of my success has been in seeing which way the pack is going to move and beating them to the punch. I'm a loner, and loners can always get the jump on a group, so long as they're not ruled by fear."

He thumbed the switch that raised his coffeepot into view. Refilling his cup, Fleiss went on, "Right now the pack is waiting for a leader to emerge and tell them which way to run. At a more stable time, this Korda would be laughed off the stage. But at this point in time, he's a threat."

"I can't believe I'm hearing you say this."

"Believe it," Fleiss said. The words held a bitter edge. "If Korda can sway the investment habits of a thousand small investors, he can do it with ten thousand. If he does it with ten, it might become a hundred. And if a hundred thousand small-time investors react to his scaremongering tactics, there's a good chance Korda's prophecies will become self-fulfilling."

Thad felt Fleiss's words push him back into his seat. "You really think it could spread like that?"

"It's already started. The reason the Philadelphia branch manager contacted us is that they've been sitting there all morning, watching people pull their money out of savings and bank-controlled fund accounts. Customers who have been with the bank for years are closing everything down. Mutual funds, IRAs, savings, college trust funds, the lot. From what they've heard, it's happening at banks all over town. According to what they've been told, the money is being channeled into put options."

Thad worked it out and said slowly, "They're betting the market is going to decline."

"All because of something this Korda's been telling them in his talks."

"He can't be having this kind of effect," Thad exclaimed. "You don't know this guy. He hardly knows how to string a sentence together. I worked with him for the six longest months of my life and never heard him raise his voice. Not once."

"Well, he's found his voice now." Fleiss motioned with his cup. "I want you to go out there and stop him."

"What, me?"

"That's right. Do whatever it takes. Find out where he is and figure out something to stop him in his tracks. The Philadelphia branch has ordered one of their guys to follow Korda and find out where he's going to be on Monday and pass the information back to us here. I've spoken with security. They've assigned a couple of guys to go along and do whatever you tell them to do. They're downstairs waiting for you."

Thad stopped his objection before it surfaced. Deep within the folds of Fleiss's doughlike face, he could see the eyes watching, measuring, waiting. Another test, this one unspoken. If he refused, he would also be turning down the job. This was what Larry wanted, he knew, someone willing to do whatever it took.

Thad forced himself to shape the words, "You've got it."

Fleiss smiled for the first time Thad had ever seen. "Take a long weekend; enjoy your first taste of New York. Then hive off to wherever they're going to be on Monday. Work fast and stop this guy in his tracks, before this thing goes any further." A second smile flitted in and out of view. "In the meantime, I'll have the office next to mine fitted out for when you get back."

⊣| TWENTY-NINE |⊢

Twenty-Three Days . . .

☐ Sunday morning found Buddy and Molly in the town of Altoona, Pennsylvania, just north of the Laural Hills. The evening was booked with another talk, the morning was free for worship. Buddy was silent as he, Clarke, and Molly drove to the red-brick downtown church. There he endured the stares and the handshakes and the overloud welcome. He entered the church and slipped into the pew, immensely glad to be able to sit and relax and listen.

His first prayer was for himself, for strength and patience and the ability to see it all to the end. Buddy stayed there through the first song as all the others around him rose to their feet. He prayed to accept his Father's call fully. To stop his objections and his foot-dragging, and to strive to overcome his own limitations.

As he was about to raise his head again, Buddy found himself thinking of Alex. His brother felt so close it was as though he had suddenly appeared to sit there beside Buddy. A burning sensation came to his heart and his eyes. Buddy experienced a gradual *joining* with his brother. In that moment all the years of distress and all the problems he had endured because of Alex simply disappeared. The exasperation and the worry and the sorrow were no longer a part of him. In their place was only love.

Buddy leaned over so far his forehead touched his hands, which were clasped together on his knees. He felt Molly's soft touch on his back—comforting and joining with him, not needing to know what he was praying for, simply wanting to join with him.

He prayed for Alex. He prayed for a healing. He prayed that the healing would start in his brother's spirit and expand to include every part of his being. He prayed that Alex would rise and accept the greatness he had been born with, that he would rise and accept his Lord.

After the service Buddy felt himself much more calm about the attention directed toward him. His heart remained full, his peace intact.

They left the church and drove back toward the hotel. As they were turning into the parking lot, a pinging sounded from within the glove box. Buddy opened the lid and extracted the cellular phone. "Hello?"

"I wanted you to be the first to know," Alex said in greeting. His voice sounded even more hoarse than usual, as though roughened by an emotion he could barely contain. "I went to church with Agatha again this morning."

Buddy knew what was coming even before his mind had fully formed the thought. He felt his entire body squeezing tight, as though the sudden flood of joy was so great that if he did not clench up tight, he would explode. He shut his eyes and turned to the window. He simply said, "Yes."

"I took the walk, little brother. I did it."

His body was trembling so hard he could scarcely whisper the words, "Oh, Alex."

"I walked up and I asked the Lord Jesus to come into my life," Alex said, whispering himself now, forcing the words out around the emotion that choked him. "I confessed my sins, and I prayed for forgiveness, and I said that if it was His will, I wanted to spend the rest of my life being His man."

□

Whey they came back from lunch, Buddy sat and pretended to read while Molly stretched out on the bed. He spent more time looking at his wife than he did his book. The travel had not just tired Molly, it had worn her down. For the first time since she had been sick with bronchitis two years earlier, Molly looked her age. She was drawn and thinner looking than before all this had begun. Yet there was an ethereal quality to her quietness, as though this, too, had been distilled by the road. She was suffused with a light Buddy felt with his heart, rather than saw with his eyes.

A half hour later she rolled over and sat up. "I want to go back and help out Trish. She's had this strep infection for nine days now. Her fever this morning was a hundred and four. Jennifer has a bad throat and a fever as well, and it looks like Veronica might be coming down with it too. Jack sounded exhausted when I spoke with him before church."

Buddy felt as though he had been waiting to hear her say the words. "I think that's a good idea, hon."

"I'm sorry to be leaving you, but not sorry to be going," Molly told him. "I need to see the leaves change color. Not these leaves. My leaves. I want to watch the elm in my backyard get ready for winter."

Buddy found himself worried that when she left, she would take the light with her. "I'll miss you."

Molly smiled only with her eyes, but it was enough. She seemed translucent, as though held to earth only by bonds of love. "I'll be talking to you every day."

"You'd better. I need to keep getting your Bible passages. They really help me, hon."

"I'm glad." She reached into her purse and came up with one of her little cards. "This is the one for your work tonight."

He accepted it and read: *Who knows whether you have come to the kingdom for such a time as this? Esther 4:14*

Buddy looked up. "This is beautiful. And scary."

Molly met his gaze with a calm brilliance, and quietly declared, "You are growing into a prophet."

The simple statement made him shiver. "I'm not so sure—"

She stopped him with a simple raising of her hand. Buddy halted, took a breath, and nodded acceptance. Molly went on. "Almost despite yourself, you *are* growing. I *see* it happening. Don't stand in the Lord's way, honey."

He did not need to ask what she meant. "It's frightening. And it hurts."

"The prophets of old were not happy men. They were forced to carry the weight of an entire nation." Her gaze was as quietly commanding as her voice. "But if you are truly chosen, as I believe you are, then the Lord must feel you are strong enough to bear up under the burden."

"I'll try."

"No, my darling." Molly reached over and took his hand. "You must *do*."

⊣∥ THIRTY ∥⊢

Twenty-Two Days . . .

☐ The security guys were about what Thad would have expected, silent and hulking and at first a little frightening. They wore matching blue blazers and crew cuts and had muscles so pumped up their shoulders remained bunched in permanent shrugs. He had asked their names and got mumbled replies he only half heard and instantly forgot. By the second hour of the early Monday drive, however, he had mentally designated them as Frick and Frack, his two silent shadows. They spoke a grand total of six words the entire trip down to Pittsburgh.

The bank's spy had done his job well. He was a nervous bespectacled kid by the name of Wesley Hadden, nine months out of MBA school and desperately eager to please. When Thad and the guards pulled in front of the Pittsburgh hotel, Hadden handed him a file containing Buddy Korda's movements over the next three days.

Thad endured the kid's business-school handshake and hearty voice, congratulated him on a job well done, and sent him on his way with a sigh of relief. He returned to where the security pair hulked, and laid out the plans he had formulated on the drive down. They accepted their marching orders with stony silence.

Thad went up to his room—the lousy hotel had only one suite, and it was being renovated. No matter. He would only be there one night. Then it would be back to the Big Apple and his office next to Fleiss. Vice president and number two trader in the Valenti banking empire. It had a nice ring. He stretched out on the bed, pleased with himself and excited about his plans.

It was a risk to stay in the same hotel as Korda, but Thad was not planning to move very far until this was over and done. Or lift a finger to do anything but give orders, for that matter. Having muscle at his beck and call wasn't all that bad a thing, when push came to shove. He laced his fingers behind his head and ran through his preparations one more time. If he had to be Fleiss's troubleshooter, this was the way to do it—separated from both the risk and the public eye, but close enough to revel in the action.

☐

The ache from Molly's absence kept Buddy company through the Monday afternoon drive. Clarke showed his usual understanding and drove in silence. The sun was a ruddy globe crisscrossed by power lines and road signs by the time they pulled into the Pittsburgh hotel parking lot. Buddy pulled his cases from the trunk and followed Clarke through the lobby and over to the reception desk, amazed that he had ever become so accustomed to the routine of checking in.

"Mr. Korda?"

Buddy looked up from signing his registration form. "That's me."

"Okay, you're in room two-fourteen." But before the clerk handed over the key card, he swiveled the form around so he could examine the signature for himself. He gave Buddy a sidelong glance, then passed over the plastic key card and said again, "Room two-fourteen."

"Thank you." Buddy walked with Clarke toward the elevator and said quietly, "What was that all about?"

"Word about you must be filtering beyond the churches." Clarke punched the button, entered the elevator, and glanced at his watch. "If we want to grab a bite before we head over, we'll need to meet in about forty-five minutes."

"Fine." Buddy walked down the hall, entered his room, dropped his bags, and went straight to the window. He swept back the curtains and flipped the window catch. He pulled, but could not get the window to open. Buddy was a fanatic for fresh air, especially in a strange room that smelled vaguely of disinfectant. He hit the catch a couple of times, but the window was jammed tight. He made a mental note to speak to the front desk about it, then reached for his cell phone and punched the number for Alex's office.

A familiar woman's voice answered with, "The Korda Trust."

Buddy dropped into a chair. "The what?"

"Mr. Korda, is that you?"

"Yes. Lorraine, what are you doing there?" But he knew the answer even before he formed the question.

"They fired me, Mr. Korda. Well, he did. Thad Dorsett. He's up in New York, and the notice came from the office of somebody at headquarters I've never even heard of before. But it was him, all right. I knew he'd be gunning for me."

"Lorraine, I can't tell you how sorry—"

"Don't let it bother you, Mr. Korda. It doesn't bother me. Agatha had already offered me a job last week. They need my help, and I love it here. She's promised me something permanent afterward." She paused and then added quietly, "If there is an after. Wait, here she comes now."

Before he could say anything more, the phone was handed over, and a cultured voice said, "Buddy?"

"Yes. I'm terribly sorry to hear about Lorraine being fired."

"Don't be. She's not. And my attorneys had a field day with the bank, warning they were going to file suit for wrongful dismissal. Got her quite a nice severance package. And we need her. Desperately."

Buddy found himself most comforted by Agatha's matter-of-fact tone. "What was it she said when she answered the phone?"

"Oh, the Korda Trust. My accountant filed the papers last week. We're spending quite a lot of money, and they wanted to set it up as a tax-deductible trust."

"Agatha, I don't like your spending so much on me."

"It's not the money. Well, it is, but it's not important. My accountant asked me to do it, and Alex agreed."

Buddy started to object and then remembered what Molly had told him about not putting up a fuss when people wanted to help. "Is Alex there?"

"No." A long pause, then more quietly, "He started chemotherapy last Friday. He goes in every third day."

Buddy felt himself drain away, all will, all energy, all desire. It was as if an unseen tap had been opened and his life was pouring out in an unstoppable surge. "How is it going?"

"He's handling it extremely well." A pause, then, "He was hoping we wouldn't even need to mention it to you. I suppose I shouldn't have said anything."

"No." Buddy tried to find strength to put behind Agatha's words. "No, you did right. He's my brother, Agatha. He shouldn't try to hide things like this from me."

"It wasn't hiding, really. He just didn't feel like you needed to worry about this along with everything else."

"It's fine. How is everything else?"

"Oh, we're moving right along here." But Agatha did not sound convinced. "Alex checked with everyone. Paul, Jack, the girls' families, me, Lorraine, Pastor Allen, the others at church. We've all bought put options through the same broker you've been using."

"That's good, Agatha." His voice sounded dull to his own ears. Poor Alex. "Please thank him for checking."

"Oh, dear. I was horribly wrong to tell you, wasn't I."

"Don't talk like that. You were absolutely right. How am I supposed to pray him through this if I don't know what's going on?"

She sighed long and hard. "I feel like I'm surrounded these days by all my mistakes and clouded motives."

"Agatha, I don't know what I'd do without you there, and that's the truth."

But it was as though she had not heard him. "You know when it hit me the hardest? Yesterday. Watching Alex go up to the front of the church. It felt as though I was seeing the most unselfish man I had ever met do what he was always destined to do."

"And you were the one who finally got him to church," Buddy pointed out.

"He went because I pestered him. He did it for me, do you see what I'm saying? And I did it for me too. Not for God. For me." Unshed tears filled her voice, but she forced herself to continue. "Just like I've railroaded the church, not allowing them to have my money unless they spent it on missions. Do you know why I've done that?"

"No, I—"

"Because my own two children have run away from God. No wonder, the way I bullied them at home. After Joe died, I used the children as a way to fill the empty days. I ruled their every waking hour, most especially on Sundays. I never let them build their own relationship with the Lord. Oh, no. I forced them to live according to *my* standards. And they did, at least until they were old enough to leave. One went to Berkeley and the other to the University of Hawaii, about as far away from home as they could get."

"Agatha, I'm so sorry, I didn't know."

"No, of course not. How could you? I pretended to all the world that everything was fine. Even when one joined a rock group and quit school and now spends his money on drugs and alcohol. And the other . . . Oh, I just can't stand the mess I've made of their lives."

"Agatha, even the Lord lost his first two children to the lures of this world. The perfect Father could not offer them freedom and then be sure they would hold to the proper course."

The sniffling slowly subsided. "I suppose that's true."

"Of course it is. You mustn't be too hard on yourself. Look at what you were up against, raising two kids on your own, trying to keep Joe's business going. You did the best you could. Yes, you made mistakes. We all do. But you cannot take their blunders on your own shoulders. Hurt for your children, yes; pray for them always. But accept that they are adults and free to find their own ways."

Agatha responded with a few moments of shaky breathing before she said, "It's strange how Alex has forced me to be so honest with myself."

"He is a remarkable man."

"Yes, he is." The words came easier now, though the voice remained an octave lower than normal. "I've spent years condemning him. I owe you as much of an apology for that as I do him."

"You don't owe me a thing."

But she did not let him stop her. "I let myself be fooled by his exterior. I saw his size and his strength, and I classed him as a drinker and a brawler. He told me about his fiancée and how he never could seem to get over being abandoned."

Buddy was so surprised he had to pull the phone away from his ear and look at it. He brought it back to hear Agatha say, "Are you still there?"

"I'm here. I'm just amazed Alex told you about that. He never talks about it. Not ever. He's not mentioned it to me once in all these years."

That gave Agatha food for thought. Eventually she said, "It's nice to think that our working together has been good for him as well."

"More than just good." Strange how Buddy could be so worried over Alex and yet so happy at the same time. "Maybe talking with you about what happened released him to go forward and accept Christ."

"Perhaps you're right." Another pause, and then, "He's a wonderful man, your brother. He has the biggest heart and the gentlest spirit I have ever known in a man."

Buddy searched for something to say and finally settled on, "I wish there were some way to turn back the hands of time and have Alex meet you earlier."

"That is the nicest thing anyone has said to me in years." Agatha's voice found a new calm. "Maybe it just wasn't time. Not until now."

"Maybe not," Buddy agreed. "I'm glad you're there now, though. Very, very glad."

⊣│ THIRTY-ONE │⊢

☐ Thad Dorsett must have fallen asleep, because the next thing he knew there was a knock at the door. He rose and checked his appearance in the mirror, straightened his tie, and swept back his hair. Then he opened the door to reveal the larger of the pair. "Everything taken care of?"

"Come on over to our room," the security guy replied, which for him was a full lecture.

Thad followed him across the hall, where the guy rapped twice, paused, then knocked once more. Instantly the chain was drawn back and the lock released. Thad followed him inside, but he halted at the sight of the two women seated on the sofa. He inspected them carefully, then said to the guard, "Nice work."

"I'm Dawn," the blond one said. She was beautiful in a hard-edged way, so long as Thad did not look too closely at her eyes.

She motioned to the redhead seated beside her. "This is Crystal."

"You're both perfect, is what you are," Thad said. He turned to watch a stranger erecting a camera tripod by the window. He demanded of the guard standing beside the closed curtains, "He knows what to do?"

"No problem." The stranger answered for himself. He wore a greasy ponytail and worked with bored efficiency. A battered metal case was flung open to reveal a huge amount of photographic equipment. He lifted a camera housing attached to a motor drive and fastened it to the tripod. Then he brought out the longest telescopic lens Thad had ever seen. He hefted it like a rifle and swung it around so the larger end was pointed toward Thad. The outer lens was the size of a dinner plate. "With this thing we'll get every wart and wrinkle in living color."

"You'd better." Thad turned to the second guard and asked, "You arranged things with the front desk?"

In response, the man turned to where his mate still stood by the door and said, "Lights." Instantly the room was bathed in shadows.

Thad walked over to where the guard was peeling back the curtains. He peeked through, excited by the voyeuristic power.

The hotel was shaped in a three-story U. The guard's room faced the narrow, inner courtyard. Overhead the sky was giving way to night. Thad followed the guard's pointed finger and saw a man knotting his tie in the mirror in the second-floor room directly across from their own. A moment's observation was enough for Thad to declare, "That's our man."

The guard motioned to the two women and commanded, "Over here."

They rose in languid motions, used to having men watch. The soft light from outside was kind to their calloused features. Thad pointed and said, "Over there. Directly across from us. What's the room number?"

"Two-fourteen," the guard tonelessly replied.

"Here," the photographer said, snapping the telephoto lens into place. "You'll get a better look through this."

Dawn leaned over, looked a moment, and said, "It's a snap."

Crystal then focused through the lens. She exclaimed, "Yeah, sure, I thought I'd seen him before."

All eyes turned toward her. Thad demanded, "Where?"

"His picture was in the paper yesterday. What's his name?"

"Buddy Korda."

"Right. That's the guy. Korda."

Dawn asked, "You read the papers?"

Crystal straightened from the camera. "Something about a speech or interview or something. Wait, wait, I remember now. The economy, am I right?"

"It doesn't matter," Thad snapped. Anger billowed in fiery waves. "All you need to know is do it when he's back from his meeting tonight and he's gotten ready for bed. Just move in and set it all up fast."

"Sure," Dawn said, weaving her way back to the sofa. "We got it, no problem."

"There better not be. You only get one chance. And remember, he's not going to want to let you in."

"I'm a big girl," Dawn declared.

"We both are," Crystal agreed, as indifferent as Dawn. "A guy like that won't stand a chance."

"And be fast with the clothes," Thad said. "We need these pictures to be hot."

"We'll be in and on him so fast the guy won't even know what hit him," Dawn promised.

"There's a bonus for getting it right," Thad said. It was going to be a real pleasure to bring Korda down. "A big one."

⊣‖ THIRTY-TWO ‖⊢

☐ The talk had tired him out more than any he had attended up to that point. Perhaps it had been the size— well over a thousand people—but he didn't think so. The crowds were growing larger with every passing day. And there were television or video cameras at almost every event these days. No, it was probably the increasing sense of pressure and juggling so much all at once—coordinating and planning and arranging and cramming more and more into every available minute.

His head buzzed with confusing bits and pieces of logistics, keeping him silent on the drive back to the hotel. When they arrived, he bid everyone a weary good night and headed for his room. His feet seemed to stumble as he plodded down the hall. He fumbled with his keycard and tried in vain to open the door until he looked up and realized he was trying to get into the wrong room. That brought an exhausted chuckle. He was tired indeed.

He scarcely managed to get into his pajamas and brush his teeth before falling into bed. He was asleep before his head hit the pillow.

The pounding seemed to come from a long distance away. Louder and louder, until he was pushed upward by the noise. The door. Somebody was knocking on his door.

He forced his eyes open. "Who is it?"

The reply was indistinct, but it sounded like a woman. He rolled over, fumbled for the lamp, and blinked in the light. "What?"

"Room service!" The pounding continued.

He rolled out of bed with a groan. "Just a minute."

He padded over, switched on the main light, and said through the closed door, "You've got the wrong room."

"Look, this is two-fourteen, isn't it?"

He had to struggle to think. "Well, yes, but—"

"Then you've got to sign for this."

"Oh, this is ridiculous." He unlocked the door and swung it open. "I told you—"

But the women were already in the room. Two of them. Beautiful and tough and *strong*. He was guided away from the door by the blond, while the redhead shut the door and then moved over to sweep back the curtains. So fast and so utterly unexpected that he could scarcely draw breath, much less speak.

Finally he managed, "Look—"

"No, buster, *you* look." The redhead wore a leer as she reached up behind and began unhooking something. "We're a little gift from a pal of yours."

"A special something you'll never . . ." The blond dropped the hand holding his arm and took a step back. "Hey, you're not him."

The redhead stopped shrugging off her dress. "What?"

"Take a look." The blond's leer was gone, her expression hard as granite. "What's your name?"

"Clarke," he stammered. "Clarke Owen."

The redhead gave him an angry frown. "Where's the other guy?"

"The other bed's empty," the blond said crossly.

Suddenly he understood, and the realization hurtled him to full wakefulness. "We changed rooms." He was no longer stammering.

The redhead's expression turned savage. "*What?*"

"There goes our bonus," the blond said glumly.

"We changed rooms," Clarke repeated, glancing from one to the other. "He likes to have fresh air at night, and this window is stuck closed."

"Great, just great!" The beautiful face held an amazing amount of bitterness. "Come on, let's go."

"Sleep tight, honey," the blond said, following her friend from the room.

Clarke stood frozen to the spot, listening to his rapid breathing, running the sequence over and over through his mind. His roving glance caught sight of the curtains. He realized with yet another startling jolt why they might have opened the drapes. As he stood there, the curtain to a darkened window across the courtyard flickered once, and was still.

Clarke closed his drapes and moved back to the door. With trembling fingers he reset the bolt. Only then did he notice the empty screw holes higher up, and realize that someone had removed the night latch. He walked over to the desk, picked up the chair, walked back to the door, and jammed it hard under the knob.

He turned off the lights and went back to bed, as awake as he had ever been in his life. He wondered if he should even mention the visitation to Buddy and decided he had no choice. They would need to make careful arrangements in the future.

Sleep was a very long time in coming.

─╢ THIRTY-THREE ╟─

Nineteen Days . . .

☐ The week was one hard push. Tuesday morning they made the six-hour drive to Akron, Ohio. Wednesday morning they moved on to Zanesville. Thursday they traveled to Dayton. It was not what had been originally planned, but very little was these days. Buddy's message was spreading far faster than he could travel, and demands for him to speak grew by the hour. The press pestered Alex and Agatha continually. They called from everywhere under the sun, demanding immediate access. Agatha turned from cool to frigid, and even Alex responded to the television bullying with a stonelike hardness.

Though tired from the week's activities, Thursday found Buddy ready for another press conference. He did not particularly want to face the press and its hard-eyed skepticism again.

But with less than three weeks left, he would do anything possible to make sure his message was heard. Despite his fatigue, he was able to trust in his newfound ability to remain steadfast to the central message. Which meant he entered the hotel conference room that afternoon, waited for the television lights to come on, greeted the gathered press while his microphones were tested, and then launched immediately into his message.

"The idea that our economy will always continue to expand, that our government can fine-tune the economy and make growth a constant, is nothing more than a myth. A sad one." He saw the smirks around the table. Such intelligent people. So certain of their attitudes and their ambitions. Buddy persisted. "All of life is cyclical. We are born, we live, we die. The same will happen with every economic cycle. There has never been a straight-line economic rise. There never will be. If you were to chart out the movements of just the last twenty years, you would need a huge graph, because the peaks and troughs are so far apart. But in peak times we tend to forget there were ever troughs. We would like to pretend that they can't happen again."

"Mr. Korda." One of the skeptical young men leaned forward. "Are you saying that we cannot learn from our mistakes? Couldn't it be possible to ensure that the next economic downturn would not be so severe?"

"In theory, certainly. In reality, no."

"And why is that?"

"Because of human nature. Because of greed." He was losing them. He could see it in their faces. Mention a moral code and their minds went on autopilot. "There is a passage in the Bible that goes, 'O foolish people, without understanding, who have eyes and see not, and who have ears and hear not.'"

He glanced around the table, saw no indication that anyone recognized the passage, and with a mental shrug returned to the central theme. "It is fairly easy to recognize that our financial system is out of kilter. Too many of the people in charge of our banks have completely lost touch with the world beyond Wall Street. They live to trade, not to serve their customers. They are after fast bucks and quick profits. Banks accept trading risks that would have been utterly unthinkable just twenty years ago.

"People look at the Great Depression as though it caught the world by surprise. Well, it did, and it didn't. I've done some reading about that time, and I've found that people were worried about the dangers five years before the crash actually arrived.

"What concerns me now, as it concerns others, is how *many* things we have in common with that period. Two of these factors have been in the press recently, the air of frantic speculation and the overly high prices of stocks. But there are other parallels that greatly concern me. I want to mention just three of them here, the three that frighten me the most.

"Back in the twenties, banks could trade nationwide. They operated in as many states as they wanted. That meant when they began going under in nineteen-thirty, their bankruptcies had a *national* effect. So in the thirties Congress passed a series of laws restricting banks to operation in just one state. Banks have been fighting to have these laws rolled back ever since.

"In the late eighties, the banks finally pulled the last remaining teeth from these laws, and now we are faced with a growing national banking network all over again.

"Second, until the depression, banks could print their own money. Supposedly this was backed up by the banks' gold reserves. But these reserves were not effectively monitored. Banks used these same reserves to back wild speculations in the markets. The result was, banks printed money backed by their good name, nothing more. When the market dropped, the banks' assets were wiped out, and their money was worth nothing.

"Banks today do not print money, but they *do* print paper credits. They print them, and they trade in them. The difference between today's paper and yesterday's money is only one of magnitude.

"Paper money is a *promissory note*. It is a freely exchangeable slip saying that when presented to the bank, the bank will produce gold or U.S. currency to cover that amount. Today's bank papers are promissory notes as well, only they're a hundred million times larger.

"Once again, these credit papers are used like currency to buy and sell businesses, support governments, cover mortgages, and run local communities. Once again, this paper is backed on nothing more than the bank's good name.

"And third, the twenties saw a huge upsurge in the amount of foreign capital flowing into the American stock and bond markets. Germany was still in ruins after the First World War, as was much of the rest of Europe. Foreign capital flowed into the only market that was booming—America. That was very nervous capital and was controlled by just a handful of huge foreign investors. When they felt the market had peaked, they pulled their money out. All at once, there was an unexpected drain with cataclysmic results. How do I know that this had such a terribly destabilizing effect? Because records show that this occurred on the Friday before Black Monday—October 26, 1929.

"Today, the Japanese market remains in severe recession. Their stock market is down *forty percent* from its level of just three years ago. Our interest rates are *nine times* higher than theirs.

"Today, Europe's economy is in turmoil. Germany and France are experiencing their highest levels of unemployment in fifty years. Their stock and bond markets are stagnant.

"Because of these and other factors, the level of foreign investment in the U.S. markets has never been higher. Once again, this is very nervous money. There is an extremely tense finger on the trigger. This gun is aimed directly at the heart of our own financial system."

□

Thad was a bitter man. Thursday morning he stared out the Dayton restaurant window as the lunch crowd began to arrive. The sunlight seemed to mock him and his anger.

"Something the matter with your food, hon?"

"What?" Thad swung back around and focused first on the waitress and then on his untouched plate. "Uh, no, I'm just not hungry."

"You're going to have to do better than that." She showed a weary smile. "Take a plate like that back into the kitchen, we'll both have to answer to the cook."

"Just bring me a coffee." He turned back to the window.

The two guards remained as silent as they had been all week. He did not mind in the least. For three days they had tracked Buddy Korda, always one step behind the man's erratic course. Plans seemed to change by the hour, leaving them utterly unable to set another trap.

Not only that, but Thad's blood was brought to a boil by the morning's papers.

The day before, according to several articles, a bulletin had flashed over the financial wires. One paper said it had originated in London, another Rome. Reuters and AP both covered it, however. The report stated that the Japanese were not going to bid on the next treasury bond offering.

Just as he had suggested to Larry Fleiss.

The response had been explosive. Bond prices had dipped by 18 percent in the space of an hour. Then a second rumor had surfaced. Because of the yen's weakness the Japanese were pulling out of stocks as well. The New York exchanges went into a paroxysm of selling, shedding one hundred ten points in fifteen minutes.

The effect was so shattering that the Japanese finance minister had been raised from his bed so that he could issue a personal denial.

The finance minister's statement had resulted in just as powerful an effect, only in the opposite direction. Bond and stock prices had soared, with the Dow closing 212 points above the previous day.

Thad ground his teeth in silent fury. Larry's jovial call earlier that morning had only poured salt in his wounds. The man had congratulated him on a great idea and crowed over the profits made by going in both directions and in both markets. Thad had forced himself to sound easy and amiable, but inside he burned with wrath over having missed the action. His idea, Larry's glory. All because of Korda botching their well-laid plans and then running across the country like a fox.

Well, this time they wouldn't fail.

When the cell phone chimed, he had it up and at his ear before the first ring had ended. "Dorsett."

It was Wesley Hadden, the kid on Korda's trail. He sounded terse, frightened. "They're giving a talk tonight at the Clarkstown community center."

"Great." Thad made swift notes. "Good work."

"They don't have hotel reservations yet." He almost bit off the words.

Either that or they were keeping it secret. No surprise, after the other night's fiasco. "If you hear something, call us back."

"This is the last time I need to report, right?"

"Probably." The kid's tone was unsettling. "What's the matter?"

A moment's hesitation, then, "I've been listening to Mr. Korda speak."

"Don't let it get to you."

"This is a lot . . ." The kid stopped, breathed hard, then demanded sharply, "Exactly how much longer do I need to hang around?"

"A day, maybe two. I'll let you know. In the meantime, stay on his case." Thad switched off the phone to find the two guards watching him impassively. "Tonight's talk is in Clarkstown. You know people there?"

"We can find them."

"Just a question of knowing where to look," the second agreed.

"Okay. Hire some muscle. Just make sure they can't be traced back to us. Can you do that?"

"No problem." Toneless, terse, not the least surprised.

"After the other night, they'll be watching for us at the hotel. So we'll make our move when he arrives for the talk. Make it look like a mugging."

"There'll be others around," one guard pointed out.

"So hit them too. I don't care."

The two hulks exchanged glances. "How hard?"

"Hard as you want. I don't just want him stopped. I want him running scared. Or I don't want him running at all."

☐

They had learned to give Buddy a little time to rest and recuperate after a public meeting, especially the press conferences. Today, however, he scarcely had time to lie down before there was a knock on his door.

When he stood up Buddy felt like he walked into an unspoken message, as though it had been draped around his bed and he walked straight into it.

Buddy opened the door for Clarke. Beside him stood the young man who had attached himself to their group back in Pennsylvania. Wesley Hadden was employed by Valenti Bank, which explained the young man's nervous air; anyone working for the bank but associated with Buddy ran the risk of losing his job. Wesley had proved to be a great help to Clarke on several occasions, traveling ahead while Clarke himself remained at Buddy's side.

"There's a problem," Clarke announced.

Buddy nodded. He knew.

"Tonight's meeting was supposed to be in a community hall, but an electrical fire broke out last night. I've just come from there. It smells like burned cork." Clarke studied his friend. "You don't look the least bit surprised. Did somebody already tell you about this?"

Buddy started to deny it, began to correct himself, and then realized it didn't matter. "Take the car and get back on the interstate. Go to the next exit. Get off and stop at the first church you see. A pastor will be out front. Ask him if we can hold the meeting there."

"Get on . . ." Clarke stepped back through the doorway. "Are you sure?"

"Yes," he said. "Yes, I am."

Clarke exchanged a glance with Wesley, who was staring at Buddy in openmouthed bafflement. Clarke said slowly, "If you're absolutely certain, I guess we'd better be going."

"Take the contact numbers with you," Buddy said. "There isn't much time."

⊣| THIRTY-FOUR |⊢

□ The breathless call came just as Thad Dorsett was checking into the Clarkstown hotel. He moved away from the reception desk as soon as he recognized the voice. "What's the matter?"

The kid tracking Korda reported, "They've changed the venue."

Thad felt awash in an icy fury. "You mean you got it wrong."

"I mean they *changed* it. There was a fire at the community hall last night." Wesley's voice was more than agitated. The guy sounded like he was approaching the edge. "If you don't believe me, go check it out yourself. I don't care."

"Calm down," Thad snapped, signaling to the guards.

"*You* calm down. I've had enough of this. I'm out, you hear me?"

"Sure, sure. Take it easy." Dorsett turned away from curious gazes cast his way. "Where are they holding the talk?"

"This whole thing is *crazy*. The guy hasn't done anything wrong. Why are you bugging him anyway?"

Thad felt another chance slipping through his fingers. "I'll discuss philosophy with you another time. Right now just tell me where the talk is going to be held."

There was a moment's silence before Wesley sullenly replied, "I don't know."

"You mean they're keeping it secret." He exchanged glances with the cold-eyed guards. Bad news.

"I mean, I don't *know*. Nobody does. Mr. Korda's told us to drive into town, stop at the first church we see, ask if we can hold it there."

"That doesn't make any sense." Now it was *Mr.* Korda. Now it was *us* headed into town. "Run that one by me again."

The kid did as he was told. "This is my last call. I can't stand this."

"You mean they suspect you?"

"I mean I don't know what's right anymore. It seemed so simple when I started. But now . . ." He cupped the phone, said something muffled, then came back on the line with, "I see Clarke signaling me." Another moment of raspy breathing and then, "I quit. That's all. I'm a banker, not a spy."

Thad punched off the phone, turned to the pair of guards, and said, "You're not going to believe this."

☐

"Are you sure we're doing the right thing?"

"What, doing as Buddy said?" Clarke laughed and shook his head. "All I can say for certain is, when he spoke there in the hotel room, it was not just Buddy's authority that I heard."

Wesley Hadden was a slender young man with a preference for suspenders and overloud silk ties. He settled his tortoiseshell-rimmed glasses more firmly upon his nose, every gesture tinged with the same nervous air that pitched his voice somewhere near a whine. "But it doesn't make sense! I mean, we're three hours from what's supposed to be our biggest meeting yet, chasing all over creation following orders that sounded, well . . ."

"Crazy," Clarke agreed. "Totally crazy."

"So how can you trust him?"

"I'm not trusting Buddy. I'm trusting God, and trusting that Buddy got it right."

"Got *what* right?" Wesley spun his head around. "Wasn't that an exit?"

"Where?"

"Back there! That side road behind us."

Clarke squinted into the rearview mirror. "I don't see anything."

Wesley spun in his seat. "I'm positive it was an exit." He slumped back around. "So now we're even more lost than before."

"Wait, there's another exit up ahead."

"So what? Mr. Korda said take the first exit." Wesley shook his head. "What difference does it make? I don't believe any of it anyway."

"Okay, here we go. No big deal. We'll just swing around and get back on the interstate going the other way." But then Clarke squinted through the windshield, and slowed the car.

"What's the matter?"

"Right up ahead, see that?"

"It's a church, so what?"

"So there's a pastor standing out there in front."

"Where?"

"Right there. By the notice board."

"But Mr. Korda said the first exit! We're on the wrong side of town!"

"Come on, it won't take a moment to see if this is the right one after all." Clarke glanced at the young man seated next to him. "Is everything all right?"

"All right?" Wesley wiped at the sweat beading his forehead. "We're off riding around Clarkstown on instructions that don't make any sense at all, and you ask me if everything is all right?"

"Have faith," Clarke said mildly, inspecting the young man more closely. Something was definitely wrong there. "In times like these, we can only find answers with the help of faith."

□

After his talk, Buddy stood listening to the pastor continue to radiate excitement over the unexpected meeting. "I had just heard that our evening speaker was canceled. Hard to argue with laryngitis. I had decided to stretch my legs while my assistant started calling around." He laughed. "I have to tell you, when your friends pulled up, I thought it was a hoax. It was only the night before last that I heard about you for the first time. A group of pastors from the area had been invited to a friend's to watch your video."

Buddy listened with one ear, still drained from the evening's meeting. Despite the lack of notice, the hall had been filled to overflowing. The meetings so often were these days. Buddy shook the hands of the last to depart and noticed that Clarke and Wesley were standing in the corner, trying to gain his attention. Buddy waved them over.

"I can't tell you how moved I was by the video," the pastor went on. "So moved I almost doubted it myself the next day. You know how it is, being swept up one moment, then caught by doubt the next. But tonight, my goodness, I have never felt such an affirming flame before."

The pastor offered Buddy his hand. "It has been an honor, Mr. Korda. And I mean that sincerely."

"Thank you." He wondered why Clarke was still holding back. Then he noticed that Wesley's face was streaked with tears.

"I will see to it personally that tapes of tonight's talk are passed throughout our city. You can rest assured of that." He gave Clarke and Wesley a friendly nod and moved off.

Clarke waited until they were alone to announce, "Wesley has something to tell you."

"I'm a spy," he blurted out. "Valenti headquarters sent me to track your movements and report them."

Buddy found himself waiting for some internal reaction, but all he felt was tired. "I see."

Clarke demanded, "Report to whom?"

"A guy named Dorsett. Thad Dorsett."

"That name sounds familiar," Clarke said.

"He was head of our local branch," Buddy offered.

"In Aiden?" Clarke stared at him. "Your boss?"

Buddy nodded and said to the young man, "Thank you for telling us."

"They promised me a promotion if I helped." The young man seemed broken by his confession. "I didn't know, I didn't realize."

Clarke's eyes widened. "The girls, the ones who came to my room."

"That was part of this," the young man confirmed. "They wanted to find some way to discredit you."

"I understand." Buddy felt more worried about the young man than he was about himself. "All is forgiven."

"Not by me," Wesley groaned. "I can't believe I've tried to hurt you. I've listened to your talk four times now, and all I hear is somebody trying to help others. You're not getting anything out of this at all."

"Nothing except the joy of serving my Lord," Buddy said, forcing aside his desire to go and rest. "That is more than enough."

"I don't even know what you're talking about," Wesley confessed. "I've watched the others at your meetings, though. I know this isn't some mass hysteria. I *know* it."

"No, it's not," Buddy agreed. It seemed the simplest thing in the world, the most natural, to offer, "Would you pray with me?"

The young man looked at him, astounded. "You'd do that? After what I've just told you?"

"As far as the east is from the west," Buddy replied. "That is how far the Lord will separate us from our own sins, if only we will confess and repent and accept Him into our lives. How can I do any less?"

Wesley nodded his head. "Teach me, then. Show me how."

Buddy reached out to draw both Clarke and the young man closer. He bowed his head and said, "Let us pray."

THIRTY-FIVE

Eighteen Days . . .

☐ Nathan Jones Turner heard Fleiss out to the end, then demanded, "You say this Dorsett thought up the rumor business?"

"The whole idea was his," Fleiss confirmed, taking great pleasure in rubbing the old man's nose in it. Losing his former number-one trader still burned. "Netted us a cool seventy-five mil in one day's trading."

"Not bad." Trying as hard as he could to sound casual about it. But Fleiss knew. The old man was seething. "Can we do it again?"

"No chance. This was definitely a once-only deal. Had to pull every string I could to get the rumors and the timing down right. Cost us some change too."

"That still leaves us down a hundred and seventy-five million," Turner pointed out. "Not to mention what I need for the second payment on the hotels. Which, I need not remind you, is almost due. I managed to put them off a week, but it was tough." Even so, the protests lacked force. Fleiss had one-upped him. Turner hated that worse than losing money.

Fleiss responded with, "A week should be long enough. Got a couple of other things in the works."

"I hope so." A pause, then, "These come from Dorsett as well?"

"One of them. The biggest one."

"Incredible that such talent would be found in a local Valenti branch."

"Sure is." Keeping his voice bland, he decided now was the time to spring the final shock. "Oh, by the way. I've decided to make Dorsett my personal number one."

"I'm not surprised, with that sort of record." Holding to his calm. But Fleiss knew and Turner knew. Another person was being moved in to shield Fleiss from Turner's spies. "Where is the wonder kid now?"

"Tracking Korda."

"Who?"

"The thorn in our side."

"Not that doomsayer from the back of nowhere."

"The very same. He's starting to have an effect on the market."

"I don't care if he's doing handstands in the middle of the Exchange!" Turner was clearly pleased to have something valid on which to hang his anger. "We've got an *emergency* here. Does the word have any meaning to you at all?"

"Sure, but this is—"

"I'll tell you what this is. It's a waste of our time, and it's a waste of our valuable resourses! Bring that man back."

"Listen, I'm worried—"

"Be worried about your future," Turner snarled. "Get Dorsett back on the trading floor. See what other projects he can dream up. Find out if he can save both your hides. And while you're at it, have him report to me. I want to meet this boy wonder for myself." Turner gathered his dignity like a cloak. "Fly him to Kennedy. I'll send the chopper. Today."

□

"Thad, this is Larry."

"Don't tell me you've already heard."

"Heard what?"

"Never mind." Thad rose from the breakfast table and carried the cell phone out into the hotel lobby. "I'm afraid we missed Korda again last night. Or at least the guys we hired did."

"Never mind that now. Where's the nearest airport?"

"There must be a municipal field outside the city. Why?"

"I don't even know where you are."

"Clarkstown. What's the matter?"

"I'm sending a jet down. Get out to the field now."

"Look, Larry, we're on this guy. It's just a matter of—"

"I told you not to worry about that. Leave the security goons on his tail. You get back here. The old man wants to meet you."

□

Early Friday morning they left Clarkstown for Flint, Michigan. Buddy had rested well and felt even more energized by the conversation he had had that morning with Molly. He waited until they had checked out of the hotel and started for the car to declare, "I'm going home this weekend. Molly's orders. It's for my health. She says she's going to shoot me unless I make it back."

To his relief, Clarke did not object. "I think we could both use a break."

Buddy reached for the cell phone. "I'll call Alex and make sure there's nothing that can't be rearranged." When he disconnected, Buddy was smiling. "They hadn't gotten anything firmed up for either tomorrow or Sunday. Amazing."

Clarke turned from the highway long enough to share his grin. "I can't believe anybody who's been through what you have would still find that word in his vocabulary."

"I suppose so. Anyway, they'll try to book us on the last flight out tonight."

"Sounds good to me."

Buddy settled back. "That was nice, praying with the young man last night."

"You know, Wesley is going to stay on with us," Clarke informed him. "He says we need to take a more careful look at security and planning."

Buddy shrugged. "We'll have to rely on God to protect us, same as always."

Clarke glanced over a second time. "You've changed, old friend."

Buddy did not deny it. "It's the Lord's doing, not mine."

The interstate traffic was a steady, aggressive rush. Buddy glanced through the morning's newspaper, but nothing he read held his attention. He settled the paper on the seat beside him and returned his thoughts to his family, anticipating the joy of seeing them again, spending a weekend together. And then, unbidden, came the old ache of worry over his brother. Buddy sighed and shook his head.

"What's the matter?"

"Alex."

"Oh." Clarke nodded slowly. There was no need to say anything more.

"We've always been so close," Buddy went on, wishing he could push the pain out with the words. "He was the one who named me. Alex was named after my father's father. When I came along, they saddled me with my other grandfather's name, Broderick."

"I never knew that."

"It's one of those deep, dark family secrets. Alex never could say it. He was four at the time, and already the most headstrong little fellow you've ever met. I had that on best authority—my mother. Anyway, he spent the better part of a day standing by my crib trying to get his four-year-old mouth around my name. Then he gave up and called me Buddy. I've been Buddy ever since."

Clarke took the first exit for Flint. When he had stopped at the light at the bottom of the ramp, he turned and watched Buddy for a long moment before saying quietly, "It's in the Lord's hands, friend."

"I know." A long sigh. "Some things are a little harder to leave in his care than others, though. Aren't they?"

The ache accompanied them through the the streets of Flint. When they stopped at a traffic light, Buddy looked out his window at a bustling scene, at people hurrying to-and-fro, caught up in worries and business and work. Construction workers in hard hats, steelworkers in blue factory coveralls, women and men in business suits, people young and old. A mother in the car next to them was tending to a baby in the backseat. Behind her

a woman in what looked like hospital whites was talking into a
cellular phone. He could feel Clarke watching him, and he struggled to put his emotions into words. "I feel like I'm beginning
to catch little glimpses of what it means to see with God's love.
I feel his sorrow for the direction the world has chosen to go."

The traffic light turned green. Clarke drove on in silence.
Buddy continued, "There will be millions who blame God for
this economic disaster when it strikes. But the truth is, He has
given us laws and He has given us a Savior. If we had followed
them more closely we could have escaped this entirely."

"If only," Clarke said quietly. "If only."

"We have nobody but ourselves to blame. But knowing this
doesn't make it any better." Buddy glanced out through the windshield. "I hurt for them, Clarke. I feel like the Lord is taking my
worries over Alex and changing them, forcing me to feel a taste
of *His* pain."

□

The seating area in the back of the chopper was empty this
time. One of the pilots came back to usher Thad in, close the
portal, strap him to a seat, and wish him a hurried welcome.
Clearly they were under instructions to make good time. Thad
sat back and enjoyed the plush surroundings.

The leather seats gave way to walls and ceiling carpeted in
the same silky covering as the floor. Seats and walls and floors,
even the frames surrounding windows and the triple television
sets, were a calming pastel blue. It gave Thad the feeling of being
both cocooned and cosseted.

As Manhattan's skyline swooped into view, Thad reviewed
what he knew of Nathan Jones Turner. The man was flamboyant

and loved the spotlight. Turner was tall and well-kept for a man in his early seventies, with deep-set eyes and a piercing gaze. He was known for his notorious temper and had the touch of a modern-day Midas. He produced movies and loved to parade around with starlets one-third his age. He owned three jets and a helicopter and hated flying. He had recently spent twenty-two million dollars on a Van Gogh. The man was a living legend.

Thad felt a twinge of unease as they passed over the Manhattan skyline and kept heading east. When a white strip of beaches disappeared behind them, Thad punched the intercom button.

"You need something, Mr. Dorsett?"

"Where are you guys taking me?"

"Didn't they say? You're being met by Mr. Turner."

He looked out the window, saw nothing but blue skies and empty blue sea. "He's got a secret island out here nobody's ever heard of before?"

"Better than that, sir. Much better." The helicopter did a slow bank to the left. "Take a look out your left portal."

Thad slid to the other side of the chopper, looked down, and gasped aloud. Beneath him was the largest yacht he had ever seen.

The pilot slid open the door separating the cockpit from the passenger quarters. A grin appeared beneath his aviator shades. "Most people do that the first time they see the boat. Gape like that."

"That belongs to Mr. Turner?"

"It does now. They built it for some sheikh who never picked it up. Turner bought it last year. Seventy-five meters, over two hundred and thirty feet. It's got about everything you could ask for in a boat. Swimming pool, diving submarine, satellite links, the works. Hang on, sir, we're coming in now."

The blond chopper hostess was there to lead him from the ship's flight deck. Only this time she was dressed in a bikini top and wraparound sarong. She led him down a set of teak stairs with what appeared to be gold-plated railings, and ushered him into a palatial-size living room.

A white-haired man rose from the leather settee, tossing aside the papers he was working on. "Mr. Dorsett. Glad you could join me."

"This is an honor." Thad did a slow sweep of the room. Anybody who went in for this kind of ostentatious luxury was looking for compliments. "And this is the most amazing place I've ever seen, on land or sea."

"Home away from home. Here, sit right down there. What will you drink?"

"Nothing now, thanks. Maybe later."

"Just say the word, and Doris will see to whatever you need." Nathan Jones Turner resumed his seat. He was a well-padded man, but the carefully tailored skipper's blazer and white trousers gave him a sleek look. "Folks told me that I should charter a boat, that I wouldn't have time to use the thing more than a couple of weeks a year. Waste of money, they called it. Know what I told them?"

"I have no idea."

"Told them to stuff it. Told them it was pride of ownership that mattered. Something most people don't understand. Or can't. Or don't want to, because they know they'd never be able to afford it." Nathan Jones Turner leaned forward and punched the air with one finger. "But *I* can. And I didn't want to *borrow* somebody else's boat. I wanted to *own* one of my own. Know how much it cost me?"

The air seemed to vibrate with the man's power. Energy pulsed from him, making a mockery of his age and his white hair. "A lot."

"More than a lot. A million and a half dollars a foot. Know what else? Got thirty percent knocked off because I paid cash. Cash on the barrel, that's the way I like to do business. Know why? Because I *can*."

Turner leaned forward again. He was always in motion, always tense and coiled, even when seated. "Only a handful of people in the whole world can command that sort of power. Not just power of money. No, sir. Power to *control* money. Have so much you can thumb your nose at the whole rotten lot. You understand what I'm saying?"

Thad felt as though he was sitting through a cannon barrage. The energy being focused his way was that strong. "I'm not sure."

"You stay there on the trading room floor, you sidle up to your trading buddy, and you'll make yourself a good salary. With bonus, we might be talking a million or more a year." Turner wiped it away with a sweep of his hand. "Small change. It's still a *salary*. What I'm saying, you want to ride free, you need a *base*. Forty, fifty million in your hand, then you can start thinking like a free man."

He was being sold. He understood that much. But why was still not clear. "Sounds good to me."

"Of course it does. You're a smart man. Couldn't have come up with that idea of yours unless you were smart." Turner inched closer to the edge of the settee. "The question is, how smart?"

"Smart as I need to be."

"That's good to hear. Because I asked you out here to make you an offer. A once-in-a-lifetime offer. A chance for you to rise above the masses and live life like it means something."

"I'm listening."

"You'd better be." Turner stabbed the air a second time, the jab so sharp Thad had to force himself not to wince. "From now on, you answer to me. You tell me everything that happens in Fleiss's office. Every last detail. What the man thinks, what he says, what he has for lunch. Everything."

"You want a spy," Thad said, finally understanding.

"I've got spies everywhere. I want me a spy who can think. Fleiss is losing it. He's past his prime. I want you to siphon off everything you can of his and get ready to take over the hot seat yourself." Turner bounded to his feet, waited impatiently for Thad to join him. "Think you can handle that?"

"Absolutely. I'm your man."

"We'll see. If you work out, we'll make every dream you ever had look like table scraps." Turner wheeled about and strode toward the stairs. "Take the afternoon off and enjoy the boat. If you need anything, you just ask Doris. She's good at getting folks whatever they want."

□

The lobby of the Plaza Hotel looked pale and public after the ship's private luxury. Thad seated himself in the corner, dialed Larry's number, and said as soon as the man came on the line, "Turner did a number on me."

"What's that mean?"

"He wants me to spy on you."

"Hang on a second." There was a squealing sound, then silence. "Okay. I've got a gizmo here that interferes with bugs and transmission devices. Can't be too careful with the old man."

Thad sketched out the conversation and used the traffic pass-ing through the lobby as his own personal reality check. Slowly he felt as though he were returning to earth from a money-clad dreamland. Strange to be thinking that while seated in the lobby of one of the most expensive hotels in the world, one where his own suite was costing the bank eleven hundred dollars a night. But after the yacht, those numbers were peanuts.

Larry waited until Thad had finished to say, "So what did you tell him?"

"I told him yes. Are you crazy? What choice did I have?"

"Then, probably none at all. Not if you wanted to keep your job." A moment of asthmatic breathing, and then, "Now is a different story."

"You got me out of Aiden and offered me my dream job." Only now the dreams felt constrictive. The power of Turner's words and his offer still reverberated. "I owe you."

"Good to hear. Well, Turner wants you back here in the office."

"Great."

"See you Monday." Another pause, then, "Thanks. You're the one with the chit to cash in now."

Thad punched off his phone, waved to a passing waiter, and ordered a drink. He had made the right decision to tell Larry. The man was sure to have figured out what went on. As it was, his options were still open. He had plenty of time to decide which way to jump.

Thad stretched out his legs and gave a contented sigh. No question about it. He was a man on his way to the top.

⊣❙ THIRTY-SIX ❙⊢

☐ It was after ten that night when Buddy and Clarke finally landed, but Molly was there at the airport to meet Buddy. She took one look at his face and enveloped him in a warm embrace. Buddy dropped his carry-on, saw Clarke accept a hug from his wife and youngest daughter, and closed his eyes on the world. Molly's arms seemed to draw the fatigue from his bones. "I want to sleep and never wake up."

"Soon," she promised. "But I told Trish we'd stop by."

"Molly, not tonight. Please."

"Everybody is finally well, but it's been hard on them. And Jennifer declared that unless she can see you tonight, she is staying awake forever."

Buddy sighed and nodded silent acceptance. At five years of age, Jennifer could be the most stubborn lady any of them had ever met. As he walked out to the car, he found himself perking up at the thought of seeing his auburn-haired angels.

Scarcely had he come through the door before his legs were enveloped by two pairs of eager arms. "Granddaddy!" Buddy lowered himself and embraced them before rising to greet his son and daughter-in-law.

He scarcely seemed to hear what he said or was said to him. What was far more important than the words was the simple joy of being back among his family, in the place where he most belonged on this earth.

Molly sat across from him, content to be where she could watch him enjoy their family. Buddy sat with a mug of lemonade in one hand, a ham sandwich in the other, and a smear of mustard on one cheek, listening to three conversations at once, as happy as he had ever been in his life.

"All right." Trish broke up the gathering with a clap of her hands. "Veronica, it's so far past your bedtime we might as well plan for tomorrow. You, too, Jennifer."

Veronica, the younger child, reached out her hands. "Take me, Granddaddy, take me!"

Buddy scooped up Veronica and started across the room. "Say good night, honey."

She nestled her face into the space beneath his chin, and waved five fingers over his shoulder. "Night-night, everybody."

His daughter-in-law started up the stairs behind him and murmured, "Be sure to notice the fish."

So he went into their room, settled his granddaughter on the bed, turned to the goldfish bowl on her desk, and exclaimed, "My, what lovely pets you've got there."

Little shoulders scrunched up in pleasure. "They're mine."

"Well, of course they are. Have you named them yet?"

"Oh, yes." A finger pointed vaguely at one of the identical pair. "That one is called Chili. And the other is Con Carne."

"Is that a fact?" Buddy glanced a question over to where their mother leaned in the doorway.

"What can I say?" Trish replied. "My baby girl is nuts about spicy food."

He went from one bed to the other, hugging Jennifer and Veronica close and listening to their prayers. When the lights were out and Buddy stood in the doorway with Trish, he found himself reluctant to go back downstairs.

"You should see yourself," Trish observed. "You look about fifty times better than you did when you got here."

"Of course I do." Buddy stayed where he was, staring down at the two night-clad figures in their little beds. "Right here is as close to heaven as I'll ever find on this earth."

□

Aiden had never looked lovelier than it did that Sunday morning. Buddy sat in his back garden watching the morning gather strength, feeling blessed by birdsong, sunlight, and every late-blooming flower. His empty coffee cup sat on the lawn beside his chair; his Bible rested open but unread in his lap. Everywhere he looked, he saw the divine.

"Buddy?"

He turned to find Clarke Owen slowly approaching with Molly. Clarke wore a strange expression. Buddy reached out a hand to his wife, and smiled a welcome to the assistant pastor, "Hello, old friend."

"I'm sorry to disturb you," Clarke said. "You, more than anyone else I know, deserve a day to yourself."

"Don't be silly. You're not disturbing anything. Pull up a chair. Both of you."

"I can't." Still, Clarke's countenance remained odd, as though the man was seeing him for the first time.

"I can't either," Molly told him. "I've just gotten a call from some people at church. They were wondering if I'd speak to the adult Sunday school classes this morning."

Buddy inspected his wife's face. He saw none of the old fear and uncertainty there, but rather a sense of calm resolve. As much for that as for the news, he said, "Molly, that's just wonderful."

"Not about your message," Molly went on. "It seems as though everyone has heard that by now. They wanted to hear my personal testimony." She hesitated and then added, "I was wondering if you would like to come with me."

Buddy did not need to think it over. "I'd be honored." He rose to his feet, very glad indeed that the morning's glory seemed to stay with him. He asked Clarke, "Is this what's brought you over?"

"No." Clarke hesitated before saying, "When I walked into the yard, it seemed as though I could actually feel the peace around you."

He started to say that it had seemed the same way to him, but decided that some things were best savored in silence. He glanced at his wife and accepted her smile and her knowing gaze. Buddy asked Clarke, "What did you want to see me about?"

"Alex has gotten a call from the organizers in Richmond. They wanted to confirm that you're still on for their rally a week from this coming Thursday."

"Of course."

"It's just," Clarke hesitated, then went on, "that's only five days before meltdown."

Buddy started back toward the house. "I realize that."

"Well. Fine." Clarke seemed to be looking for some further reaction. "They're estimating eighty thousand men will be there."

Buddy nodded acceptance of the news, more concerned with the grace that accompanied him back into the house. He said to them both, "Give me a second to get on a jacket and tie."

□

The feeling of being embraced by the morning held him throughout the drive to church. It left him quietly isolated even when people began coming over and greeting him and welcoming him back. Buddy seated himself and watched as Molly was guided toward the front of the largest chapel.

Once at the podium, she glanced down to where her husband was seated, smiled a greeting to those gathered before her, and began, "Throughout these weeks of watching my husband share his message, I have not had a single experience of the Spirit. For that matter, I have never felt much of anything throughout my entire life's walk in faith. But the absence has bothered me. Then one night while I was traveling with Buddy, I asked him to pray over me. Nothing happened that night either, but the next morning I awakened with a sense of having been granted a message cloaked in the mystery of silence, the same silence I have known from God all my life."

Buddy could scarcely believe his ears. He leaned forward, wondering if anyone else in the entire audience realized what an effort this was for his wife, what it cost her. Yet as he watched, he began to see that it was costing her nothing at all.

Molly's voice held to its normal quietness, yet the assuredness with which she spoke was utterly new. "I have spent a great deal of time over these past couple of weeks wondering just what this silence means. And I've come to recognize that it is not an absence of God. All I've had to do is look out over the auditoriums and churches and meeting halls and see that God is there with us. I've come to see God's silence as *essential*. It has also occurred to me that this is often the way God deals with us. In *essential* silence.

"Imagine, if you will, a grand heavenly orchestra. The conductor raises his baton. The entire orchestra is poised, ready, *silent*. God forms such an essential silence in us so that our ears can become more carefully tuned. We are being prepared to receive His message. We are being invited to still our busy minds and our hyperactive lives so that we can hear the heavenly host sing out in eternal glory, 'Hallelujah! Praise His holy Name.'"

Buddy fought back the misting which threatened to cloud his vision. He did not want to miss an instant of this. He gave the pews to either side quick glances, just enough to see that the people were concentrating with a rapt silence of their own. He turned back to the front. He was so proud at that moment that he felt he would positively burst.

"What God communicates in faith," Molly continued, "is far greater than by vision and rushing wind. My isolation from these experiences has been an immense blessing. Otherwise I might have begun to *limit* my faith by grasping for them. I might have started to live for the *experience* and not for God.

"A mystical experience is not the defining moment. There should be affirmation from others within the church. And the written Word of God must confirm." Molly stopped there. She reached over and touched the closed Bible beside the podium.

Buddy strained to keep his vision clear. It was strange how such a simple act as his wife reaching out and touching the cover of the Book could affect him so deeply. Yet she seemed to be reaching across the distance that was separating her from God simply by reaching for the written Word.

Molly raised the Bible and held it to her as she went on. "I did not want to join Buddy as he took God's message and went on the road. I have always loved my small town, my little responsibilities, my stable world. Yet God has drawn me out from my comfortable routine. He has drawn me farther and farther along His chosen path with His silence.

"My expectations were not enough. My horizons were too small. I said to God, I like it here. God said to me, I want you *there.*

"In accepting His message of silence, I have come to see a larger directive, one that has consequence for all of us. The ninety-fourth Psalm calls death the 'land of silence,' the place where God is absent. Yet Jesus goes into death, the farthest recesses of empty silence, to seek and to save. He has shown us that His love is greater than sin or eternal death. He accepts our darkness, our death, and our well-deserved everlasting silence upon Himself. Through Him we have been given the glory of never-ending life. Through Him we may hear the eternal song of praise."

Molly bowed her head and said, "Let us close with a moment of prayer.

"Lord Jesus, You are the light that drives out darkness and saves us from the endless silence. You are the light that draws us to holiness. Help us make this day a living hymn of praise. Teach us to appreciate the moments of silence, that we may better hear Your call."

THIRTY-SEVEN

Thirteen Days . . .

☐ Wednesday morning found them in Decatur, and that was where the storm started growing fiercer.

The previous Monday morning they had flown to Indianapolis, where Buddy had given a luncheon address that filled the city's largest church to overflowing. Then it had been on to Lafayette for a press conference, a speech, and a too-short overnight stop. Tuesday had started in Kokomo, then across the state line to Champaign, Illinois. A morning speech in Urbana, then a fast drive to Decatur. His luncheon address drew almost a thousand people. Buddy had long stopped thinking about the numbers.

The newspapers were becoming increasingly vociferous, such that Clarke did not even mention them unless he felt it was something important for Buddy to see. But after the Decatur meeting a man approached, introduced himself as a local broker, and asked if Buddy was planning on changing his dates.

"Of course not."

"Don't get me wrong, brother." The man was both sincere and nervous. "I've heard about you from a dozen different people. Today's gathering only made me more certain that what you say is right. But do you realize the date you've set is less than two weeks from today?"

"I am counting the hours," Buddy replied fervently.

"But the market is stronger than it's been in years!" The man pulled a handkerchief from his pocket and wiped his palms, then his face. "I've got people calling me from all over the state, friends I've known for years. They're selling everything they own and putting their money in options."

"This is good news," Buddy said.

"Is it?" Another swipe, and then he nervously stuffed the handkerchief away. "If the market doesn't move as you're predicting, and on the day you say, these people are going to lose a lot more than they can afford."

"Other than the fact that the Lord reigns in heaven above," Buddy replied, "I have never been as certain of anything in my entire life as I am about this."

"And the date is set?"

"In stone," Buddy confirmed.

The man gave a grim nod. He offered Buddy his card as he said, "Call me if anything changes, will you?"

Buddy watched him walk away, then he moved to where Clarke stood comparing schedules with Wesley Hadden. He asked, "What are the papers saying?"

Clarke shook his head. "I've stopped worrying about them."

"And you don't want to know," Wesley Hadden agreed.

"Tell me."

Wesley expelled his breath in a rush. "Well, the small-town dailies are split. Most of the editorials can be pretty hard on you, but every once in a while there's somebody who claims that you are sounding an all-important wake-up call. They've usually attended both a press conference and a gathering of the faithful. They talk about the evidence you give, but they also mention the power of your message."

"And the others?"

Wesley glanced toward Clarke before reluctantly saying, "The closer we come to the date, the worse they sound."

"Show him the cartoon," Clarke said.

Wesley looked pained. "Why?"

"He wants to know. Let him see it."

Wesley reached into his briefcase, pulled out a magazine, riffled the pages, and said, "It's in this week's *Time*."

One glance was enough. The political cartoon showed him in a long white beard and three-piece suit. The cross hanging from his neck was so big it dragged in the dirt. He carried a sign that said, THE END IS TUESDAY. Tuesday was crossed out, and Friday scrawled beneath it, and Monday beneath that, and on down until he ran out of room.

Buddy handed it back, gave a thin smile, and said, "It looks a lot like me."

"That's all you have to say?" Clarke was astounded. "This doesn't bother you?"

"Why should it, when we're seeing the crowds get bigger every day, and we hear that people are acting on the message?"

"No reason," Clarke agreed, exchanging a glance with Wesley. "None at all."

Wednesday evening they drove to the airport and checked in for a flight to St. Louis. Buddy could feel eyes watching him as they checked in. He tried not to let it bother him. The crowds were growing, the word was spreading, and time was running out.

As he went through the boarding process, Buddy reviewed their plans for the final days. Alex and Agatha were condensing as much as they could. Alex sounded increasingly tired every time they talked, but so did everyone else. Buddy's hurried conversation the previous afternoon with Agatha confirmed that Alex was doing as well as could be expected, and that his brother continued to hold up under the chemotherapy. Buddy let it go at that. The rest could wait until after. Everything had to wait until after. The countdown became an unspoken chant they all shared. Just thirteen days to go.

Christian radio and television networks were organizing live feeds to stations around the country. Alex had agreed without even discussing it with Buddy, hoping the message's power would carry over the wires and through the air.

They were working straight through this weekend; Buddy knew he could neither object nor beg for another time at home. It was a flat-out race from here to the finish.

□

Buddy settled into his seat on the airplane and was busy with his seat belt when a voice said, "Mr. Korda?"

"That's me." Buddy looked up to find two men in business suits and briefcases hovering in the aisle. "Can I do something for you?"

"You already have." The older man offered a meaty paw. "Just wanted to thank you for what you're doing."

Buddy accepted the hand. "Thank God, not me."

"I do, sir. Every morning and every night and sometimes in between."

The other man said, "I heard your message on a tape they played in our Sunday school class last weekend. I've never seen people get so excited over something on a cassette. Went out and invested every cent I had into put options, just like you said."

"That's good," Buddy said. "Now make sure your friends don't just listen, but also act. Tell them to remember the road to hell is paved with good intentions."

"I'll do that, sir. I surely will."

When the pair had shaken his hand a second time and moved off, Clarke leaned over and said, "Now is as good a time as any, I suppose. You've been invited to appear on national television. *Lonnie Stone Live* wants to do two segments with you, one next Thursday night and one the following Monday."

"Fine," Buddy said, and it was. "Tell them yes."

"Buddy, these television people," Clarke hesitated, then willed himself to say it aloud. "They want to set you up, then once the date has passed, they want to shoot you down."

"I don't care what they want." Buddy turned to meet his friend's gaze full on. "Thursday night and Friday morning of next week will be the last chance we have to get the message across."

Clarke mulled that over, then asked, "And the following Monday?"

"I have to tell them to take their money and get out," Buddy explained. "Before it's too late."

⊣| THIRTY-EIGHT |⊢

Eleven Days . . .

☐ By that Friday Thad was beginning to feel secure in his position, and much more at home in New York. He was still housed in the Plaza, still living as a visiting exec on the company's expense account. But that was about to change.

From his suite high in the Plaza Hotel, New York's mythical image seemed almost true. The skyscrapers looked factory fresh as they reached up with beckoning arms to wish him a good morning.

The sordid reality was all too clear, however, down at street level. Even from the back of a limousine there was no disguising the beggars, ten to a block. The crazies were also out in force that morning. Two weeks in the place and already Thad knew to waste no time on the dregs scattered everywhere, clogging every alley and doorway, hands out like a ragged chorus line, begging for change. Ignore them all. It was the only way to survive in this town. Live like they weren't even there. Thad had already decided the city burned so bright because the darkness ran so deep.

Even so, the view from the back of a company limo wasn't all bad. The street life was as entertaining as a new Broadway musical. New Yorkers were constantly auditioning for roles they had already won, where the world was their audience and the admission was free. Laughter was canned and loud enough to carry. Everything was done at full speed. People even relaxed in high gear.

The city's energy amplified the closer he drew to Wall Street. He spent the remaining minutes of the drive going over the documents delivered from his Realtor that morning. Thad had put in an offer on a brownstone at Ninety-third and Park. Those who lived closer in called this area the hem of Harlem. He didn't mind. It was still Upper East Side, and it was a building that would soon be all his.

The objective for most New Yorkers was to rise to a higher floor. The lower down one lived, the greater the threat of being impacted by too many other human bodies. So everybody was on the move, trying to go from the first floor to the fifth, from the fifth to the twelfth, from the twelfth to the penthouse. Then it was time to keep the penthouse and buy the weekend place in Connecticut, which was as far as most New Yorkers' umbilical cords would stretch.

Thad was still enough of an outsider to prefer a bit of green to a more spacious view, and so he was looking to buy a house. The place he had selected came with a postage stamp of a garden surrounded by a thirty-foot brick wall topped with electrified barbed wire. All the comforts of home.

Upper East Side was the place of wealth in action. For about thirty blocks north and south and four or five east to west, it was a high-rent island for the wealthy. The greatest competition was over making an elegant impression. Money was less critical than the time to spend it. The pets were as decorative as the paintings on the walls. Here it was possible to believe there was nothing wrong with either New York or the world. It was a great place to have money and want to flaunt it, which was exactly Thad's aim.

He set the real estate papers back into his briefcase as the limo pulled up in front of the Turner Building. Thad bounded up the stairs, gave the receptionists a quick greeting, ignored the myriad stares that tracked his movements toward the elevator.

Upstairs Thad stopped by his soon-to-be office and checked on the workers laying the new carpet. The old carpet had been fine, but he had changed it anyway, selecting the most expensive silk-and-wool spread he could find. It was good to give the office rumor mill something big to chew on. His private sanctum was a declaration of having arrived.

The contract negotiations with the Valenti lawyers had been predictably vicious. But Thad had stuck fast, and Larry had backed him up. In the end he had gotten everything he had wanted. The day after signing, a mysterious payment had appeared in his newly opened account. That same afternoon a courier had delivered a pound of beluga caviar, a new solid-gold Rolex, and a note from Turner saying, "Glad to have you on board." Thad reported the early bonus to Larry and then used it as down payment on his brownstone.

He entered the trading floor and did a quick scouting. Activity remained at the same fever pitch. Everybody was on edge, stretched by positions that shifted from tenable to terrorizing in the space of a few minutes.

A guy whose name he could not recall looked up from his calculations to grin as Thad passed. Thad slapped the offered palm and asked, "How's it going?"

"Awful. This market needs a daily injection of Tylenol. It's one giant headache. Been that way for weeks." He swiveled to track Thad's progress past his desk. "Hey, what's the scoop for today?"

"Not a chance."

"Come on, be a pal."

Thad arrived at the final desk before the door leading to Larry's private sanctum. He dropped his case and turned to grin at the guy and feast on all the other eyes following him. "If you need a pal, go buy a dog."

In fact, Thad was working on his third idea for Larry. It was a major deal, one that would have been impossible to get by the bank's senior monitors had the market been any less nervous. As it was, however, nobody was making much money and losses were mounting. The sort of alternatives he had offered Larry his second day here were one of a kind. There was no chance to repeat them, not without risking being caught by the SEC. No, what he needed was a new way to guarantee profits, one that remained within legal boundaries. Barely.

As it was, the trading floors were structured along fairly normal lines—equities, currencies, futures, options, and so on. Thad opened his briefcase and pulled out the copy of a file he had left with Larry the day before. His plan was not to add, but rather to restructure on a massive scale. What he wanted was to shake up the entire trading operation, to put his stamp on the bank and its future in a major way. The great secret of New York was, take a chance. Thad was planning to do just that.

The over-the-counter derivatives market was bigger even than the one for money futures, and far more dangerous. Here, companies could hedge against any risk they cared to name, and for any amount. It remained almost entirely unregulated, as it essentially comprised contracts between two private parties. The crowning glory was that it was also completely legal.

Thad had watched its rise for years. He knew this sort of legalized piracy could spell major profits for years to come.

Over the previous eighteen months, OTC derivatives had suddenly started growing at an electric rate. Even so, many banks were afraid to touch them—Valenti included. Thad proposed to change all that, drawing a hundred traders from other less profitable areas and concentrating them on these ventures. The bank's first entry had already started, a project Thad had managed personally in interest-rate swaps. He was two days into the deal, and the bank already had a paper profit of $2.2 million.

If his proposal was accepted, Valenti would soon be doing a roaring business in trades whose names were a foreign language even to most bankers—caps, flaws, spreads, captions, flawtions, spreadtions, and even more exotic fare. Caps set an upper limit on the interest rate paid. Swaps typically changed a fixed rate of interest for a floating rate, or vice versa. For clients it could be a cheap insurance—or an expensive gamble. For everyone seeking to cover a risk, there was another party looking to take a chance.

Most often, people in positions of decision-making power gradually became hooked into playing the derivatives markets like others did the casinos. Metal-working companies, pension funds, insurance houses, utilities, local city governments—all were involved and actively courted by the traders. It only took one person with a penchant for fast profits and the authority to sign checks to open the company to risks it would never in its wildest dreams consider taking in its normal course of business.

If things went wrong, the results could be horrendous. Orange County lost over two billion dollars in thirty-six hours on a derivatives deal gone awry. The largest German steel company went bankrupt after just one bad trade. The oldest bank in England lost more than a billion dollars through one rogue trader and was forced to close its doors after 250 years in operation.

These and a hundred other companies had vanished without a trace, more grist for the gossip mill that circulated among derivatives traders. Here this morning, bankrupt at midday, forgotten the same afternoon. Thad was not the least bit concerned. He had no intention of being on the losing end of anything.

The magic to OTC derivatives was, there were no rules. None. Traders related the price of oil to the value of the Japanese yen to the cost of unmined Indonesian aluminum. Not even the traders themselves understood some of the risks they were setting up. Nor did it matter, so long as they got in and out fast enough. All they needed to see was the potential to win.

And if they did win, the payoff was huge. Twenty million dollars on a quarter-million-dollar hedge, payoff time of less than three days. That sort of thing was commonplace. Those who tapped out simply vanished. Their places were taken the next day. There were always more people out there clamoring to take the plunge.

Wall Street had a name for these high-risk derivatives. They were called nuclear waste.

□

The red light at the top of his bank of phones finally blinked a half hour after Thad's arrival. He picked it up and said in greeting, "The market's gyrating like a kid's yo-yo."

"When this volatility finally gets a direction, it's either taking off like a shuttle launch or dropping like Niagara Falls," Larry agreed. "Every day we don't have a direction is just adding to the explosive tension."

"Still looking for a leader, just like you said."

"Right. Come in here."

"On my way."

When he arrived, Larry pointed him into a seat and said, "I like your plan."

"Just like that?"

He closed the file and scribbled on the cover. "Something this big will have to be reviewed by the board and okayed by Turner himself. But I want you to go ahead and start implementing the changes."

Thad could not repress his grin. "Fantastic."

"Just one thing." Fleiss reached for his mug. "Korda."

"I know." The morning's high diminished. "The guy's becoming a bigger nuisance with every passing day."

"The *Journal* called him 'a phenomenon' this morning."

Thad's gut took a bitter twist. "I missed that."

"On the editorial page. Responding to some press conference in the back of beyond, I forget what the city was called. Made the *Times* business page yesterday."

His gut tightened even further. "I missed that one too."

"Just as well. Apparently it was more of the same. The twenties all over again, a major drop on the way, stuff we've heard a hundred times before." Fleiss hit the button to bring his coffee apparatus into view and refilled his mug. "Only now he's getting national play."

Korda remained the only dark spot in Thad's rapid assent. "I saw he got a mention in *Forbes* this week."

"And *Business Week*." Fleiss shook his head. "The man's gone from being a clown to a menace."

"Just like you said."

"Yeah, well, being right but being in the red doesn't get a win. I got a call from the old man this morning. He wants to know why we haven't done anything about this guy. After he ordered me to drag you off the case last week, it was a little hard to take."

"But you didn't tell him that."

"No, what I said was you'd be back on it. Seems our goons from downstairs have had trouble pinning Korda down."

Thad nodded. He knew all about that. Wesley Hadden had become a turncoat. He was acting as a one-man security detail, on duty night and day. "Nowadays Korda's schedule is a national secret. His hotel and airline reservations are being made under block bookings. His movements are impossible to track in advance."

"Not next Thursday." Fleiss picked up the other piece of paper resting on his immaculate central table. "I got word from the guards this morning. There's been major advance coverage of some rally he's addressing. You heard about this?"

"No." Thad did a quick calculation in his head. "But next Thursday is only five days before Korda's going to disappear all on his own. The following Tuesday is going to arrive and the market's going to surge despite all his sour predictions. Korda will be good for one round of Jay Leno jokes before he's buried for good."

"Doesn't matter. There's too much chance he'll push back the date a week or so. That'd just give the cycle more time to build." Fleiss glanced at the paper in front of him. "Next Thursday Korda's one of the scheduled speakers at this rally in Richmond."

Thad rose to his feet, reached for the paper, and said, "I'll get started on the changes around here and then go take care of Korda personally."

"Stay well back. You're there only to make sure things get done right this time. I want to get Korda out of the picture, not to lose my number-one trader." Fleiss's flat gaze followed him to the door. "'Just make sure the man disappears.' Those were Turner's exact words. The man is to vanish from the face of this earth."

There was no way he was going to sit this one out. "Don't worry. In a week's time Korda is history."

THIRTY-NINE

Five Days . . .

☐ Thursday morning Buddy gave what he hoped would be his last press conference of the week. He spent the time between breakfast and the conference reviewing the whirlwind that his life had become. Their Friday and Saturday itinerary had called for St. Louis to Dallas, Oklahoma City, and Wichita, and then a long leap to Omaha and Des Moines. On and on, pushing harder and harder, moving farther and farther from home. Television lights and reporters had begun meeting them at the airports, and with each stop their questions became more mocking. Yet the crowds had grown ever larger, and the message's power had continued to resound.

Sunday had been Seattle and Portland; Monday, San Francisco and Sacramento and San Diego; Tuesday, a flight halfway across the nation to Little Rock. In his daily conversations with the home office, Alex and Agatha had sounded increasingly like robots. Every day Buddy heard more voices in the background, more telephones and excited chatter filling the spaces between words with his brother. Buddy had known better than to even ask what was going on. Wednesday had been Atlanta and Charlotte, and that night the drive to Richmond. The entire way up Clarke and Wesley had chattered excitedly over the Richmond rally scheduled for the following afternoon. Buddy had spent the hours drifting in and out of a strange half doze, never really connecting with anything that had been said. In their nightly conversation the previous evening, Molly had offered to join him for the final push. Buddy had told her not to bother. He missed her, but he could not ask her to endure the road. Besides, it would not be long now.

When Buddy arrived at the hotel's grand ballroom that morning, he discovered waiting for him a crowd of journalists larger than the first few groups who had gathered to hear his message. He did not mind the number. He scarcely saw them. All he could think about was that the countdown continued. Tomorrow was the final chance for people to make their investments. He wanted to pound the podium and scream the words with every shred of energy he had left.

Instead, Buddy found the words were there waiting for him when the television lights flashed on. He began without preamble, "Analysts are now saying that there is every reason for the market to sustain its climb for years to come." Buddy shook his head. "I have been a banker for more than thirty years. I can still remember the late seventies, when the Dow was stuck below a thousand for over three years. That particular generation of analysts claimed that the market had permanently anchored itself.

That was the expression of the time. It was permanently anchored, and there was no reason to believe that it would ever rise again.

"Now we are looking at a Dow that has broken every record a dozen times over. Now we in our wisdom can look down our noses and say how wrong they were." Buddy gripped the podium, leaned forward, and said, "But how will the next generation of analysts view our confident assessment that this unprecedented rise in the market will continue for years to come?"

He gave them a moment, hoping and praying that the message would get through. But there was no response from the field of faces, just a sense of staring out at silhouettes rather than people. "No nation on earth has ever experienced growth without downward slides. Never, in all of history. Why? Because there are too many factors underpinning any economic rise. We tend to forget them when all is going well. But the truth is, if two or three of these structural factors fall in tandem, there is every likelihood that the entire economy will decline as well.

"Let us talk about one of these vital unseen factors that help to hold up our economy—our nation's banking structure. Never in recent memory has the banking system been as unstable as it is now. And the reason for this is the current trading craze. It is, in my opinion, a cancer eating at the heart of our nation's financial system.

"Before I explain why trading is so hazardous, let us take a look back at the Great Depression. After the Crash of 1929 on Wall Street, the world's economies crumbled like a house of cards. Poverty struck like a worldwide plague. Nobody thought it could happen. But it did. Wall Street's collapse was caused by gambling, pure and simple. People borrowed to gamble, because the returns were great. The more they made, the more they gambled.

Their debts rose just as fast as their incomes, sometimes even faster.

"After the Crash of 1929, the government instituted financial reforms that were supposed to make this gambling impossible. And it stopped things for a while, or at least slowed things down. But now two related markets are sidestepping these laws. These are the new trading markets that I say hold a disastrous level of risk for all of us. One is called *futures*, the other *derivatives*. Ten years ago, the market in financial futures barely existed. This year, the Chicago financial futures market will have a turnover in excess of *fifty trillion dollars*."

Finally, finally, he saw a few of them stirring. A few were leaning toward their neighbors, a few were making notes. Buddy felt a note of desperation enter his voice. He pleaded, "These modern-day traders dress their actions in fancy jargons and glossy brochures, but the bare truth is that they are simply buying and selling *risk*. The world's financial underpinning is based on a gambling pit unlike anything seen since 1929.

"America's top five banks hold on average three trillion dollars in derivatives on their books, and from this obtain almost half their total profits. This means they hold *ten times* more in high-risk paper than they have in total equity capital. Ten times. These banks have no choice but to ride the tiger.

"The biggest worry for the banks is not that they might have gotten things wrong. No. The biggest danger is that they have customers who will lose big and then not be able to cover their losses. One such major loss would be enough to wipe out a bank's total cash reserves. That could happen in the space of just one day. The bank would be insolvent. Everyone who has placed their money in one of these banks, everyone who is relying on these banks to meet their own financial obligations, would lose every cent.

"Worse than that, the big banks do an enormous amount of business with each other. When it comes to derivatives, all of the world's major banks are holding hands. So if one starts to sneeze, they could all catch colds.

"If one major dealer could not make good on its commitments, a dozen others could be threatened. Another participant might then withhold payments. If that happened with a dozen, the system would enter meltdown.

"And the eruption could take place in three or four hours. This situation becomes much more serious because of how concentrated the wealth and this risk have become. One third of the world's total monetary wealth is controlled by just two hundred funds.

"In offices around the world, twenty-four hours a day, these fund managers hear the same news, hedge their bets with new risk derivatives, and prepare to jump at a moment's notice. Everyone is trying to catch the market swing and move in the right direction. Everyone is watching the other. Two hundred players is not so many that one can move with much secrecy. This means that if one jumps, chances are others will too.

"To have this much money all jump at once means that whatever swing the market begins to make will be amplified beyond all logic. A relatively small number of investors, mutual funds, investment banks, and Wall Street firms might see a new risk develop, and so they move together. The market reacts with a big dip. This notifies others of a move. The others rush out. The market dives. Panic ensues."

Buddy stopped. For once, the gathering of press and media seemed genuinely attentive. A voice from the back said, "Then what, Mr. Korda?"

"Go look at the newsreels from the thirties," Buddy said, wanting to weep with a sudden wave of frustration over his inability to do anything about it all. "Look at men selling apples on every street corner. Watch ten thousand people riot when fifteen jobs become available. See people harnessed to horse carts because working a man to death is cheaper than paying for hay or gas. Ask an old-timer to describe what it was like trying to feed a family. Then try to imagine what it might be like doing the same for your own loved ones."

⊣| FORTY |⊢

☐ Thaddeus Dorsett slipped the leather thong down tighter on his wrist. He had never held a cush before. That's what the guard had called it. A strange, soft-sounding word for something so deadly. The instrument was about a foot long, with a springy handle ending in a bulbous, fist-size club of steel and lead, all bound in leather to make it easier to hold and quieter to·wield. Thad's other hand still burned from where he had slapped the weight down a little too hard. He whipped the handle and heard the humming sound as it sprang back, hungry and vicious.

The guards had orders not to use guns. Too much noise, and not personal enough. He wanted Buddy Korda to see who was doing this. He wanted the man to see what it meant to cross

Thaddeus Dorsett. He wanted Buddy's last few minutes to be full of terrifying regret.

The alley was perfect. Thad could not have asked for a better place to spring their surprise. There was only one route for Korda to walk the three blocks from his hotel to the Richmond stadium. One narrow road. What was more, the entire downtown sector was strangely subdued this Thursday afternoon. As though the entire city's attention was focused on the nearby stadium.

The stadium crowd had been loud and quiet in strange turns. Occasionally faint snatches of song or voices could be heard. Thad had watched the guards exchange nervous glances over this. Which was very strange. He would have thought those goons could be bothered by nothing at all.

A guard came sprinting back from the hotel, confirming that Buddy had not left his room yet. The guards had brought in some extra hands to handle anybody who was unfortunate enough to walk to the stadium with Korda. Thad observed them leaning against the alley's opposite wall, a trio of goons with the dull-eyed blankness of people who would do anything for money.

Thad's blood surged at the thought of finally getting his own. "Remember," he hissed, "leave Korda for me."

No one bothered to respond. He had said the same thing a half dozen times already.

Thad checked his watch once more, wondering how much longer he could stand the waiting.

The guard by the alley's entrance chose that moment to turn and wave his hand over his head. They were coming.

Thad's heartbeat surged to an impossible rate. He glanced at the faces around, saw no sign of tension or excitement or anything beyond hard-edged boredom.

He accepted the black stocking mask handed out by the security guard. Thad watched how the others shifted the masks around so that the eye- and mouth-holes pulled down correctly. He felt a strange, stomach-twisting surge at the thought of what those guys had done to make this motion seem so natural. For himself, the mask felt tight and sweaty.

His breathing sounded overloud in his ears as he started toward the alley's entrance with the others. Up ahead, the guard raised his hand, the fingers extended, the thumb cocked back onto his palm. Four. There were only four of them. A piece of cake.

His heart pounded like a blood-soaked gong in his ears. He raised the cush, ready to pounce as soon as they appeared. The road stretched out empty and void in front of them. He heard the scratch of approaching footsteps, the murmur of quiet voices.

Out of nowhere, a fog drifted in and enclosed them, a mist so thick he could not see the wall he was touching. One moment all was clear and ready, and the next he could not see a thing. One of the thugs grunted in surprise. He heard someone else hiss for quiet.

If anything, the mist grew thicker, tighter. Breath was hard to come by, as though milky fingers were reaching out and closing around his throat. The feeling was so strong that Thad reached up and ripped a larger hole in the clinging mesh, clearing it farther from his mouth. Still, it was tough to draw a decent breath.

The footsteps were almost on them. Thad stepped forward, wanting to be the first to strike.

Shadows coalesced in the fog, but from the *opposite* direction. They were coming from the *stadium*. Thad backed up in alarm. The shadows followed, far too tall to be Korda and his men. They looked like warriors carrying shields, which was impossible. Shields and clubs. Or swords. Warriors standing a full foot taller than Thad, and broader than the goons.

A guard jostled him on one side. Or perhaps it was one of the thugs, backing up with him. Thad pulled off the mask. He could not breathe in this mist. Then he felt a wall behind him. He must have swerved sideways in the mist. Then the wall *moved*. Thad spun around and felt his heart squeeze shut at the sight of another shadow *behind* him. This one was bigger than the others, a behemoth looming over him, the club raised over his head longer than Thad was tall.

"*We're surrounded!*" The shriek was alien, even though he could feel it rip from his own throat. "*Run!*"

"They're everywhere!" The guard's voice was as hoarse as his own.

"Get me *out* of here!"

Thad felt a burning sensation on his hand, as if acid were seeping off the leather strap. He peeled skin off his wrist with his fingernails in his terror to get the cush off.

He dropped to his knees. Yes. That was the answer. Get down low and let the others take the heat. He sank lower, crawling and scrabbling on his belly through the damp filth coating the alley.

He heard shrieks and cries behind him. The sounds only made him crawl faster, through the blinding mist, wriggling on his belly so hard his clothes were shredded by the gravel underneath, finally catching a glimpse of light up ahead, as if he was approaching the end of a suffocating tunnel.

Thad gasped a sob and stumbled to his knees. His fine Armani suit was drenched and filthy with tatters flapping from his elbows and knees. He did not even notice. He scrambled to his feet and fled in terror.

⊣| FORTY-ONE |⊢

☐ Richmond that Thursday afternoon was experiencing a late heat wave. But it was not the temperature that made Buddy stop as he walked up the concrete runway and entered the stadium. Beneath a brilliant sun spread the largest crowd he had ever seen, much less addressed. Every seat in the bleachers was taken. Faces and colors spread out in every direction until they became distant blurs.

The playing field itself was lost beneath a seething mass of bodies. From the thirty-yard line back stretched row upon row of folding seats. Between them and the front stage, thousands of people gathered and stood and knelt and prayed.

Clarke moved up alongside. "Is everything all right?"

"Fine." It was a noisy, joyous, fervent cauldron of people and spiritual power. The Spirit was there and moving among the family of believers. "Just fine."

"Mr. Korda?" A harried young man wearing a badge and carrying a walkie-talkie scurried over. "Greg Knowles. Great that you could make it." He took Buddy's arm and began leading him forward, down the stairs and across the single patch of green not filled with bodies. "There's one more speaker before you. He'll be about a half hour, maybe forty-five minutes. We like to leave time for the Spirit to move at will."

"I understand." Buddy mounted the stairs, shook a couple of hands, and seated himself on the stage's back row. Strange that he could look out over such a gathering and feel no nerves. His fatigue and travel stress had gradually eased. Here and now, the outside world could not enter. Here and now, he was home.

When it was his time to speak, a distinguished gray-haired minister known throughout the nation gave the introduction. "By now, most of you have heard of Buddy Korda. This past week the press has been full of reports about how this one man has begun to have an effect upon the stock market. How there has been an unprecedented buying of futures options by people who would otherwise never be expected to enter this high-risk market. Huge numbers of people. Phenomenal numbers. That is the word I have read over and over this week. *Phenomenal*. It is phenomenal, the papers and the television pundits say, that one small-town banker can have such an impact upon people. They claim that it is simply a sign of the times, that people are nervous and willing to follow anyone who claims to know where the market is headed.

"Well, I am here to tell you that I have heard a tape recording of Buddy Korda's message. And after that I saw a video. I imagine that many of you out there have. And both times I was completely thunderstruck by the power of God moving through this man.

"We have a bank of television cameras out here in front of the stage today. Those of you who have attended our gatherings know this is not normal. But from what I have learned in a conversation with his home office this morning, today is the final day of Buddy Korda's message. Tomorrow is the last day we can act on his advice.

"I have every confidence that his message is correct, so much so that I have put all of my savings into something I did not even know existed before last week—something called put options. I am staking my reputation and my family's savings that Mr. Korda carries a message from God. And if his message is correct, Monday is too late. Brothers, hear what I am saying. More important, listen to Mr. Korda himself. And if you agree, if you feel the Spirit's direction, then I urge you to act. That is why the cameras are here. So that as many people as possible can hear and act." He turned and nodded toward Buddy.

Buddy approached the podium and the bank of microphones, greeted the crowd, and began. "I wish I could leave unsaid what I'm up here to tell you. Because what's most important is what you've been hearing from the speakers before me, that Jesus must reign in your minds and hearts. He is truly the way, the truth, and the life.

"But I can't stop there. Not today. I feel called to be where I am. Yet what's important is what you hear the *Spirit* say to you, not what words I speak. Remember that. I need to be the

Lord's messenger, and you need to hear confirmation from the Lord, not from me."

□

"This way, Mr. Korda. Here, let me take the towel."

"Oh, thank you." It was Thursday evening, and Buddy was in the Washington offices of CNN. As he removed the makeup towel from around his neck and handed it to the production assistant, he glanced around. Here everything seemed to run at double time. People did not walk, they scampered. Voices were tense and high-pitched. All the expressions looked vitally important, immensely serious.

Buddy allowed himself to be shepherded through a series of doors and into the side wings of a large soundstage. At its center was the familiar backdrop for *Lonnie Stone Live*. The production assistant pointed to a large screen situated to one side of the empty stage and said, "Mr. Stone is in New York today. You'll be able to see him on that feed. The questions will be passed to you through a speaker set in the desk, see it there?"

"Yes." Buddy felt nervous tension transmitted from everything around him. Cables littered the floor. People moved lights and cameras about, barely casting a glance in his direction. He was simply the day's product, to be spotlighted and handled and monitored, and then moved aside for whatever was hot tomorrow. There wasn't time for anything else.

"Okay, let's just fit your mike into place." The production assistant stepped aside as a sound technician clipped a tiny microphone to his lapel, ran the wire under his jacket, and gave him the control pack to slip into his back pocket. "Would you say something so they can adjust the sound level?"

"I have never been on television before."

"Fine. That's great." She returned a thumbs-up through the control room window and ushered him toward the desk. "All right, let's adjust your coat so it doesn't bunch around your shoulders." She gave the back of his jacket a hard tug and tucked it farther into his seat. "Try to hold to one position through each question, Mr. Korda. If you want to move, do so when Lonnie is talking."

"I understand." The makeup was constricting, and under the lights it left his skin feeling as though it could not breathe. "How long—"

"Eight minutes until you go on, and we will probably play this for five minutes today." She glanced at her clipboard. "You're back with us next week, do I have that right?"

"On Tuesday," he confirmed.

"You'll be an old hand by then, won't you?" She gave him a practiced smile and moved back beyond the reach of the lights. Immediately a camera rolled forward and fastened its great square eye on him.

Buddy gave a swift prayer for guidance and received the same response as at press conferences—a simple determined foreknowledge of what needed to be said.

The minutes dragged on until the production assistant waved at him, counted down, and then pointed to the monitor. Buddy saw the seasoned smile and heard the famous voice say, "And joining us now from our Washington studio is Buddy Korda, a name that has become increasingly familiar, and in a remarkably short span of time. Mr. Korda, it's a pleasure to have you with us today."

"Thank you for having me."

"Mr. Korda, do I have it right that you are predicting a major economic downturn to strike sometime next week?"

"On Tuesday," Buddy affirmed.

"You'll excuse me if I say that it seems a little strange. The markets are booming. The latest economic figures, released just yesterday, indicate that the nation enjoys the best economic health it has seen in years." Stone picked up a sheet of paper and read, "Unemployment is down, wholesale purchasing is up, factory usage is at an all-time high. Today the market hit another record level, with the Dow climbing almost two hundred points." He let the paper drop. "It seems as though the economy is not agreeing with you, Mr. Korda."

"There are a number of factors that could change that almost instantly."

"So you are suggesting, are you not, that people who hear your message should risk everything they own by going against the market, flying in the face of every pundit on Wall Street, and betting the lot on the market falling? Isn't that right?"

"Yes."

"Are you perhaps interested in changing your deadline, Mr. Korda? Perhaps give yourself a little breathing space?"

"There is no need." Buddy looked straight at the camera and put as much emphasis as he could on each word. "The reason I came into the studios today was to urge those who have heard my message and feel it is true to *act*. Tomorrow is their last chance."

"The markets will be open for business on Monday as well," the interviewer pointed out.

Buddy shook his head. "Monday will be too late."

The interviewer gave his familiar, hoarse chuckle. "I wish I was as certain about anything as you appear to be about this. Tell me, Mr. Korda, do you have any idea just how far the market will fall?"

Buddy felt the door open. Not for emotional impact, but rather for a response. One given in astonishing clarity. "The Dow Jones average will close next week at less than nine hundred."

It took Lonnie Stone a moment to recover. "That is a drop of over eighty percent."

"Yes, it is."

"In one *week*?"

"That is correct."

Another moment, and then, "Mr. Korda, all I can say is, I hope you are wrong."

Buddy felt an overwhelming sorrow, a sadness for the people, the businesses, the nation. He shook his head. "I'm not wrong."

⊣⊩ FORTY-TWO ⊩⊢

Four Days . . .

☐ Friday morning Thad Dorsett returned to the office a broken man.

He sat at his console, watching the markets open with the speed of a grand prix roaring into action. He saw nothing but a blur.

He started when the red light at the center of his phone console began flashing. Thad sat a very long time, trying to formulate a plan, struggling to draw his shattered parts together. Then he reached and picked up the receiver and punched the connection. "Dorsett."

"So how'd it go?"

The question brought a first sign of hope. Clearly Fleiss had not caught the interview with Korda, which CNN televised nationwide. Thad ventured, "Not too bad."

"That's good, sport. Real good. The old man will be pleased."
The voice sounded like a robot's voice in a human body. "Say,
what happened to the two security guys? They never checked
back in."

Thad heard the flatness of his own voice, knowing the dead
sound matched Fleiss's exactly. "I guess they must still be celebrating."

"Yeah, well, they deserve it. Say, you seen the market this
morning?"

"It's rising," Thad guessed. It had been setting new records
all week.

"Like a skyrocket. We're going for the stratosphere, you
mark my words."

"Time to grab hold and ride the bull." Thad mouthed the
words, but felt nothing.

"You got it. Heard your new office is gonna be ready first
thing Monday. You still moving into your brownstone this weekend?"

"Tomorrow," Thad confirmed, searching inside himself for
a shred of pleasure over the coming step, the arrival of all his
dreams. All he found was a gigantic void.

"Good timing, kid. Nothing I like to see better in a trader."
Larry's chuckle sounded machine generated. "Well, back to the
trenches."

"Right." Thad hung up the phone and returned to staring
sightlessly at the flickering screens.

He would leave early, as soon as he was certain the market
was going to continue its ride into the wild blue yonder. Monday would come soon enough, then Tuesday, and with it Korda's
downfall. As soon as the world saw that Korda's predictions

were wrong, Thad's failure to take the banker down would not matter.

He struggled to draw the screen's numbers into focus; he saw that the prices continued to rise. He sat back, deaf to the screaming pandemonium rising around him. His lie was indeed intact. The market was going to rise, and Buddy Korda was soon to be history.

⊣| FORTY-THREE |⊢

Three Days . . .

☐ The Saturday morning papers were vicious. The market had broken all records on Friday afternoon. The pundits who mentioned him at all made Buddy out to be a disgruntled former bank employee who had turned against everything and everyone.

The weekend editorials read like obituaries. They were putting his time in the spotlight down as another of those unexplainable aberrations, symbolic of how people preferred to follow their hearts rather than their minds. With words as brooms, the papers and the radio and the television all pointed at the market's continued rise, then swept Buddy Korda into the back room of oblivion.

Buddy did not budge from his backyard. At his request, Molly had gone out and returned with as many papers as she could find. She delivered them with a set mouth. When Buddy asked her what the matter was, she simply said, "Stay where you are."

The day was warm and the sunlight strong in a cloudless sky. Buddy felt the light reach down and work to release the cold and the tension and the weariness trapped inside his bones. Through the open windows he heard the phone ringing continually. It awoke him from his brief naps, jerking him awake with electric jolts. He would reach out, as though still in some distant hotel room, still pressed for time, still driving himself and his friends to bone-weary exhaustion.

And for what?

He knew what the phone calls were saying. He knew people were calling, panic-stricken over having done as he had said. As he thought the message from heaven had said. But did he have it right? How could he be sure that he had listened to the right voice?

He had no answers. His prayers felt like dust rising from the emptiness of a spent and overworked heart. God remained silent and distant. Buddy had nothing to offer those who called, or the few who stopped by. His little back garden was a refuge from the world.

Saturday night they disconnected the phones. Sunday morning Buddy brought his coffee cup outside and sat looking out over an unseen lawn.

He did not even turn around when he heard Molly's swift steps swishing through the grass. "Aren't you coming with me to church?"

"You go ahead." Buddy sipped at a cup long gone cold. "If Monday goes like Friday, I doubt I'll ever move from this garden again."

The expected reprimand did not come. Instead, Molly's hand reached over to stroke his cheek. "My poor man. You've given everything you have to give, and you're afraid."

"Terrified." Buddy swallowed hard, fighting down the terror and the despair. "What if I was wrong all along?"

Molly squatted down beside his chair, gripped his arm with both hands, and said, "It's not time to worry about that yet. One more day. Can you hold out that long?"

He jerked a tight little nod. "Say a prayer for me."

"I always do, my husband." She kissed his cheek and rose back up. "The children wanted to come over after church. I didn't have the heart to say no again today."

"That's all right." Buddy turned now, looked up, and stiffened. For the first time he could ever remember, Molly wore her collar open. The scar was partially covered with makeup, but it was still there for the world to see. "Honey, what are you doing?"

She gave the open collar a nervous pat, as though unsure herself if it was right. But her voice was quietly resolute. "I've hidden behind my walls for too long."

"Molly, I . . ." Buddy struggled to his feet. "Wait and let me get on a tie."

"No, you stay here and rest." Molly guided him back down. "This is something I want to do on my own."

□

He must have fallen asleep, because the next thing Buddy knew, Alex was dragging one of the other lawn chairs over next to his own. "How you doing, little brother?"

"All right." But Alex deserved more than platitudes. "Tired. Scared."

"Sure you are." Alex seated himself, reached into his Sunday blazer, and brought out a slip of paper. "Clarke asked me to give you this."

Buddy accepted the paper, unfolded it and read:

> The LORD lives! Praise be to my Rock!
>   Exalted be God my Savior!
>
> You exalted me above my foes;
>   from violent men you rescued me.
> Therefore I will praise you among the nations, O LORD;
>   I will sing praises to your name.
> Psalm 18:46, 48-9

Slowly, carefully, Buddy refolded the paper and inserted it into his shirt pocket. "I wish I was as sure as he sounds."

"I guess you'll just have to let us be sure for you then, won't you?"

Buddy looked in helpless appeal at his brother. "Are you really so certain?"

"More certain of that than I have been of anything in my life." Alex's eyes held a burning light, one that seemed to touch Buddy as not even the sun had been able to. "I have discovered a love that will never abandon me. And I know that you serve the Master. I *know* it."

Buddy took a breath, drawing in Alex's confidence as well. "This is like a dream."

"Wait, it's about to get a lot better." He turned to where Agatha was hesitantly approaching and reached out a hand in greeting while rising to his feet. She walked over, allowed Alex to slip his hand into hers, and gave Buddy a shy smile. Alex turned back and beamed. "Little brother, we've got ourselves an announcement."

Buddy felt it coming before he knew what it was. He struggled to rise from the chair.

Alex watched him with an ever-widening grin. Molly was hurrying over, wiping her hands on her apron. When they were all together, Alex announced, "Agatha is going to make an honest man of me."

"You're already honest," Agatha said, the edge totally gone from her voice. "But I have agreed to marry you."

Molly said for them both, "This is wonderful."

"I didn't want to ask her," Alex said. "Can't even say how many days the Lord has left for me on this earth."

"None of us do," Agatha countered. "But whatever days we have left, I want to spend them with Alex." She looked at him with shining eyes and said with strength and quiet conviction, "Whatever comes."

"Praise God," Buddy whispered. He reached out and gripped Alex's hand with both of his. "Whatever tomorrow brings, I now count this whole trial a grand personal success."

⊣‖ FORTY-FOUR ‖⊢

One Day . . .

☐ A rascal wind greeted Thad Dorsett as he stepped from his new house Monday morning. Grit lashed at his face and tried to sneak in around his sunglasses. The air was far too hot for October. His skin felt dry as parchment and his tongue overlarge for his mouth. He nodded a silent greeting to the limo driver and slipped gratefully into the back.

Though not yet eight o'clock in the morning, the financial district throbbed with tension and activity. The communities of Riverside and Soho and rejuvenated Tribeca divulged their battalions of Wall Street warriors. They marched in their legions, racing toward the battle zone.

Thad took the elevator to the top trading floor. He stopped in the doorway of his new office, surveying with deep satisfaction the wood-paneled expanse and navy blue carpet. Looking around the room, imagining where he would station his desk and the conference table, and seeing himself enthroned by the window went a long way to restoring him.

The weekend had already done much to renew his confidence and enthusiasm. His new house was fantastic. The move had given his exploits a new sense of reality. Other than a series of jarring nightmares, moving into the top realm had been everything he had dreamed of.

But the nightmares had been vile. Thad Dorsett had woken time after time, bathed in sweat, chased by fiends taller than the Wall Street skyscrapers. Last night he had decided to take no chances and had swallowed a double dose of sleeping pills. The nightmares had been reduced to vague phantoms that he had managed to push away. Most of the time.

As the din from the trading floor began to build, Thad entered the main hall and slid into his seat. His last day among the peons. His furniture was scheduled for delivery by mid-morning. On the desk in front of him was the folder containing the outline for his proposed changes. A note from Larry clipped to the outside said that the old man had given his approval.

Thad laced his fingers behind his head, leaned back, and returned greetings from people he scarcely saw. Hearing the envy and the awe in their voices helped make the day truly complete.

□

At ten minutes to ten, Thad looked up as a sudden silence gripped the room. The floor manager had the ability to draw major news bulletins off the top board and flash them on every screen at every trading desk. If any news bulletin ever deserved being called major, this was it.

Maurichi Securities was the largest financial institution in southern Japan. It controlled a full one-third of Honshu Island's total wealth. It employed 39,000 people worldwide. It had over eight hundred offices, including trading operations in Sydney, Hong Kong, Calcutta, Paris, and New York.

Thad sat joined with all the other traders in stunned silence and watched the words race remorselessly across his central trading screen. The chairman of Maurichi Securities had called a press conference and announced that undisclosed positions on the international derivatives market had cost the bank nine billion dollars. The bank's cash reserves were depleted. The bank had no choice but to close its doors.

The moment seemed to stretch into eternity, frozen by a universal desire to ignore the bulletin, to refuse to accept what it meant. Then Larry Fleiss's voice crackled through the intercom, shrieking at a level Thad had never heard before.

"Sell yen!"

The trading floor erupted. Thad was grabbing phones and punching buttons and screaming with the others, dumping every yen-based position the bank held. Or trying to. Everywhere around the world, traders were scrambling to do the same. Thad's screens began flashing new rates so fast Thad could not find a strike price.

Fleiss's voice sounded overhead once more, instantly freezing the clamor. "Okay, listen up. We're getting a feed on the stocks and bonds held by Maurichi. They're coming up on your screen now. Dump them fast. Take any price."

Like most Japanese banks and security firms, Maurichi had concentrated its U.S. holdings within the range of companies known as blue chips. These were the largest and most stable earners within the American economy. Yet earnings and price-share ratios and future profitability meant nothing at this point. Maurichi would be forced to dump all its assets in order to meet as many of its outstanding positions as possible. Prices were going to hit the basement and keep falling. It was vital they get out, and get out fast.

By two o'clock in the afternoon the Dow had dropped 850 points from its Friday close. A thirty-minute breathing space had been imposed when the market was down 500 just before noon, but the instant it reopened the frantic selling resumed. By mid-afternoon the traders were hoarse, exhausted, and sweat-stained. Thad had taken to drinking tea laced with bourbon and honey to hold on to what voice he had left.

Ninety minutes before closing, the next nail was set into the coffin. The chief official of the Japanese National Bank issued a formal statement declaring his "grave concern" over the state of the U.S. market. Ten short words, but enough to transform the traders' panic into sheer unbridled terror. Ashtrays and coffee cups went flying in every trading room around the world as dealers sought frantically to unload anything and everything tied to the dollar.

The U.S. treasury secretary lashed back thirty minutes later in a hastily declared press conference, accusing the Japanese bank official of "shock tactics in idiotic revenge for his own financial institution's precarious position," and declared that the weight of the entire U.S. government would go into supporting the dollar and the American financial markets.

The markets reacted with a violent about-face. The dollar leaped from the basement to the attic, rising seventeen yen in seven minutes. The dollar climbed 20 percent against its low of the day, just 5 percent down from Friday's high. But the stock market continued to drop. There was nothing that hit share prices like uncertainty.

When the closing bell sounded, traders stumbled about like shell-shocked victims of a bombing attack. Thad staggered to the back pantry for another cup of something he would not taste. His feet scuffled through paper and tear sheets three inches thick. Two traders he knew vaguely were sprawled on the floor, phones dangling by their sides. As he picked his way over their limbs, Thad happened to catch sight of a Reuters news flash streaking overhead. The Dow's final position was down one thousand, four hundred seventy-five points. A one-day decline of 19 percent.

⊣‖ FORTY-FIVE ‖⊢

☐ The press began arriving about three o'clock that Monday afternoon. The first few teams had the temerity to ring their doorbell. Molly appeared on Buddy's behalf, quietly refused their requests for interviews, but said he would make a statement later.

That was enough to galvanize the gathering. By five the street was blocked solid from end to end with television vans. The police had been called in, the front lawn cordoned off, and a semblance of order restored. Molly had given permission for the media to position microphones by the front steps, but otherwise the throng was kept well back.

Still the crowd grew. People who drove found themselves parking as far as three blocks away. There was no need to ask directions, not even for those arriving from out of town. The steady stream of people all took the same route.

Buddy appeared at six. There was a stir of recognition, and instantly the bank of television lights switched on. Buddy stood on his top step, endured the flashes from the photographers, and simply waited through the screaming flood of questions.

He spent the time looking out beyond the horde of press to where the gathering continued to grow. He nodded to a few familiar faces. They, in turn, were silent, somber—the exact opposite of the journalists and their shouted, aggressive questions. He stood there and waited, content to look out.

Once the journalists finally accepted that he was not going to respond, the tumult gradually died away. When all was quiet, Buddy stepped up to the huge bunch of taped-together microphones. "I have an announcement to make," Buddy said. "I will not answer any questions, because I do not want anything to take away from the critical nature of this message."

A reporter shouted, "Will the market continue to fall?"

"I will not answer questions," Buddy repeated, and waited until he was sure the silence would hold.

Then he looked out to the cameras, bunched on ladderlike tripods behind the reporters. He focused all the power he could muster and said simply, "This message is intended for all the friends and brothers and sisters out there who have heeded the directive I was told to bring.

"This message is, *SELL*."

Buddy tried to look *through* the camera, wanting to communicate directly with the people, make them understand how vital this was. "Sell your put options *now*. Sell first thing tomorrow morning. There is no telling how long the market will hold together. Do not allow greed to hold you in place. Sell it *all*.

"Then convert everything you have, everything you can transfer, everything you can withdraw, *everything* into cash. Not cash in a bank. Cash in your hand. Gold would be good. If not gold, then dollars. But cash."

He waited through a long, silent moment, and then said again, "*Sell now*. That is all I have to say."

A voice from far back in the throng shouted, "Thank you, brother!"

"Thank God," Buddy replied, turning away. "Good night."

─‖ FORTY-SIX ‖─

☐ At Buddy's request, Alex called and simply informed the national networks that Buddy would respond via a feed set up at the Aiden television station, and would be interviewed by Lonnie Stone alone. They had no choice but to agree. By this point, Buddy Korda and his on-target predictions were making headlines right around the globe.

When it came time that evening to leave for the local station, they had to call in the police once more. A phalanx of bodies was necessary to clear a way to the cruiser assigned to take them downtown.

The car was just beyond the drive when a man wrestled his way through the cordon and threw himself on Buddy's window. Buddy backed into Molly as the man clawed at the glass and screamed, "You did this! You! You cost me everything!"

Two policemen pried the man loose, but not before he shrilled, "It's all your fault, Korda! I hope you hang!"

"Hold on tight, folks," came the laconic order from the front seat. The patrolman began steadily accelerating away.

"Don't pay him any mind, sir." The patrolman in the passenger seat turned around. "I heard you speak on a video my church played last week."

"We heard the Spirit is what we did," his partner corrected.

"Yeah, well, anyway, we went out and did just what you said, stuck it all in those put options."

Buddy tried to still his nerves. The man's contorted features felt branded into his mind. "Get out first thing tomorrow."

"Yes, sir, we've already got the message through to our broker. He says he's gonna do it for everybody who did like you said."

"He said we're gonna be millionaires by this time tomorrow," the driver added. The flashing lights turned his solid features into multicolored stone. "Can't hardly believe it. But we're gonna take half of whatever we get and put it in the church fund. Don't know what we'll do with the rest. Bury it in the backyard, I suppose."

"That's good." Buddy felt himself steadied by the policemen's solid assurance. "That's very good indeed."

There was yet another crowd waiting outside the television station. As soon as the patrol car slowed, press and television camera lights flashed on full. The second patrolman said, "Looks like somebody tipped them off we were coming."

"There's an underground garage around back," the driver said, flipping on his siren and plowing steadily around the building.

Through the back window Buddy watched a horde race behind them, shouting and jostling and trying to keep up.

Even before the motor was cut, a nervous figure appeared in the garage's elevator and frantically waved them over. The driver said, "Better head on out, Mr. Korda. We'll hold the fort down here."

"I'll just sit right here," Molly said, leaning over to give his cheek a kiss. "I think this will be a much nicer place to pray."

"The Lord go with you," the driver's partner said, as Buddy slipped out. "We'll be saying the words with your wife."

Buddy rushed over, spurred to speed by the noise pushing in through the garage doors. The young woman greeted him with, "Mr. Korda, great. We hoped that'd be you. New York has been calling every five minutes, asking if we could move this up."

"Let's go," Buddy agreed, watching the doors shut just as the first figures raced into view.

The woman raised the walkie-talkie she was carrying and said, "Have security get down to the garage. We've got a riot in the making. And don't let any of those people inside the offices."

Upstairs, Buddy's reception could not have been any more different from the last time he visited a television studio. This time, the station president was there to shake his hand, thank him for coming, usher him personally into the makeup room. He was asked if he cared for coffee, and was then informed that Lonnie Stone himself was on the telephone, wanting to discuss the program.

"There's no need," Buddy said, waving the receiver away. "Just tell him I'm ready whenever he is."

His progress to the studio was followed by silence and stares. Everyone stopped to watch, study, and observe, knowing without saying that they were witnessing something they would tell their grandchildren about—the passing of a real live prophet.

The hookup was completed while Buddy was still being placed into the seat normally occupied by the local news anchor. As soon as the monitor came on, he saw and heard the world famous interviewer say, "I see we're finally hooked into Buddy Korda at the local Aiden, Delaware, station. Thank you for coming, Mr. Korda. I have seen the second part of your message, as has almost anyone in this country who has a television. Would you care to repeat it here?"

"I would," Buddy agreed, and again focused with all the force he could muster upon the camera. "All those who have acted upon my message, for your own sakes, do not let greed rule you now. Do not wait for the market to bottom out, hoping that you might profit even more.

"Others must be able to cover these obligations in order for you to gain from your investment. Tomorrow afternoon the people holding your paper will begin to fold. Therefore I tell you, *get out now*. First thing tomorrow morning, sell every put option you are holding. Convert it into cash and gold. And give thanks to God."

There was a moment's pause, a breathless hush that extended far beyond the monitor and the camera and all the shadow figures gathered just beyond the lights' reach. Finally the interviewer asked, "Are you saying that the market is actually going to crash, Mr. Korda?"

"I am making no more predictions. It is too late for that. I am simply telling these people to *get out now*."

"Too late?" Lonnie Stone adjusted his glasses, leaned across the desk, and said, "The president has announced a press conference for a half hour from now. He is expected to place the entire weight of the Federal Reserve and the United States Treasury behind keeping our markets open and stable. Would you like to change your position?"

"Not at all. Everyone who has taken heed of my message and purchased put options is urged to sell everything as soon as the market opens, and convert all their holdings to cash and gold."

"What about those who did not do as you said, Mr. Korda? Do you have any advice for them?"

"Yes, I do." Again Buddy forced all the power at his command upon the camera lens. "The kingdom of God is at hand. Repent. He who believes in the Son has everlasting life."

He stopped, half expecting to be cut off, but the production staff were all locked in the same breathless silence. So Buddy kept his gaze steady on the camera and went on, "Those who focus upon the world see these happenings as all that matter. But those who follow the Lord Jesus know that these events too will pass. They are *not* the end, not even the beginning. For the Scriptures tell us that all this will pass away, and in its place will come that which is more glorious than anything we can imagine. The twenty-fourth chapter of Matthew's Gospel tells us, 'And He will send His angels with a great sound of a trumpet, and they will gather together His elect from the four winds, from one end of heaven to the other.'"

Buddy paused again, this time simply to give thanks for the chance to serve, for the chance to have seen all that he had, for the opportunity to have grown as he did, and for it now to be drawing to a close. Then he finished with, "The door is open, the Lord is waiting to receive you. Come and join the living."

FORTY-SEVEN

Meltdown

☐ The next morning, chaos struck like a physical blow as soon as Thad Dorsett entered the trading room. Through the night, U.S. stocks had continued to trade around the globe, falling in every market worldwide. When the New York Stock Exchange began trading, the Dow Jones opened 917 points below the previous day's close. Trading was suspended for almost an hour. When the market reopened, it continued to fall steadily.

That afternoon, the market went through a brief rally. Then came the bad news. The Chicago Merchant Bank, the nation's eleventh largest, was closing its doors. Traders raced through the book, checking their positions on anything that might have been tied to Merchant and for which payment was now frozen. The result was grim despondency. Merchant's tentacles spread through the entire market structure, from options to currencies to every stock market to Fannie Maes to gold futures. The Chicago exchanges had bundled a huge amount of their trading work through them.

When the red light began flashing at the center of his phone console, Thad wanted to stand and flee. He picked up the receiver as he would a snake. He could only think that Fleiss would accuse him of lying, of not taking care of Korda as he had claimed. "Yeah?"

But clearly Fleiss had decided there was no time to waste on the past. "Take a look at our position. I'm putting it up on your screen now. Second channel. See it?"

"Yes." Thad stared at the screen, unable to believe his eyes. The numbers Valenti Bank were sustaining on the debit side were too big. These current positions were impossible to sustain. "What happened?"

"We hit the iceberg, is what happened." Fleiss's customary hoarseness was worn down to a leathery whisper. "We're gonna make the sinking of the *Titanic* look like a toy boat going down in a bathtub."

Leveraged positions that yesterday had made perfect sense now threatened to push the bank over the brink and into insolvency. And not just his own bank. "This can't be happening."

"It's happening, all right. Unless something major takes place and we find a way to hide the dirty linen until it does." A moment of heavy breathing, and then, "It's not just us, for what it's worth. I've been checking around. The whole market's sliding toward the falls."

The fingers holding the receiver felt numb to the elbow. "What do you want me to do?"

"Do what that Korda character's been saying. Go short. Buy every put option you can get your hands on."

Thad kept staring at the screen. "But we don't have the collateral."

"You think I don't know that?" The hoarse tone rose to a shrill whine and then subsided. "We're so far in the hole it doesn't matter any more. Buy everything you can. Bet the load on the market heading farther south. Pledge anything you can think of. I'm giving you everybody on the floor. No limits. Buy as fast as you can."

Thad sat staring at the silent phone until he spotted the floor manager hustling over. He stood, loosened the knot on his tie, and prepared for battle.

□

Finally at two-thirty the SEC chairman stepped in and closed the exchange. Trading was suspended on all the nation's markets. A breathing space was declared.

But none of the traders moved.

A half hour later, London and Paris opened. They promptly responded to the growing crisis by closing down all markets for twenty-four hours. Tokyo was deluged by so many conflicting orders that it had no choice but to follow suit.

Traders finally departed for the night with shattered nerves and shell-shocked expressions.

When Thad walked out on the street, his limo driver was nowhere to be found. He found himself too overwhelmed to care. He walked the length of Wall Street, seeing his own dread mirrored on every face he passed.

⊣ FORTY-EIGHT ⊢

☐ Buddy spent most of Tuesday in the back garden playing with his grandchildren, visiting with his family, and making idle chatter with Alex and Agatha and Clarke Owen and a few others that Molly permitted through the front door. The police kept the cordon in place, although by now most people had other, more critical things to fill their days. Even the number of journalists dropped to fewer than a dozen.

From time to time they returned to the living room, where they watched the drama unfold on CNN. The reports grew steadily grimmer. Even when the news flashed of a sharp rise in the market, not even the announcer seemed to believe that it would continue. Business reports from the balcony overlooking the New York Stock Exchange showed unbridled bedlam on the floor below.

When news broke of the Chicago Merchant Bank closing its doors, the normally unflappable business reporter looked ready to cry.

"Buddy," Clarke called from the door. "You're still coming to the worship service tonight?"

The church had decided late the previous afternoon to hold a meeting that evening. Before Buddy could decline, Molly appeared in the kitchen doorway and replied for him, "He'll be there. We all will."

"Good." Clarke gave him a single nod. "See you around seven."

When the door had closed behind him, Buddy turned to his wife. "Molly . . ."

"Don't you even start." She planted her hands firmly on her hips. "This is the church that raised you and stood by you through it all. You need to go, Buddy. It's time."

"Daddy!" Paul, his older son, called from the living room. "Get in here quick!"

He and Molly raced across the hall and stopped where his two sons and their wives stood before the television. He heard the business reporter announce, "Unconfirmed reports claim that it is not just Chicago Merchant facing dire straits this afternoon. According to sources close to the management, if the Valenti Bank were forced to cover all its trading liabilities today, it would be short almost seven billion dollars. A spokesman for the bank has called this ludicrous scaremongering. However, the bank had no comment regarding the accusations that it had lost heavily in tradings over the previous three months.

"On a related development, word is just coming in of a catastrophe at sea. Billionaire Nathan Jones Turner, owner of Valenti Bank, has reportedly fallen overboard and disappeared. While no one at the bank or at Turner's Connecticut office will either confirm or deny the reports, the Coast Guard did receive a frantic Mayday call from the Turner yacht, reporting a man lost at sea. We will have more on that as it comes in. We return now to our coverage of the Valenti Bank."

The camera panned out over the looming edifice of the Turner Building. The announcer continued, "Like many U.S. financial institutions, the Valenti Bank has poured massive amounts of its own and its investors' capital into the futures markets. During this recent era of rapid expansion, Valenti's worth has skyrocketed. However, sources claim tonight that this increased valuation was used as a basis for further highly leveraged tradings in what are known as derivatives."

The camera's perspective switched back to the reporter's face. "If what our sources claim is true, apparently this bubble is on the verge of bursting. What is certain is that given the current state of the market, Valenti's stock and bond assets are plummeting in value. This has undermined the bank's deposits, which in turn hold up its outstanding loan balance."

Molly said, "I don't think I understood any of that."

Buddy did not take his eyes from the television screen. "The bank is in trouble. That's really all you need to understand."

The announcer concluded, "Such a shortfall would only be aggravated by the rumored losses in the international currency and futures exchanges. Whether or not this institution can survive, if the rumors are indeed correct, is anyone's guess. This is Alicia Newstone for CNN News, reporting from Wall Street."

Molly's gaze followed Buddy as he backed slowly away from the television. "It's happening, isn't it?"

Buddy could only nod. The weight of sorrow for all those he had not managed to touch threatened to crush him.

⊣| FORTY-NINE |⊢

☐ Such was Buddy's distress that he kept his face lowered the entire trip to the church. He had not wanted to come at all, but Molly had insisted. The rest of the family tried to hide their unease with small talk. Buddy scarcely heard them.

Then Molly turned a corner and exclaimed, "Who are all these people?"

From the backseat Trish asked fearfully, "Is it a riot?"

"They look too well dressed for that," his son Jack pointed out. "And too calm."

Buddy raised his head and saw strangers milling about, surrounded by a darkness as complete as that which shrouded his heart.

"Look, Mom, the guy with the flashlight. He's waving you to the curb."

"We can't be expected to park here," Molly cried. "We're six blocks from the church."

Buddy squinted and focused on the man. He was indeed pointing them into a parking space. He heard his son say, "We've never had to park this far away."

"Where are the others?"

"Right behind us, Mom. I see them."

Molly cut off the motor. "Stay together, everybody. I don't like the looks of this."

Buddy opened his door and sighed as he got to his feet. The crowd was noisy but in a disjointed, comfortable way. Buddy sensed no threat. "Come on, everybody."

Then he jerked his head back as a light flashed into his eyes. "Buddy?"

"Point that thing in another direction, will you?"

"Sure." The flashlight dropped away, but the voice raised to a shout. "It's him!"

"Where?" A hundred voices eagerly picked up the chorus, demanding to know where he was. Then a hundred more. Buddy felt the first inkling of real fear. Then Molly was moving up beside him, taking his hand, and calling back, "He's right here."

Alex stepped up on Buddy's other side. "Make way, everybody! We've got a date with God!"

The man with the flashlight moved up in front of them. Buddy recognized him as Lionel Peters, the fellow church elder. "We've been waiting for you folks to get here. Come on, Buddy, I'll make a way for us."

The crowd did not press against them. Instead, they opened up a path toward the church and simply stood and watched as Buddy and his family walked through. At least at first.

Buddy turned a corner and spotted the distant shining steeple when the first woman crossed the invisible line. In the flashlight's glare her face was streaked and shimmering with tears. She grabbed his arm and cried, "Bless you, Brother Korda."

That was enough to burst the dam. People began flowing forward, reaching across, patting his back, his arms, trying to grab his hands. A thousand voices shouted thanks, cried in glory, yelled messages that were lost to the night.

Buddy allowed Molly and Alex to keep moving him forward, numb with shock.

Then they turned the corner, and Buddy realized what he had seen up to that point was only the tip of the iceberg.

The six-lane intersection in front of the church was packed solid with people. As was the lawn surrounding the building, the church steps, and the parking lot. Shouting and crying and waving, the noise was a commotion that followed them across the street and pushed them up the stairs.

Buddy caught sight of Clarke helping a group of young men arrange loudspeakers around the front pillars. He waved in Buddy's direction and pointed overhead.

Buddy looked up, and saw that a hand-painted banner had been strung from the eaves. It read: *The stone which the builders rejected has become the chief cornerstone. This was the Lord's doing. And it is marvelous in our eyes!*

Alex pressed his face close enough to Buddy's to be heard. "Ain't this something?"

Buddy turned to his brother and was greeted with resolute hope. "Who are these people?"

"Friends!" Alex shouted back.

Molly pressed close to his other side and said, "It is the harvest of your work, my husband. I am so very proud of you."

Alex settled a powerful arm across his brother's shoulders and pressed him up the stairs. "Come on, let's go praise the Lord!"

About the Author

Before becoming an award-winning author, T. Davis Bunn earned a Master's degree in international finance and worked as an international business executive. His books include the best-sellers *Another Homecoming* and *Return to Harmony* (both co-authored with Janette Oke), *The Quilt, The Presence, To the Ends of the Earth*, and *One False Move*. As a result of *To the Ends of the Earth*, he was named the Novelist in Residence at Regent's Park College, Oxford University. His most recent novel for Thomas Nelson Publishers is the Christmas story *Tidings of Comfort and Joy*. He and his wife, Isabella, live in Oxfordshire, England.

OTHER GREAT BOOKS FROM T. DAVIS BUNN

To the Ends of the Earth

A compelling historical tale of political, and personal conflict during the rise of Christianity. The favorite son of a Carthaginian merchant journeys to Constantinople to find riches and power. But when he finds ruthless government ruling in the name of Christendom, he risks losing his faith as well as his life.

0-7852-7214-3 • Trade Paperback • 408 pages

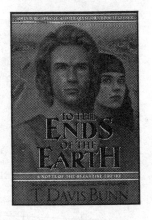

One False Move

A young investigative reporter makes a troubling discovery about a new cyberspace game and designer drugs. As she investigates, she is partnered with a slick business executive, and both are racing toward answers and mortal danger. A blend of techno-thriller, mystery, and romance that will keep a diverse group of readers turning the pages.

0-7852-7368-9 • Trade Paperback • 400 pages

Tidings of Comfort and Joy

The story starts with an old photograph—one of Marissa's grandmother taken during World War II, younger and more beautiful than she had ever seen. But the officer who was embracing her with such passion—he didn't look like her grandfather. As the questions begin, an extraordinary story unfolds. A story of love and loss and caring, of separation and reunion, this novella is destined to become a holiday classic as well as a wonderful family story.

0-7852-7203-8 • Hardcover • 240 pages